GLORYBOUND

Guss's yellow eyes were stricken, the vertical slits nearly oval. Both tips of his forked tongue had gone numb. He felt hot. And cold.

He saw himself as he truly was, a solitary figure in the vast universe who, alone, had been delegated the task of saving the world of humans from utter destruction.

The mental picture was so dramatic, so poignant, he almost wept.

If he lived, he decided, he would write a book about it. Perhaps even a play.

Also by Ward Hawkins
Published by Ballantine Books:

RED FLAME BURNING

a novel by
Ward Hawkins

SWORD OF FIRE

BALLANTINE BOOKS ● NEW YORK

A Del Rey Book
Published by Ballantine Books
Copyright © 1985 by Ward Hawkins

Library of Congress Catalog Card Number: 85-90752

ISBN 0-345-32348-3

Manufactured in the United States of America

First Edition: October 1985

Cover Art by Ralph McQuarrie

CHAPTER 1

Bissi, the god-spider, came back just before daylight, as Guss had known he would. The first two victims had been taken at intervals of about three hours, and now Bissi had returned to take the next-to-last meal from his larder.

The meal was going to be another Jassan, a worker who had strayed unknowingly into Bissi's domain. And three hours after that meal, Guss knew only too well, the god-spider would return for the only meal that was left.

There could be no escape. He was bound in a strand of spiderweb wrapped around and around in a cocoonlike shroud he could not hope to break. He could only wait in mind-shattering terror while the fate of his fellow Jassan was played out before his eyes.

The victim's name was Lasso.

He was screaming.

In his mind only.

More reptilian than mammalian, Jassans had no vocal

ability, but evolution had given them telepathic powers even greater than voice, and the fright-filled mental screaming was almost impossible to endure. The keening vibration, high and thin, set every cell in Guss's brain afire in sympathy, adding to his own mortal terror, tempting him to scream just as wildly.

But he had not screamed.

Not yet.

Bissi, the god-spider, was hideous. The enormous creature was covered with a furlike coat that was black for the most part, with a striping of yellow bands around its bulbous abdomen. It stood easily two meters in height, when it chose to erect itself on its four pairs of walking legs, and spanned twice that when in a walking posture. There were four eyes in the head. The two larger eyes, spaced close together in the center, seemed to be windows to the creature's mind, while the other two, smaller and placed higher and wide apart, seemed to serve as sentinels, watching the perimeters. The mouthparts beneath the head were serviced by two leglike appendages, one on either side, and were dominated by the fangs, arched daggers, each carrying enough venom to paralyze or kill instantly, as the god-spider chose.

Bissi came through the archway and stopped in front of the two bound Jassans; erect, he stared at both his victims, silently, as if indulging in the luxury of the choice of which terrified Jassan to take first. Or perhaps the increase in terror, the stimulation, would add flavor to the food after the digestive juices had reduced the flesh and organs to fluid—Guss didn't know. He did know he could not become more terrified if the god-spider were to torment them thus for a hundred days.

Guss had never claimed to be courageous. He was a sissal-player, and sissal-players were supposed to be creative and sensitive, not brave adventurers. And when it came to that, he was very good at what he was supposed to be. Exceptionally good. What was it the human, Harry Borg, had called him? "The Elvis Presley of Jassa!" And if that meant adulating fans thronging to his every performance to savor the symphony of fragrances as only he was able to produce them, then the description fit perfectly. He had what Harry called charisma. And in addition to that he was an exceptionally handsome performer.

Wasn't he?

He was tall for a Jassan, always elegant in dress and bearing. His eyes were quite large, rather more gold than yellow, and the pupils could vary from thin, vertical lines to almost round, dark wells of sympathy and understanding. His forehead was higher than most, his muzzle was shorter, and his nostrils had an aristocratic lift that set him somewhat apart from the working classes. Not that he ever placed himself above anyone; it was just that he had the look of being finer goods. Due to his sissal-playing, his eight-fingered hands moved with an easy grace, and through years of testing odors, the movements of his forked tongue had developed a unique fluidity—creating exquisite fragrances was, after all, the way he entertained.

How then—and why hadn't he asked himself this in the beginning—could he possibly have perceived himself as the one destined to save what he had come to think of as "Harry's World" from total obliteration?

He was certainly not cut out of the same bolt of hero-cloth that Harry Borg was. Harry Borg was a giant, powerful, swashbuckling human, capable of feats of great daring, totally unafraid. And why then had Guss, a gentle artist by profession, even tried? Stupidity? A deep and burning sense of obligation? A genuine affection for the *Homo sapiens* he had come to know? Most probably it had been a combination of all three.

Commendable? Perhaps. But utterly foolhardy!

The god-spider, Bissi, finally approached the madly screaming Lasso. The short appendages on either side of the god-spider's mouthparts reached out to grip the bulging-eyed, gape-mouthed victim in a firm grip. The twin daggers that were his fangs were then gently, yet inexorably, inserted into the poor victim's chest cavity; as Guss watched, his own yellow, wide-slitted eyes bulging, Bissi injected just enough poison to paralyze. Lasso stopped squirming and screaming. But Guss could see that Lasso's eyes had lost none of their awareness as Bissi lifted him, cocoon and all, and carried him away.

Guss moaned in torment.

His insides make better soup, if he's alive when he gets injected, he thought hysterically, flooded with black terror. Only the very best for Bissi!

Why in the name of time had the Jassans made gods out of such awful creatures? The giant spiders should have been exterminated eons ago! Instead, those distant ancestral Jassans, motivated by the *if you can't beat them, worship them, and they might not hurt you* kind of reasoning had made gods out of them. *Gods?* Out of *spiders?* The most *un*godly of all creatures? And over the centuries the spiders had become an unshakable curse destined to plague the thinking Jassans forever!

Oh, they could be useful at times. Like being made the guardians of this place, which housed the only known portal to Harry's world. The once-beautiful, now age-worn estate had belonged to Guss's family for centuries. Guss only lately had been able to reclaim it from the government by paying an enormous tax bill—only to have it confiscated once again upon the discovery of the only entrance to Harry's world.

Though the portal had been sealed, Guss had managed to learn how to open it, but he hadn't known that the guardianship had been given over to Bissi, the god-spiders! And that ignorance was going to prove fatal. In about three hours.

With the horrible presence of Bissi gone, along with the nerve-wracking screams of Lasso, Guss sagged limply in the spiderweb coils that bound him. He did not quite lose consciousness, but he was as close to fainting as he ever had been. And while in this in-between state of consciousness, his whole life did not pass before his eyes, only the recent part that held the events that had brought him to this most awful predicament.

It had begun the night of the concert in Cressna, after the final curtain...

He was in his dressing room, the thunderous telepathic applause still warming his mind, when his friend Los Ross came to him, tentatively and afraid, with most awful news. One of the few scientists left, he had been assigned the task of monitoring Harry's world, and he had discovered evidence that had convinced him that Harry's world was going to suffer the nuclear holocaust Harry had feared— not five years from now, as Harry had so often predicted in moments of gloom-and-doom, not ten years from now: within days from now.

Days!

Within days, all animal life was going to be extinguished, Ross said. Most plant life would go with the animals. And possibly the world itself.

"You can't mean it..." Guss's telepathic voice was a whisper. "You can't possibly *know*!"

"I mean it," Ross answered. He was suffering pain along with Guss. Ross had met the humans when they had been in Jassa a hundred days ago, first as captives and then as saviors, and he had learned to like them just as Guss had. "And I know."

"How could you?"

"Mean it? Or know?"

"Know."

Ross moved to make sure the dressing room door was locked. Then he came back to sit next to Guss at the dressing table, to speak to Guss's image in the mirror. He had become a worried conspirator, keeping his telepathic voice low.

"We have instruments," he said. "We found them put away in museums. Marvelous instruments, capable of marvelous things. One of the things one of the instruments can do is detect the presence of materials the humans need to make nuclear weapons. We have found a lot of it. And I, personally, have found some that is *illegal*, clandestine!"

"No! Really?"

"No one knows I've done it." Ross looked guilty. "I mean that I've found the *illegal* material."

"How could *you* find it, and the others *not* find it?"

Ross looked very guilty now. He glanced nervously at the door, as if to be sure it was locked. He moved closer. "I can read their minds," he said.

"Name of Osis!" Guss said, shocked. "That *is* illegal! The penalty is death!"

"For *us*, yes!" Ross said quickly. "For one of us to force the protective block of another *is* death—as it should be! What madness would result if we could read each other's minds at will! But these are bassoes, Guss. Humans, if you will."

"And that's not illegal?"

"I didn't say that! Of course it's illegal—if it were known."

"So you haven't told anyone in our government?"

"I dare not! I would have to tell them I had been reading

minds, and that would mean—" He choked, his eyes going wide.

"Death," Guss finished for him.

"Almost surely."

"But—wait! We can't read human minds! That's why Sassan gave Harry his brain implant. Without that, how could you even touch a human mind, let alone read it?"

"With another of the marvelous instruments I spoke of—from the ancient museum. Very old, clumsy, but effective. It records the brain waves; a computer interprets them—" He lifted his hands, pleading. "Take my word for it, Guss. I know what they are thinking, planning. And they are planning to detonate a nuclear device that will destroy them."

"Son-of-a-gun!" Guss whispered, shaking his head.

"What does that mean?"

"Something Harry used to say—a curse. It means amazement, apprehension."

"He must have meant a very great deal to you."

"He did! He does!"

"Oh, siss," Ross said in sympathy.

Los Ross was a thin Jassan who wore spectacles the way the surgeon Sassan wore them—always crooked on his lean muzzle. Also like Sassan—was it the way of all intellectuals?—his clothes were always awkward and loose-fitting. He had thin shoulders and wore a worried, puzzled expression always in his large, yellow, vertically slitted eyes. But he was a sincere person, a very responsible kind, who troubled himself, sometimes to extremes, about the troubles of others.

"Is there *any* chance—any *tiny* chance—you could be wrong?"

"None," Ross answered miserably but with absolute certainty. "The bomb is being constructed in a seaside village they call Hoboken. In an old warehouse. It is to be detonated in their capital city, Washington. And on a day when two branches of their government are to meet together."

"Osaris help them!" Guss whispered.

"I don't think he will."

"Then they will all be destroyed?"

"Yes."

"Zat! And it's all to go off—when?"

"Within six days of this moment."

Guss needed another moment to assimilate the awful news of the proximity of the disaster. Then he asked, "Who—who knows about this?"

"You and I. And my assistant, Dosis. You know her."

"I like her. And no one else at *all* knows?"

"No one."

"And in six days!" His mental voice climbed. "Six *days*?"

"That would be next Wednesday, their time."

"Will it affect us? Here, on Essa?"

"No. We exist in different dimensions, in different times, different spatial zones. The zinial process requires the tenth orcass be elevated—"

Guss lifted a hand to stop him. "Whatever," he said. "I just play the sissal." He got to his feet and paced about his dressing room. He still could not accept, as a final, inescapable reality, all that Ross was telling him. In the first place, the reality was too enormously evil to be acceptable. He did not *want* to believe that anything so evil could happen, anywhere, to anyone.

He went on long moments, fighting it.

Then his basic honesty made him admit a truth.

When he didn't want something to be, he would usually try to ignore it, or try to convince himself with endless arguments that the "something" did not exist, that the "something" was a lie manufactured by someone for some selfish purpose. He knew he was capable of the most marvelous self-deceptions to protect himself from no more than merely unpleasant truths. What could he invent to hide from a truth as overpoweringly dreadful as the news Ross had brought? There was really no limit. But he knew he must not let that happen. This time he had to face the truth, however terrifying.

"I don't believe it," he said, turning to Ross.

"Guss!" Ross said imploringly.

"No. No, Ross. I know what you're thinking."

Guss returned to sit again, this time facing Ross. He laid one of the eight fingers of his left hand on Ross's arm. "You're thinking, I've scared the tuss out of him. He's going to try to hide behind a lot of self-deceptions and pass them off as truths. Isn't that what you're thinking?"

"I know you very well."

"You're right. You scared the tuss out of me. Harry's kind is going to destroy themselves and their world? That's totally unbelievable. Even if I were not a moral coward— and I'll admit I am one—I wouldn't believe it. But it's not for cowardly reasons that I don't believe it."

"All right," Ross said. "What reasons?"

"I came to know Harry Borg very well. And I came to know his females and his young male fellow humans very well. Will you concede that?"

"Conceded," Ross said.

"They are very strong creatures, those human beings. And I don't mean physically, though they were certainly that. Mentally strong, that's what I mean. They are survivors! All of them. We Jassans, when faced with what seems absolute defeat—death, for example—are known to quit, to give up, to accept death. And to die. Isn't that so?"

"Yes, it's so."

"But not Harry Borg! *He* will go on fighting until after the last drop of blood has been drained, the last breath taken. He's proved that. He's actually done it, literally— to the last drop, to the last breath! And only Sassan could have brought him back to life. He is a fighter! And so are the others, all of them. Agreed?"

"Agreed. And what has that got to do with this?"

"Will you agree that most others in his world would tend to be like the humans we came to know?" Guss said carefully, trying not to fall into the trap of rationalizing in ways that would *only* suit the conclusion he wanted to be the truth.

"Yes, I will."

"Keeping that in mind, then, wouldn't you say it was highly unlikely that a Harry Borg, that the millions upon millions like him, billions, as a matter of truth, would contemplate mass suicide—*total* suicide—for even a millisecond of time?"

"More than unlikely. Impossible."

"Well, then?"

"We're not talking about suicide."

"Ross! It would be mass suicide!"

"No, Guss. Suicide is a voluntary act. This is going to be murder. Mass murder on an unbelievable scale."

"Semantics be damned! Suicide, murder—what difference, if they're all going to die?"

"A big difference—and you know it!"

"Show me!"

"Harry Borg, and the millions and millions like him, don't *know* this is going to happen. If they did, they would stop it!"

"How could this be?"

"That he doesn't know?"

"That *you're* the only one who *does* know. It's their world. I would think *they* would know, if you knew. Or even before you found out about it. *They live there!* And you're only eavesdropping from another world, another dimension!"

"The Dissa-two is an instrument they do not have, and probably won't have for another thousand years," Ross said patiently. "That's one reason."

"Make it two."

"As I told you, this act, which is going to result in the holocaust, is thought to be only a political statement. It is secret, of course, known only to the several humans who will perpetrate it."

"No!"

"Yes, Guss."

Guss was anguished with disbelief. "Great Essnia, Ross! What possible gain, political or other, would come to them if they destroyed it all? You see?"

"See what?"

"The error in what you're telling me. Even the greatest of fools wouldn't for a moment dream of destroying everything to make a political point. There would be nothing—no one—left on whom to impose their political views."

"*They* don't *know* they are going to destroy everything. The perpetrators—I think they call themselves terrorists—think it will all stop after the initial act. But what they *don't* know is that they are being used."

"Used?"

"By someone, some power, some force—I don't know who or what—to fuse the final holocaust. Now *don't* ask me what being, what power, or what force. Or why he, or they, or it wants to destroy them all. Because I don't know!"

"Ross! It still makes no sense!"

"I agree wholeheartedly!"

"And yet?"

"*You* could go through that hole again; you know the

way, you know the other side. You could warn Harry
Borg—"

"Ross!" Guss interrupted. "What are you saying?"

"Don't you want to help them?"

"Osis, yes! I want to help them, but—"

"But what? You're a coward. I'm a coward. We both
know it. But this goes beyond bravery or cowardice. It's
something that *has* to be done! And you're the only one
to do it."

"But our government has forbidden any interference!"

"That's right."

"Then—then I'd face a death penalty!"

"Right again."

"Ross, for the love of Isoris!"

"If you don't go, they will die. You are the only one
of us who can talk to Harry Borg, the only one he would
believe. There is great risk for you, yes. But how much
do they mean to you? Ask yourself that."

"Zat! Double zat!" Guss felt himself fly into fury, a
stupid, useless, foolishly dramatic fury, and he was unable
to prevent it. He began raging, cursing. He made senseless
accusations. He described Ross in very unflattering terms.
He asked Ross to consider his, Guss's, career. Didn't
Ross put any value at all on Guss's life? Didn't he have
any regard for Guss's audience? The Jassans who depended
upon him for entertainment and a relaxation that bordered
on ecstasy?

It was an arm-waving, tongue-waving tirade he was to
remember, afterward, with shame. And Ross sat through
it all, stubbornly silent, suffering, until Guss, exhausted,
slumped in his chair at his dressing table again.

Guss looked at Ross and shook his head weakly. "You
didn't even mention that billions of our kind—lizards,
snakes, turtles: Harry called them reptiles—would die in
a holocaust, along with the humans."

"I knew I didn't have to."

Guss looked at him steadily a long moment. "You think I've given in? That I'll go?"

A hint of what could have been a smile crept onto Ross's face. "If you haven't, I'll go back to the beginning and try to influence you all over again."

Guss tipped his head back and waved his forked tongue at the ceiling, a gesture of final capitulation. He moved the gray third eyelid across his eyes and sat for a moment in silent self-searching.

"I don't think I can do it," he said finally.

"If you try?"

"If I try."

"Why not?"

Guss moved the membrane back, revealing golden eyes that reflected severe inner doubt, the vertical pupils almost round now. He looked at Ross with pain. "The doorway is guarded, you know."

"So I've heard."

"The guards are instructed to arrest any who try to pass." He tossed his hands. "To kill, if necessary."

"So I've heard."

Slowly, Guss fixed his gaze on Ross's eyes. "That means *I* would have to kill the guards," he said slowly. "Ross, I can't kill anyone!"

"I know it would be hard."

"You still think I should try?"

"A few of ours, or *all* of them," Ross said quietly.

"Zat!" Guss said. "You don't give up!"

"There's no need for me to give up," Ross said quietly. "You'll argue with yourself endlessly, just as I have argued with myself, but you'll come to it, just as I did." He tapped Guss's arm with a finger of his own. "It's something we both know has to be done."

"Yes, it does," Guss said wearily, defeated.

"Good!" Ross stood. "I'll have more detailed and precise—up to the minute—information for you by tomorrow evening. The coordinates of that warehouse in that seaside village, for example. I'll also have some small things—weaponry, protective devices, whatever I can find—to take along. I'll bring them to you at your place before the sun sets tomorrow."

"Bring one thing, above all else," Guss said.

"What's that?"

"Courage," Guss said. "I seem to be in very short supply."

CHAPTER 2

Guss had been alone in his sleeping quarters for the best part of two hours. As promised, Los Ross had collected a few things "that might prove useful," and Guss had been sorting through those items with shaking hands.

Small nuggets of high explosive! Sarsiss forbid! Imagine carrying those around in your pocket! Kill yourself before you killed anything else. Gas pellets, guaranteed to asphyxiate a dinosaur. A mile of unbreakable strand compressed into a palm-sized reel. A gun that could, depending on the setting, paralyze or kill a bassoe. A slim cylinder that would produce a metal-cutting flame. "Carry this in a body orifice," Ross had suggested. Disgusting!

And there were other nasty devices, some to extricate oneself from difficult situations, others to put humans in inextricable situations. Name of Osaris! He wanted to think of himself as savior, not as an assassin! He was not organized for the kind of a bloody business Ross was apparently sure it was going to be—that was the simple

15

truth of it. He was a creative creature! Not a destructive one!

He shouldn't go—he knew that!

He was standing beside his sleeping pallet, the gadgets Los Ross had brought him scattered on the cover, staring at the tiny vial cupped in his palm, his eight fingers trembling as if he were playing vibrato.

"Instant death!" Ross had said. "I included it because I know you won't want to face torture."

"I'm to carry that in my mouth?" Guss had asked, shocked.

"Best way," Ross had replied comfortably.

Scientists! Brave as tigers—as long as it was going to be somebody else taking the risks.

He picked up the hand weapon last of all. Scarcely bigger than his hand—he could, in fact, conceal it with fingers closed—the little nastiness could make a hole the size of a fist in a plate of targa ten times without reloading. What would it do to a Jassan guard?

It was too awful to contemplate.

"Then how am I going to kill?"

How was he going to walk in and cold-bloodedly shoot an unsuspecting fellow Jassan? He couldn't! It was impossible! Never could Guss Rassan, the sissal-player, the lover of all things living, commit such an act of utter cruelty. He held his hands up outspread and watched them shake, mute testimony to the truth of that.

And yet it looked as if he was going to have to.

"There you are!" Sissi's voice interrupted his thoughts.

He turned to find her in the doorway, and his golden eyes suddenly bulged. She was wearing the camouflage green and brown uniform of Harry Borg's troops, the Red Flame Brigade. "Combat fatigues," Harry had called them, and he'd ordered a uniform made for her—as a gesture of affection, certainly not for any serious purpose. There were even emblem patches sewn on the shoulders and overseas cap! She was wearing a weapons belt with a hand weapon holstered on one side, a short sword on the other—just like Harry had worn.

"Why are you dressed like that?" Guss asked, his thought-voice gone squeaky.

"I'm going with you," Sissi answered calmly.

She looked very attractive in the uniform. Hardly shoulder height but very shapely, she had the loveliest golden eyes in all creation—Guss was willing to testify to that—softly luminous, with pupils that could be vertical hairlines or wide, round wells a Jassan could drown in. Her muzzle was rather short, her nostrils were pertly tipped upward, and her velvety forked tongue, to Guss's absolute knowledge, could persuade the most determined male into enjoying the most forbidden delights.

But she was not a warrior!

"You're not going anywhere," he said.

"Oh, yes I am."

"Oh, no you're not!"

She was not at all disturbed by the unequivocal ultimatum, delivered with all the male authority, power, and certainty of which he was capable. He was disturbed. Ultimatums, especially to beautiful females, were not his way of going. They drained him, physically and emotionally.

But she was not disturbed. Nor was she drained.

She turned, rather casually, away from him to check her appearance in a full-length mirror, twisting this way and that, adjusting her weapons belt to a slightly more appealing slant, smoothing a wrinkle in her blouse.

"Just why am I not going?" she asked, still more interested in her appearance than in his reply.

"Do'you want to die?" he asked.

"Don't answer questions with questions." She adjusted her weapons belt again.

"It would be death!" he said, his mental voice rising to the human equivalent of a yell. "The guards are ordered to shoot to kill! Is that what you want? You want a blast to cut you in half? You want to lie in two pieces, bleeding?"

The picture scared *him*. He began to shake again. "Well, is it?"

"Of course not, silly."

"That's what would happen!"

"I don't think so."

"Oh, yes?" he exclaimed, exasperated. "Why not?"

"You wouldn't go if that were going to happen." She gave him a sweet smile in the mirror. "You're not that brave."

He glared at her. Then he turned his back to her. "All right. I'm not that brave. I admit it."

"Good for you."

"I didn't want to tell you what's really going to happen."

"So now tell me."

"I'm—I'm—" he couldn't say it. "I'm going to have to—ah, immobilize the guards."

"Kill them, you mean."

Guss jumped as if poked by a cold finger. "Sissi! Great Essnia!" He turned and looked nervously about. "You shouldn't talk like that! You know me better, anyway. I wouldn't—*couldn't*!—in cold blood kill anyone!"

"*I* knew that," Sissi said. "I didn't know you did."

Guss leveled a finger at her reflection in the mirror. "You know what you are?"

"Tell me."

"You're what Harry Borg called a wise-ass!"

"Is that a compliment?"

"It is not!"

"Then I reject it."

Throwing up his eight-fingered hands, Guss waved his long, forked tongue in huge exasperation. "Osaris, help me!"

"Nobody else will," Sissi agreed.

Trying to get control of himself and of the conversation, Guss paced the length of the room, then turned back. "The guards are not the real problem," he said in a quieter tone.

"What *is* the real problem?"

"The going!" Guss said. "The penalty for crossing is death! And that's whether anyone is hurt or not. Death! Do you hear? Death! And probably not a fast one."

"Only if we're caught."

"They'll catch us."

"Only if we come back."

"Come back? Are you thinking of *not* coming back?"

"Aren't you?"

Guss sputtered. He hadn't, he realized now, given the return much thought—any thought. Zat! He hadn't been able to work his way through all the problems of *getting there*! Getting back had been too far ahead. But he thought about it now. With a sinking sensation. "We—I couldn't stay there," he said weakly. "I've got—responsibilities! My audience—well, I—"

"We'll have to stay there, Guss."

"But—"

"For a time, at least," she said, making it a comforting equivocation. "We'll work something out."

"Not *we*!" Guss shouted the thought at her. *"Me!"*

"Us," she said, smiling gently.

Guss clapped his hands to the sides of his head, holding it as if he thought it was going to burst. Females could be so damned frustrating! And the thought, even frantic as it was, brought him a new line of reasoning.

"You're nothing but a female!" he said.

"Why, so I am!"

"I mean, this is not your—a female's—kind of an expedition. It's dangerous. It calls for strength—and daring—and courage. That's it! A steady hand in the face of danger. A cool mind! Resourcefulness!"

"Right on!" Sissi said.

"What d'you mean, 'Right on!'? You're talking like a human now."

"Like Harry's staff?" She rolled her golden eyes. "Those young males! Woweee!"

"Sissi!"

"They were some kind of men!" Sissi lolled her tongue out lasciviously. "Made me wish I was human."

"Osaris help me!" Guss pleaded toward the ceiling. "I'm talking life and death and she's talking sex!"

"I'll talk sense," Sissi said suddenly, "if you will."

"If I will—"

Sissi went to sit on the edge of the sleeping pallet, her back very erect, her manner serious, waiting.

"Sissi." Guss was more uncomfortable now than angry or frustrated. "Sissi, I—well, look." He went to sit beside her, to take one of her hands in his. And when he spoke again, it was, it seemed, more to her hand than to her.

"If you were to be killed, that—I mean, that, alone, would, well—it would be the end of me. You see, you— you mean so very much to me." He paused to draw a deep breath, a male about to take a very high dive. "I— I haven't said this to any female before—but you're the first, the only one I ever felt this way about." After a long moment, he asked, "D'you believe this? What I'm trying to say?"

She covered his hand with hers. "I believe you."

"I didn't know I felt this way before now."

"I did."

He turned and embraced her. He found he was moved almost more than he ever had been, and he tried to make light of it. "Well, hey! You might have told *me*."

"I knew you'd find out, sooner or later."

Their tongues entwined, tying the beautiful love-knots that said more to each other than thought-words ever could. And after a long moment, Guss held her at arm's length and looked earnestly into her lovely golden eyes. "Now you see why I can't let you come with me. I just can't let anything happen to you. Do you understand?"

"I understand," Sissi said.

"Good!" Guss said, with relief. "That's settled."

He started to rise, but Sissi held him back.

"What now?" he asked.

"Don't you want to hear why I *am* going?"

"Why you're what?"

"Going with you," Sissi said quietly. "I am, you know."

"Sissi!" Guss's thought-voice was beginning to rise.

"Listen to me now!" Sissi said sharply.

Guss shoved to his feet.

"You gave me a lot of reasons why I shouldn't go," Sissi said, "and I listened patiently. Now you've got to listen to the reasons why I *must* go with you."

Guss glared at her silently.

"Fair's fair! Isn't that what that little human female, Tippi, used to say?"

"All right, then!" Guss said, arms akimbo, sternness in every line of his face and body. "But I've got to tell you, I have very little time. I've got to leave here in—" he looked at his watch "—thirty minutes."

"Will you sit down?"

"Not by you. Not where you could—"

"Over there, then."

He backed into a recliner, never taking his eyes from her. If there was one person he trusted less than Sissi, it was himself. His mind had a way of straying from the topic at hand to gentler things, and he couldn't let that happen now.

"Have your say," he told her sternly.

"I'm just as capable as you are," she said.

"At what?"

"At almost anything. And in some things, more capable. I can think faster than you can, for instance."

"Oh, no! I won't concede that!"

"Bluster will get you nowhere!"

"But—"

"You're too emotional. You're not practical. You're a 'Don't feed it and maybe it will go away!' type."

"And you're not?"

"I'm not." She tipped her head. "I caught you, didn't I?"

"You could have gotten me in jail!" he stormed, suddenly angry. "I told you a hundred times we shouldn't! It was against the law! You were too young! And I didn't have a permit. But you wouldn't listen." He glared at her. "You're oversexed! D'you know that?"

"Aren't you lucky!"

"I—" He struggled against saying what honesty required, which was "Dosis, yes!" and finally said, "That's got nothing to do with what we're talking about!"

"You brought it up."

"I take it back!"

"All right," she said calmly. "But you have just proved I can talk circles around you—" she held up eight pretty fingers to forestall a protest "—and that could be important. Talking, I mean. Circles around others."

"You've got more reasons?" he asked grimly.

"I can face death better than you can."

Guss winced in spite of himself. "So can a million others."

Sissi didn't elaborate on that point: No logical proof could be offered to support the contention, and the argument would be unnecessarily cruel to Guss. She instead offered a more easily debatable point.

"Females fight as well as males to protect themselves—or to protect others."

"Now that's where you're wrong!" Guss said, taking heart. "You're half the size of the average male. You've got muscles of twill! Six like you couldn't overpower me, let alone a human like Harry Borg!"

"Male ego!" Sissi said. "Male stupidity!"

"What's that supposed to mean?"

"In my hands," Sissi said, drawing her sidearm, "an esso is just as lethal as it would be in the hands of a giant. And more lethal than it would be in your hands, because you would have to think three times before you pulled the trigger." She pointed the small, terribly destructive weapon at Guss. "I can pull it the instant I need to."

She pretended to pull the trigger.

Guss almost fainted. "Sissi!" he yelled.

She put the small, pistollike weapon back in her holster, her point made, obviously, because Guss's forked tongue was hanging out like a long, red, split-ended ribbon, a sure sign of extreme fright.

"If I go with you," she said while he was still recovering, "neither one of us would be alone. Me, to die of loneliness, knowing you would never be able to get back without me to help you. You, to give up without me to support you—I mean, emotionally—to give you love, comfort."

"Sissi! That's not fair!"

He got up to stride away again, trying to clear his mind of her appeal to his emotions. He was vulnerable to that kind of an attack, and he knew it. He turned again, well away from her, to make a real effort to regain his stern masculine stance.

"I want practical reasons, Sissi! No mushy nonsense!"

Sissi became suddenly very incisive. "I've got one."

"What's that?"

"'A beaut!' as Harry Borg would say."

"Don't play games!" Guss said, becoming wary.

"You're what Harry called a klutz—that's the reason."

"Wait a minute—"

"You're a klutz, Guss. In your heart you know you are. You can't do anything right the first time. And hardly ever the second time. If it's important, you'll find a way to do it wrong twice before you finally get it done right."

Guss withdrew his long tongue, clamped his jaws tight. She had touched on a very sensitive point. Instead of making a heated defense, he went to a drawer that held odds and ends and began searching through it while she continued to elaborate.

"Think about it." She was quietly, insistently, drilling the thought into his mind. "With me beside you, you can be spared doing the wrong thing, or making a mishmash out of the right thing."

Rummaging in the drawer, he said, "And you could tell me how to do it right the first time? Is that it?"

"That's it."

"And I *am* going to do everything wrong?"

"No, Guss."

"Just the important things?"

"Guss!" Sissi exclaimed, suddenly sharply alert.

Guss had found what he'd been looking for—a length of stout cord—and he was advancing on her with a very determined look in his golden eyes. She tried to scramble out of his reach. He dived the last few feet and caught her, pinning her down on the sleeping pallet.

"Guss, you fool! Stop that! You can't—"

"I can. I've got to."

He used his superior weight and strength to pin her down, then to turn her on her stomach and pull her arms behind her back. While he held her, still struggling, kicking and cursing, he tied her wrists together.

"Sorry, my love."

He tied her ankles, then turned her over. He looked down at her, panting from his effort, apologetic.

"You can't go, and that's final," he said.

She was silent, staring up at him.

"The servants will find you in the morning."

Quickly then, avoiding her accusing eyes, he began packing a traveling case with the items Los Ross had brought him and personal clothing. When all was ready, he started for the doorway, case in hand, with absolute determination. Then he turned and came back to bend over her, to look into her golden, still accusing eyes.

"You really are," he whispered. "I mean, the only female I have ever loved."

His tongue reached out to caress her tightly closed lips. She remained silent, still accusing. He turned and hurried through the doorway and, he was quite sure, out of her life.

Guss's hands were shaking badly when he stowed his traveling case in his personal aircraft, a fast, sporty two-seater Cassal. Saying good-bye to anyone, at any time, had always been an emotional wring-out for him. He was, and he knew it, a sentimental slob. Give him anything with emotional depth—kindness, love, generosity—and tears welled. Give him the loss of a friend and tears spilled. Give him the loss of a loved one and tears rained inside of him like a waterfall.

He could hardly see well enough to get the Cassal started, let alone fly the cursed thing. Saying good-bye to Sissi had been the hardest thing he had ever done.

"Up to now, anyway," he said, snuffling.

He took the Cassal skyward with an almost foolish velocity, pinning himself down in the seat with the force of great weight. He watched the dark, light-dotted land recede beneath him; long moments passed before he let the horizon creep upward into his line of sight again. He was, in a very real sense, fleeing not only from Sissi and all that she meant to him but from a life he loved, as well.

There did not seem to be any real possibility of ever coming back once he'd stepped through the door into Harry's world. He had begun to face the reality of that now. While the thought brought an almost overpowering depression to him, it did not cause him to falter. Rather, it made him squeeze the accelerator with a savage ferocity, to speed the very fast aircraft to the very limits of its ability in what was, even to him, a recognizable effort to destroy any urge to turn back.

He came in high above the estate that held the only portal, the Gateway, to Harry's world. And even as he spiraled in, slowing, to search the grounds, he had time to think with a plaintive bitterness, Why me? Why here? On the whole planet of Essa, why did it have to happen at *my* place?

He had just—finally—regained ownership of the old estate, and then, while looking around, fixing, he'd hammered a hole in the wall in the master bedroom. The supreme klutz-up, Harry had called it. All right! But what kind of enormous klutz-up of fate and misfortune had put the thin skin dividing Harry's universe from his universe—that dimension from his dimension—in *his* master bedroom? Why not the royal palace? Why not in a jungle someplace where no one would notice? Or in a rest room in a tube station in downtown Larissa?

"No! It's got to happen to me!"

The grounds below were strangely silent and deserted-looking in the early-night darkness, and that brought Guss's mind away from mental complaining and back into sharp focus.

"Where are the guards?" he asked aloud.

The main building, lighted only by the soft reddish glow of the built-in luminescence, stood tall and silent on grounds where the shrubbery, planted and replanted times beyond counting, was overgrown again. Nothing moved. And how could that be? This wasn't just any estate. This was the site of the most remarkable occurrence in the recent history of Jassa. True, the government wanted it kept secret. But this? Nothing visible? Nothing going on?

"It can't be!" he said.

But it was.

There should have been vehicles of various kinds. And aircraft of the federal police on the landing pad. But there were none. The landing pad was deserted. The roadways were empty. It was enough to make his skin crawl. He brought the Cassal in to a quiet landing and waited. He could see no movement. He could pick up no communications of any kind, though he focused his mental receptors to their very sharpest.

"Got to be guards," he muttered. "Got to be!"

He decided they had to be inside.

"Maybe drunk," he said. "Maybe playing games."

He got out of the aircraft and stood a moment, feeling the touch of the soft wind. It was not indecision that held him now. He was using the moment to build courage. He knew what he was going to do. Since killing the guards was out of the question, he had decided he would use trickery.

And persuasion.

He was, after all, Guss Rassan, the very famous sissal-player. He would be known to the guards beyond any doubt, and they would be delighted that he should appear. But not surprised. It was his place, after all. He owned it. And he was the one who had discovered the Gateway, wasn't he? Right! So it was not beyond belief that he, for some mawkish, drunken reason, should come here to get something he had left behind. And if that something had been left on the far side of the Gateway, where it could be gotten in only a moment or two, why not let him through to get it? Who would be the wiser? He wouldn't tell if they wouldn't. And they would have passes to his next five concerts that they could use or sell for a considerable sum as they saw fit. Nothing wrong with that, now, was there?

Of course not.

And once through, he needn't come back. It was a perfectly reasonable scheme.

There was the small fact the scheme required he go empty-handed into Harry's world, leaving behind the case containing the nasty devices Los Ross had provided. But that seemed a reasonable alternative to cold-blooded murder. And so, leaving the travel case and the nasty devices in the Cassal and imitating the wavering stride of a fairly intoxicated celebrity, he made his way to the entrance.

The inside, faintly illuminated, was silent.

"Hello!" He sent the communication with the slightly muzzled tone of a drunk. "Anyone here?"

There was no answer.

Puzzled but not daring to drop his pretense of drunkenness, he wavered his way through the foyer and down the hall that led to the master bedroom. He came, finally, to stand across the room from the Gateway, which was plainly visible in the soft luminosity, a clearly described rectangle of targa, indestructible and impassable without the knowledge-key.

Guss was frightened now. The emptiness of the place was weird.

All he had to do was cross to the door, communicate the number-code to the locking device, and he would be able to walk through! How lucky could he get? He was thinking he should go back for his travel case, for the personal clothing if not for the devices, when he was struck in the back and knocked flat by the impact.

Bissi had taken another victim.

And now, wrapped in his shroudlike cocoon of spider webbing, Guss watched the archway through which Bissi would come when the god-spider returned for the last meal in his larder, which was to be none but himself, Guss Rassan, the famous sissal-player. He watched with a fixed, bulging-eyed stare of total fright. His forked tongue was again that long, red, split-ended ribbon that hung limply from his sagging jaw, and his golden eyes, pupils widened to near circles, held an expression close to idiocy.

He knew he had given in to fear and that he had given up as well. He was ashamed of it. Being less than brave had been a stigma he had kept concealed most of his life. When he had admitted cowardice, it had been always in a half-joking fashion few, including himself, ever took seriously. Perhaps he had hoped, deep within himself, that when the final moment came he would prove, miraculously, that he had had great courage all along and had just not been able to recognize the fact, that he could accept death with a flippant joke, a casual gesture of his hand.

But he could not.

The thought of that great, ugly, nasty four-eyed monster coming back through that archway ... approaching him, stopping in front of him to look him over ... then reaching out with those two armlike front legs ... to hold him steady for the slow insertion of those swordlike poisonous fangs into his chest ... to inject him with a poison that would only paralyze him, hold him helpless ... until the moment, sometime later, when the great nastiness injected into his body the stream of enzymes that would turn his insides into a soupy mixture that would be sucked out, while he was still alive, and eaten ... *Yaaaaak!* ... had terrified him out of his mind. No jokes. No flippant wave of his hand.

He had wet himself. But he hadn't screamed. Not yet. *There it was!*

Sarsiss! It was early! He should have another hour! At least an hour! He wasn't ready! For the love of Sarsiss, he wasn't ready!

Bissi came into the room without haste. The eight legs, moving with a slow, effortless rhythm, spanned an area three meters across. They were tipped with a single claw and covered with thick, black hair. The shorter, armlike appendages that serviced the mouthparts wiped the spider's lower face, as if in anticipation of a savory feast. The large central pair of eyes, many-lensed, faintly shining, were intent on Guss, while the upper two, set widely, looked indefinitely elsewhere.

Guss's eyes had focused on the monster's fangs. Shining, arched, they reared out of the upper mouthparts and curved down, becoming needle-sharp at the tips, some sixty centimeters in length. The hairy foreparts polished the wetly gleaming instruments of death as the god-spider approached. Guss could see two drops of clear liquid already at the tips of fangs.

The poison!

Bissi stopped, the central eyes not two meters from

Guss's own, staring at Guss. Guss moaned. "No! No! No!"

If the god-spider heard the desperate mental communication, it gave no sign. Instead, the wet inner mouth-parts worked in busy anticipation.

Still, Guss did not scream. He held fast now, braced. *Thank Sarsiss! I'm not totally craven!* And there was a weird kind of joy for him in the discovery.

Bissi reached out with the black, hairy forearms. They took a firm hold of Guss, standing helpless in the spider-web bonds, held him, seeming to enjoy prolonging the taking of this last victim.

And it was at this, the last possible moment of life for Guss, that the flash came.

Then another—and another.

Bissi shuddered. And then blew apart.

Guss, dazed quite out of his mind, watched in shocked disbelief as Bissi's bulbous yellow and black abdomen exploded, sending a great gout of yuck splashing across the room. Legs fell off, thrashing wildly. The head was there in front of Guss one moment, and the next it dissolved utterly, struck by another flashing beam. Bissi was dead!

And beyond the still thrashing legs, the oozing remnants of the abdomen, standing in the same archway through which Bissi had come, was—Great Osaris! It was—*who*? *Sissi?*

He couldn't accept it, couldn't believe it.

But it *was*!

It was Sissi, dressed in her combat uniform, the hand weapon pointed now at the floor. Just as she had said, the esso had proved to be as lethal in her hand as in the hand of a giant, and, just as she had said, she had wasted no time in using it.

"Sissi," Guss croaked. "Thank Sarsiss!"

They stood as they were for long moments. Guss was unable to move, since he was wrapped in spider webbing. But nothing restrained Sissi. She stood motionless, staring at the still feebly waving legs of the monster she had destroyed, her golden eyes fixed, dazed. And more long moments passed.

"Sissi!" Guss finally called. "Cut me loose!"

"I—I can't!" she finally responded.

"Why—why not?"

"I can't move!"

"You can't move?"

"I—I'm scared to death!"

She began to shake, slightly at first, then uncontrollably. The esso fell to the floor, her head tipped back, and her tongue waved toward the ceiling. Guss was sure she was going to faint.

"Sissi! Sissi!" He sent her name at her with the loudest yell his mind could manage. He knew hysteria had hold of her. "Stop it! Stop it!"

"I can't—I can't!"

"Sissi! There's another Bissi around! There's got to be!"

That got through. Control of sorts came to her. She searched wildly for the esso, found it at her feet, caught it up, and looked everywhere around her.

"Cut me loose!"

Guss's voice penetrated Sissi's panic. She ran to him, drew the short sword, and began cutting through the web. The moment he was loose, she began to shake again. Guss caught her just as she was about to fall.

"Sissi! Sissi, sweetheart! It's all right!"

"I—I can't stand spiders!" she wailed.

She was limp in his arms, her eyes closed. He lifted her and carried her out of the room. In another room he found a pallet and put her down. But he did not give her long to recover. Almost angrily, he kept at her until she, truly angry, slapped him away.

"Stop pecking at me!"

The threat of another Bissi had not been idle. There were usually more than one in any area, and that they could communicate with one another was a known fact. They ran together to get Guss's traveling case, and Sissi's—for now there were two Cassals on the landing pad. During the effort they found breath for a hurried exchange:

"How did you get here? I left you tied."

"You're a klutz, remember?" she answered.

"What's that mean?"

"A klutz is a klutz is a klutz! You can't tie a knot that would hold a gift package together, let alone a stubborn female!"

Running, it was hard to argue. Guss managed, "It wasn't good rope."

Her reply to that was a gasping profanity, short but precise.

"Glad you did," Guss said. "Got here, I mean."

"I bet. You'd klutzed up again!"

"I was trying not to kill anyone, and I—"

Another profanity expressed her opinion.

"You don't have to swear!"

"Y'got a better answer?"

They ran back into the building and went straight to the master bedroom and the Gateway. The portal to Harry's world was unguarded now. The question of whether Sissi was going to go with him through the Gateway had somehow become moot.

At least it hadn't come up again.

Guss stood in front of the doorway. Sissi, waiting impatiently at his side, looked at him. "Go on!" she said. "Open it!"

"I'm going to!" Guss said. "Don't rush me!"

"Who's rushing? I'm asking!"

"Let me get my mind together!"

"Zat!" she said.

"Sissi! Stop it!"

Sissi was looking behind them, the weapon in her hand again, her golden eyes wide, her forked tongue a frantic blur.

"Come on! Come on!"

"Shut *up*, will you?"

"Have you gone klutz on me again?"

"I'm trying to think!"

"Think? Zat on think! Open the damn door!"

Guss hit the side of his head with a hard palm. "I've got to think three symbols and five numbers! In the right order! Will you shut up so I can get them straight?"

"What are they? The symbols, the numbers?"

"A rectangle. A pyramid. Two sevens. A circle. A four, a nine—and a two. Or is it pyramid—one seven—then a circle? No, that's not it. It's two sevens, then a—"

"Guss!" Sissi squealed. "There's another one!"

"One what?"

"Bissi!"

"Now you've done it! I can't think at all!"

"Holy zat!" Sissi said.

The Bissi had appeared briefly in the doorway, just long enough for Sissi to have seen it. Then it had pulled back. The god-spider, having seen the corpse of the other, knew the intruders were armed. It would summon help— armed Jassan guards—that would come quickly. Sissi ran to the door.

"Think, damn you!" she yelled.

She found the Bissi across a wide inner room, crouched against a wall. She didn't faint. She didn't hesitate. She didn't aim. She began shooting. She destroyed half the far side of the building before the wildly aimed beams finally blasted the second Bissi into an explosion of flying spider parts.

"Sissi, I have it!" Guss's thought-words were thin with a crazy, hysterical glee. "By Scoss! I think I have it!"

When she turned, she saw that he did, indeed, have it. The door stood open.

They both caught up travel bags and ran through the invisible barrier, felt the *snap* as they made the change from one dimension to another, and almost fell on reaching the other side. Guss turned and sent the code that closed the door with the solid *thunk* of a bank vault.

He grabbed Sissi in a violent hug. "I made it!" he said. "I made it!"

She looked up at him, exasperated. "*We* made it," she said.

Guss looked down at her, still enfolded in his arms. "That's right. You *are* here. You came with me."

Sissi, again at a loss, pushed away from him and looked about to discover where and what "here" was. She was not impressed. She was in all truth shocked. Even repelled.

"This?" she said. "*This* is Harry's world?"

Guss was looking around, too. It was Harry's apartment, just as he'd remembered it. Dull, drab, almost ugly compared to his home in Osis. But most depressing was the unlived-in look. Neither Harry Borg, nor anyone else, had been in the apartment in months.

Sissi's tone was accusing. "This—this is a dump!"

"Well, it's not—much."

"You told me Harry's world was great! Really fine! You call this fine? I wouldn't keep troggies in a place like this!"

"But it's not all like this—"

"And where's Harry?"

"I thought he'd be here."

"Nobody's been here in ages!"

"I can see that!"

"Well? What're we going to do now?"

"Let me think."

"Take too long," Sissi said. "I'll think for you—"

"Now, wait a—"

"We're stuck!" Sissi was on a roll, furious. "We're stuck in a strange world! We can't go back! We can't go forward. We can't go anyplace! We can't—"

"Sissi! Listen—"

"—talk to the natives! They use percussion; we use telepathy. They don't have communicators! We look like their *lizards*! They'll think we're from outer space! They'll lock us up. They'll kill us!"

"Wait a minute! Wait a minute!"

"Wait? You talk of wait? We've only got five days! Five days until they blow themselves out of existence! And us, too! *You and me, you bonehead!* Five days— that's all we've got! And you talk of wait? Listen, I—"

Guss grabbed her. He clamped a strong eight fingers around her muzzle, locking in her flashing forked tongue, and he held her, a small, quivering bundle of outrage, until he was sure he had her attention. Then he spoke with a firm resolve.

"I'll think of something," he said.

CHAPTER 3

"The bastard!" Harry Borg whispered.

Ahmed Hassad had severed the finger at the second joint, and now it lay in a crescent curve in the box: the first joint, the nibbled-back nail, the small, rounded tip. It was—had been—Tippi's little finger. He had known that at once with a shocked, aching certainty. The little finger of her left hand, carefully washed, without blood, packed in cotton. But hers. He had never ached so badly in his life. God! How could any man, however depraved, sever the finger of a child and send it as a threat?

"You're going to pay for this," Harry Borg whispered.

He was sitting in the pub of a very old inn. Oak and stone and slate roof that had withstood centuries of storms on the Irish headlands above Saint George's Channel were holding at bay yet another storm; heavy rains were lashing at the leaded windowpanes just at Harry's shoulder. But the low-ceilinged room was snug enough. A peat fire was burning on the hearth. The smell of mulled wine and stout,

37

fine tobacco, and wet woolens made breathing good. The soft light came from old brass and smoky glass fixtures, and they lighted here before him, on the scarred, age-darkened oaken plank table, the severed finger of a child.

"Come now!" the message, open beside the finger, ordered.

Or within an hour, the message said, the next finger of the left hand will be sent. Then the third after another hour, and after each hour following, a finger—until all the fingers are gone. Then a hand. Then another hand. Then an ear. And another ear. And then a nose . . .

Harry found himself cursing steadily, fiercely, deep in his chest, his huge hands curled into rocklike fists. He was helpless to defy them, and he knew it. He knew he could not let them take even one more finger from that child, no matter what the risk, no matter what the cost.

He folded the finger back in the tissue that had wrapped it, placed it carefully, tenderly, back in the box, folded the wrapping paper around the box, and put the box in the pocket of his raincoat. Then he stood, pushing back from the table.

He was a striking figure of a man, hard-muscled, wide of shoulder, lean of hip, with long and powerful arms and legs. His hair was dark brown, curled tight to this head. A close-cropped beard, more red than brown, covered a hard, square jaw. A generous mouth was now drawn flat with cold rage. On either side of a short, straight nose and beneath heavy brows, his eyes were a burning fury of deep, dark blue. A single band of solid gold was clamped on the lobe of his left ear.

The three elderly locals in the pub, drinking their evening pints, smelling of soaked wool and farmyard, looked at Harry Borg with silent stares. One, a glass halfway to his lips, paused without drinking, then set the glass down carefully, as if afraid a sudden noise might detonate a bomb. Another scrubbed the back of his hand across his mouth and sat back, though Harry was the width of the room away. They watched Harry write in a notebook, then tear the sheet and fold it; they watched him tighten the belt on his coat, give the folded paper to the barkeep, speak a word, then stride to the door. When the door had closed after him, shutting out the fury of the man, the locals breathed sighs of relief.

"I think I've seen the devil," one said softly. Then he drank what was left of his pint straight down.

"Aye, that you have," said another.

Outside the door, the rain pelting unnoticed on his bare head, Harry Borg set the collar of his coat against the wind and strode away from the tavern door to the center of the road. There, he called to his cadre, the young men who had served with him in the country of Jassa, in that other-dimension world, Essa.

"Can you hear me? Any one of you! Come in!"

He did not use his voice. Since they had all been equipped with thought-transmission implants by the Jassans, there was no need for sound. They could communicate telepathically over greater distances, sometimes as much as a kilometer, but at this moment, he could not reach any one of them, even though he sent his thoughts roaring into the wind at the top of his mental powers.

He waited, then tried again.

There was no still answer.

Harry Borg bent his head and began striding along black pavement that led, distantly, to that ancient Irish city of Drogheda. The dark, wind- and rain-swept highroad was barely discernible as it followed the coastline where the waves of the Irish sea battered and spumed endlessly.

Walk north, the instructions had said. Alone. We'll find you.

He paused. Was that a whisper of a thought? He waited, head and beard streaming wet with rain, face taut. No. All he could sense was a distant humming, as if from a telephone line, but no thought-words, no intelligence, nothing.

And it was not their fault. It was part of the plan of this night that the young men would be at a distance, out of sight, there to remain until they heard from him. They knew the lives of Lori and Tippi might well depend on strict obedience; nothing would induce them, Harry knew all too well, to add to the peril of the two they loved almost as much as he did.

If there was fault, it was his own.

There had been no time to plan carefully. He had panicked—he would admit that now, grimly—when he'd learned that Lori and Tippi had been taken from their Dublin hotel room and spirited away. But the panic had turned to a shaking, murderous fury when he'd opened the package delivered to him at the pub by a rain-soaked slip of a girl, who'd taken his five-pound note, curtsied, and vanished back into the storm.

Harry knew how he had failed: He had not known Ahmed Hassad.

Not all of him. Not the depths of him. He had not seen the horrors of utter savagery that lay just beneath the cool, agreeable surface of the man. It was as if he had come upon a coin, a perfectly minted coin of great value, and then, turning it over, had found the other side to be seething putrescence, stinking, slimy, rotten.

Owner of shipping lines, oil cartels, gold and diamond mines, vast shale deposits in America. Maker of conglomerates. Timber baron. World banker. The maker and breaker, the earthshaker. Ahmed Hassad, rich beyond guessing, yet so black of heart, so utterly without con-

science, that he would sever the finger of a young girl to
gain an immediate end...

Unbelievable!

But true. The proof was in Harry's pocket. The left
little finger of a small girl. A girl who nibbled her nails,
whose sweet gamine's grin could steal your heart, whose
love of life, of everything living, beautiful or not, was
utterly without end.

Harry Borg cursed and spat as he strode in the dark
and rain. All he could hear was the wind-carried sound
of the rugged Irish shore where the storm-driven seas
were breaking. His thoughts matched the night: raging,
black, almost demonic.

What had Hassad meant, there was no time?

"No time to bargain," he had said. He would have Vec-
Power now, this night, he had said. If Harry did not give
it to him, he would take it by force.

By force?

From Harry Borg?

And Harry had roared with laughter.

Then.

Not now.

Then.

Each stride, each strike of his heels on the pavement,
jarred a new word or phrase out of the seething fury that
filled his mind, making fragments of his thinking.

He hadn't known Hassad then, as he did now. He
hadn't realized that he himself had an Achilles heel, an
easily reached weakness that, when found, would disarm
him in a single stroke. His Achilles heel had been Lori
and Tippi. Taking them had rendered him defenseless,
had made him Ahmed Hassad's to command.

Harry's hand closed around the small package in his
pocket. Hassad's to command!

He swore an oath. A solemn oath, sworn by every god

he had ever known. However rich, however highly he was regarded, however well he was protected, however far he might run, Ahmed Hassad would pay for what he had done this night.

He would pay for what he had done to the small girl. For what he had done to Lori, the girl's mother, who must have suffered equal pain or more. For what he had done to Harry Borg, who loved both mother and child beyond life itself.

By all the gods, he would pay!

Harry strode on.

He did not know he had been watched through an infrared spotting scope, until the sudden shaft of a powerful hand-held beam of white light suddenly reached out of the darkness ahead to blind him. He came to a halt and stood, brace-legged in the harsh glare. The light held, then went beyond, searching, making doubly sure there were no followers the infrared scope might have failed to discover.

Then a loud-hailer sounded. "Hands on your head!"

Harry complied.

"Come ahead—straight to the light."

Harry strode forward, blinded to all save the glare of the spotlight. He came finally to the rear end of a heavy black sedan parked on the shoulder of the highway. A door stood open, and beside the door he could make out the hulking dark shadow of the very big man who was holding the light.

"Hands on the car!" The man's voice was harsh. "Spraddle the legs!"

Harry did as he was told.

A second man came from the far side of the car and gave Harry a thorough search, digging into every body crevice that could possibly conceal a weapon. He found none. The search finished, Harry was about to straighten

and turn when he was struck a fierce blow on the back
of the head.

A moment of stunned blindness, then Harry roared
with anger, turned.

Another, harder blow from a swinging club caught him
on the temple. Blinded again with waves of darkness laced
with pain, he sagged to his knees. A faint impression of
the face of his assailant—high cheekbones, wide-set
eyes—was for a moment in his mind. Then he was struck
a third blow that brought total darkness.

His recovery was a nightmare of booming pain, of frag-
mentary moments of lucidity, of disconnected thoughts—
reality, memories, old scenes, present scenes—fading in,
fading out. He became aware that he was in the back seat
of the car between two men, his hands cuffed behind him.
Two more men were in the front seat, their hats and
shoulders black shadows in dim light. He heard windshield wipers beating. He smelled wet clothes. He heard
voices.

"... coming out of it."

"God! I hope so. Our necks if he dies."

"Y'near killed 'im!"

"Said soften 'im up, didn't he?"

"Didn't say kill the sucker."

"Said scare hell outa 'im. Make 'im want to talk."

"Talk? With his brains scrambled?"

"There, he's goin' out again!"

"God damn it!"

"You fool! You killed 'im..."

The voices faded from Harry's mind.

They were replaced by fragments of remembered times
and places. The faces of Lori and Tippi, the mother and
the child, beautiful, loved. That other world, Essa. That
other country, Jassa. Guss... Sissi... forked tongues and
golden eyes... beloved friends...

A moment of consciousness. Pain.

Distant voices.

Clack-clack. Clack-clack.

Windshield wipers.

Shimmery images again.

"We've got to keep all we've been through a deep secret." His own words, spoken in his apartment after their return from Jassa—he heard them again. He saw their faces again, as they listened to him. Lori, Tippi, Illia, Chad, Homer, Ernie, Arnie, Sam.

He heard himself as he told them there were millions to be made for all of them, if they played it right. They agreed again in his remembering. He saw their faces again, looking back at him. Sober, intense faces. Good people. His people. They trusted him.

He was conscious again. Handcuffs were biting his wrists.

"He's coming out of it!"

"Careful, he's a tough son of a bitch!"

"Better believe it!"

A warning voice: "Steady, damn you!"

Rough hands gripped his arms, heavy bodies held him. He surged against them, swelling his chest, drawing air deep into his lungs to fight the pain, fully aware now. The two men sitting with him in the back seat were struggling to hold him down. One of the men in the front seat had turned; he held a short club upraised, ready to strike. High cheekbones, wide-set eyes. Harry forced his straining muscles to relax, letting the two beside him force him deep into the seat.

"Hit 'im again, I'll bust your face!"

The one with the club sniggered. "Friend a yours?"

"He's half dead now—that's enough!"

"Is it okay to go in?" the driver asked.

"Yeah."

"Hassad's gotta be wonderin' where the hell we've been."

"Be mean as a snake."

"Get movin', then!"

Harry had been able to follow that conversation, and awareness was getting easier with every moment. He could remain conscious now. He was beginning to feel stability, confidence. He watched past the shoulder of the men in the front seat, saw the headlights find a gateway and turn and follow a drive that curved upward along an aisle of yews that were bending and whipping in the wind and rain.

He knew where he was and where they were going. He had been there yesterday.

That bloody bastard, Ahmed Hassad!

Harry had sought out Hassad, the incredibly rich financier, with a legitimate business proposition. He had wanted financing for an invention he had named Vec-Power. There had been no need to say that he had not really invented it, that he had really brought it with him from Essa, the world of the Jassans. He had thought a model that demonstrated what a combination of anti-gravity and fusion power could do, without revealing the secret of the power modules, would be enough to interest the man who could provide unlimited capital to develop it.

He had been right.

God blast it! he thought now. I botched it! He moaned to himself. And I called Guss a klutz!

"Leave the model with me," Hassad had said, smiling. "Let my men check it. I'll get back to you in a day or so." The best of all friends, they shook hands. "If it is as it seems to be, I'm going to offer you a good deal. A very, very good deal, believe me!"

Ahmed Hassad. Was the man a monster?

"Believe it!" Harry said the words under his breath, a curse.

When he had returned, he had found that Hassad's "very good deal" was no more than a privileged theft. Hassad had wanted Vec-Power, wanted the secret of the power module, and he had wanted it immediately. There was no time to dicker, he had said. And Harry had realized that the replica of a medieval Irish castle Hassad had built here on the east coast of Ireland was being stripped of artworks—tapestries, paintings, sculptures, armor—even at that moment. Hassad had given Harry one day to agree—and to bring his woman and child, and young men, if he wished, and to return to what Harry had seen would be a life of servitude.

Harry had telephoned his refusal.

Hassad had offered to reconsider. If Harry would meet him on neutral ground, the Cup and Boar, they would discuss it further.

And that had been no more than a means of decoying him away from Lori and Tippi so that they might be kidnapped and used as a means of persuasion.

The headlights picked up the stone facade of Castle Gonagh, as Hassad had named it. A formidable bulwark, though counterfeit, towering, topped by battlements, entered through an archway. The heavy sedan stopped before wide stone steps that led to a huge oaken door.

"C'mon, you." The men yanked Harry from the car and shoved him, still with his hands cuffed behind him, up the stone steps. Harry's strength had returned, but to cover whatever small advantage the deception might provide, he pretended great weakness, staggering, mumbling vaguely. The four men cursed him as they all but dragged him through the door and into the great front hall.

"'Soften 'im,' Ahmed said! Didn't say turn 'im into spaghetti!"

"Sucker's a weaklin'. Can I help it?"

They half dragged Harry down the length of the great hall that only two days before had been lined with fine armor and weaponry of the Middle Ages, and now was stripped, echoing to the sounds of dragging feet and cursing.

They lurched, finally, into a vast central room that might well have been a setting for the Round Table of King Arthur's time: walls of mortared stone, vaulted ceiling, heavy tables and benches and thronelike chairs, an enormous hearth in which logs were burning. Two days before, priceless tapestries and works of Raphael, Rembrandt, and Vermeer had hung on the walls. Now, only a few swords, shields, pikes, and maces lay scattered at the base of the walls, waiting to be packed.

Ahmed Hassad seemed unaware that a sagging, stumbling Harry Borg had been brought in, nearly unconscious, by four men, all dripping wet with rain. He was dining with guests. And dining in Hassad's castle was ceremony rather than repast, with himself as high priest. He was at the moment offering one of his guests a special viand.

The guest, on Hassad's left, was Tippi, her left hand bandaged.

Lori was on Hassad's right.

Both Lori and Tippi were strangely silent, eyes vacant. Seeing the vacant eyes, Harry knew why he had not been able to contact Lori and Tippi telepathically—there was no mind working behind those eyes. But he had to try again.

"Lori!" he called silently. "Lori! Lori! Wake up!"

There was not even a whisper of a response.

"Tippi!" he called. "Tippi! Hear me! It's Harry!"

Nothing. Just the hum of emptiness.

"Bloody bastard!" he roared at Hassad.

That earned him another blow that buckled his knees

again. Sagging, he knew he had to keep his tongue silent or he would never recover. When a measure of steadiness returned, he gave his attention to another of the guests.

Opposite Hassad sat a woman whose name was Soo Toy. Strikingly beautiful, as any woman of Hassad's had to be, Soo Toy had a wealth of black hair, great dark eyes, a thin and perfect nose, a mouth that was full and sensuous; she might have been Chinese, but Harry had met her on his previous visit and knew that she spoke English perfectly, with just a hint of a French accent.

She was ignoring Hassad and his other guests, as her eyes searched for and found Harry's eyes and held them with studied intent. Harry could not read her expression. She could be an ally. She could be a lethal enemy. Harry couldn't tell.

He sent another loud telepathic call. "Chad! Homer! Do you read me?"

There was still no answer.

Harry stood silently as the dinner went on. Servants brought course after course, their movements careful, formal, precise—they might have been serving a banquet in Windsor Castle. Hassad carried on a steady conversation that went without response from Lori and Tippi, though, dutifully, Soo Toy responded when there was need of it. And, finally, the charade ended.

Brandy was served Hassad. A thin cigar was lighted for him. He pushed his chair back from the table and got to his feet with the air of a man well satisfied.

"Chad! Homer!" Harry called telepathically again. "Come in, damn it! Come in!"

There was still no response.

Hassad stepped down from the raised dining area and crossed the room to stand before Harry. He was a big man, as tall as Harry and perhaps a little heavier; a powerful man. Huge biceps bulged the sleeves of his perfectly tailored dinner jacket when he lifted his arms; his chest strained fabric and buttons when he breathed. And he was handsome beyond reason. He had lustrous black hair, well barbered; large, dark eyes beneath strong brows; perfect white teeth; and a small cleft accented his chin.

On first meeting him, Harry had thought Hassad looked more like a matinee idol than the man some called the richest individual in the world. Just now, looking at Harry, there was nothing but good humor in his eyes. He lifted his cigar and pushed the glowing tip firmly against Harry's cheek.

Harry did not wince, did not blink.

Hassad was impressed. "Good man," he said. "I think we're going to have a long and amusing time persuading you to tell us your secrets."

Harry, staring at Hassad, his face expressionless, was sending an urgent telepathic call again. "Chad! Homer! Where the hell are you?"

"On the road south of the castle!" The answer was sudden. And surprisingly clear. "We picked up your note. We're rolling."

The sudden glow that burned in Harry's eyes was caught by Hassad. But he misunderstood it. "What is this? You're looking forward to our diversions?"

"You want diversions?" Harry said. "I've got a suggestion."

"And what would that be?"

"You're going to beat on me, right?"

"In a sense, yes," Hassad agreed. "But I have something more sophisticated than clubs in mind. We're going to attach electrodes to various sensitive parts of your body and apply current."

"I'd rather have your men beat on me," Harry said, "if you'll take the handcuffs off and let me have my licks at them at the same time." He showed Hassad a hard grin.

"It'll give you a chance to see if they're worth the money you're paying them."

Hassad took a moment and found the idea had merit. He looked at the four men who had brought Harry in. "What do you say?"

What could they say?

"Hell, yes!" they said, almost as one.

They had to pretend they thought the idea that Harry could last more than a moment against them was ridiculous. Even laughable. And they may have even believed it. At Hassad's nod, they set about clearing space.

"Gonna love this, sucker!" one of them said to Harry.

They took the handcuffs off Harry's wrists, and Harry, hands free at last, began the slow business of taking off his coat and shirt, while tending to the more urgent business of telepathy.

"Do you read me, Chad?"

"Loud and clear."

"Where are you?"

"Just approaching the driveway to the castle."

"I'm a prisoner here. About to be tortured."

"Can't let that happen."

"I'll copy that."

"You're in the castle—where?"

"The main room. Lori and Tippi are here, too. They're doped out of their minds."

"We'll be careful."

"And there are armed men. Four. Or more."

"No problem."

Harry was watching the others.

The huge black had stripped off his coat and shirt. Enormous muscles were plaited across a massive chest. More muscles were like snakes under the skin of his huge arms. His neck was a massive column, narrowing to support a small, bald, glistening head.

Formidable!

The men had decided there was no need for the four of them to attack Harry at once. How would that look to Hassad? Four of them against one man, however big? No way! Each one of them would have to prove able to take Harry alone—or be out of a job.

Hassad had returned to his chair, turning it so that he had a good view of the area that had now become an arena. He was sitting comfortably, a cigar in one hand, a brandy in the other.

Harry tossed aside his shirt. He took a deep breath that swelled his equally impressive chest, then flexed his shoulders. He suddenly felt good. No, dammit! He felt fine! He was about to collect on a debt that was long overdue.

"Chad!" he called telepathically.

"Sir!"

"Give me fifteen, twenty minutes. Okay?"

"Fifteen or twenty minutes, sir!" Chad responded.

Harry heard Homer say, "What the hell's he talkin' about? They're gonna torture him, and he wants fifteen or twenty minutes! That makes a lot of no sense!"

"Must make sense to him," Eddie said.

"His kind of sense," Arnie said.

And Sam said, "Which ain't like any other."

Harry grinned at the exchange.

Then he took a hitch at his belt, lifted his big hands, spat into the palms, and rubbed them together. He gave Ahmed Hassad another hard grin. "I'm savin' you for last."

Hassad tipped his head in amused assent. "If you're still alive," he said.

CHAPTER 4

After having promised Sissi that he would "think of something," Guss Rassan had done his best to live up to the role fate had pressed upon him by thinking up an absolutely astonishing plan for overcoming all the difficulties that confronted them. But all he had to show for it, after two hours of trying, was zilch.

That was another of Harry Borg's expressions. It meant zero. Nothing.

But he hadn't told Sissi.

She had spent the two hours sitting before the primitive communicating device Harry had called a TV, watching humans go through some of the most idiotic rituals ever imagined, her firm little jaw clamped shut, her lovely red forked tongue a prisoner, her large, yellow, vertically slitted eyes burning, all sixteen of her fingers laced together in a tight double fist. She was, all in all, in the combat fatigues of the Red Flame Brigade, a monument of silent fury.

"Mad as hell!" was the way Harry would have described her.

But Guss couldn't help it. He couldn't think.

Panic had a lot to do with it—he would admit that to himself, if not to her. When he became as frightened as he was now, the chances were better than good his brain would go skittering around like a leaf in a whirlwind. And the less he could think, the more afraid he would become, which meant he would be less able to think, and become even more afraid, and—Zat!

The time was near midnight. Soon, the night would be gone. And perhaps even sooner, the Gateway would open to spew out soldiers of Jassa, looking for him and Sissi.

To kill them.

Or to take back to be executed slowly.

Every second that passed brought the awful moment closer. And that didn't even begin to take into account the fact that this entire world, Harry's world of humans— he and Sissi included, if they somehow managed to escape the soldiers of Jassa—was going to be consumed by a nuclear holocaust within, as soon as midnight passed, five days!

Unless he could get the word to Harry Borg, so Harry could stop it.

And he didn't even know where Harry was! Or when he would come back to this hovel. If he was ever going to come back. And he did not have the faintest idea of how to find Harry if he did not come back. Or even where to look!

Double zat!

How could he go looking? To the natives, he would appear to be what they called a "lizard," a huge one, walking on two legs, with scaly skin, with vertically slitted yellow eyes and a forked tongue. Just one look at him— handsome Jassan though he might be—would scare the

wits out of the first human to see him, and send the poor
creature screaming.

Triple zat!

His mind was a writhing, seething mass of uselessness.
His usual pink-touched gray, lightly scaled skin had gone
sickly pale, he saw on catching his reflection in a mirror.
His yellow eyes were stricken, the vertical slits nearly
oval. Both tips of his forked tongue had gone numb; opening his mouth wide, he could see that his throat was irri-
tated. He felt hot. And cold. His condition could be very
serious! He wondered if Sissi had any idea how unwell
he was. She would probably feel differently if she knew.
Perhaps even sympathetic. He cast a quick glance at her
reflection in the mirror.

She wasn't even looking.

She was still hunched, staring at the TV, a ball of sup-
pressed fury. He moved away from the mirror, despairing.
No, she didn't know he was unwell, perhaps even desperately unwell. Most likely, she didn't even care. He was
alone with his problem. Alone, deserted, abandoned with
this enormous burden on his shoulders. He saw himself
as he truly was, a solitary figure in the vast universe who,
alone, had been delegated the task of saving the world of
humans from utter destruction.

The mental picture was so dramatic, so poignant, he
almost wept.

If he lived, he decided, he would write a book about
it. Perhaps even a play.

The television screen in front of Sissi suddenly presented a new picture, and she reached out to turn a knob.
The screen blank, she stood up. "Well?" she asked.

She straightened her belt, positioning the short sword
on her left hip, the deadly short-barreled esso on her right,
clearly finished with doing nothing, ready to do something.

"Well, what?" Guss asked nervously.

"Have you decided what we are to do?"

"I—I'm still working on it."

"You've had almost two hours!"

"It's not easy, Sissi!" He waved his hands. "It takes a lot of study, of balancing this against that!"

"This against that!" Sissi's tone was one of huge disgust. Small she might be, frail in appearance, delicate when that was needed; but when she had to, she could turn into pure plass, the unbreakable, unbendable stuff of the ancients.

"Consider this 'this'!" Sissi waved her hands in a circle. "No one has been here in this place in months! No one is apt to come here in more months!" She pointed a finger where the Gateway would be if it were visible. "And consider that 'that'!" She put her fists on her hips. "They *will* come after us! They are *overdue*!"

"Sissi! Wait!"

She didn't seem to hear him. She went on, ranting about how they had to get out, but Guss had stopped hearing her. He had suddenly seen the answer. He didn't know where the answer had come from. Out of his subconscious, perhaps, where it had been lurking all the time, the true measure of his ability to think clearly under fire.

"I have it!" he said.

To Sissi, he looked as if he had been struck by a current of high energy. His eyes had lighted up like yellow fire. His color had gone from sickly ash to warm, pulsing gray. He was full of life, eagerness in every quivering line.

"What have you got?" she asked cautiously.

"An absolutely astonishing plan for solving our problem!"

"A *what*?"

"The plan I've been looking for!" he said, triumph as well as relief in his tone. "I knew I could find it! There wasn't a moment's doubt in my mind. It was just a matter of carefully balancing—"

"I know!" Sissi said impatiently. "This against that!"

"Well, yes."

"And just what is this astonishing plan?"

He stared at her, rather disappointed in her inability to recognize the drama of the moment. "*I'm* going to do it," he said.

"Do what?"

"Save this world of Harry's!"

He had let his eagerness be replaced by a calm air of confidence, and now it was Sissi's turn to stare again. She couldn't believe it. He was serious! He, Guss, the klutz, the sissal-player, was going to save Harry's world? Her tongue became gentle, coaxing. "My love, if you'll sit down for a little while, I'll get a cold compress—"

But he wasn't listening. To judge by the light burning in his yellow eyes, his mind was forming plans, like a ribbon machine making ribbons. His tongue was whipping around in a blur; he was smacking one hand into the other.

"My big mistake," he said, pacing, "was I kept thinking I had to find Harry, and that without him we were lost! Ridiculous! I have the coordinates of that village. Hoboken, wasn't it? I can go there and find those—what do they call them? Terrorists?—and I can stop them, just as well as Harry could!"

Sissi's mouth fell open. Her tongue lolled out like a long red string.

"Are you *serious*?" she finally asked.

"Of course I'm serious!" He was offended.

"Have you any idea, any idea at all, of how impossible that is?" she pleaded.

"Ah-hah! See?"

"See what?"

"How negative you are?" He pointed a finger at her.

"That's a female trait! Negativism! It would get us nowhere! Thank Osis, I'm a male! A male with vision. With initiative. Like Harry! I see problems! I see solutions! I get answers! I move!"

He grabbed her arm. "Come on!"

"Guss! You've gone bassier than a—" But she couldn't seriously resist. The alternatives were even more ghastly.

A few moments later, they were moving furtively in the dark alley behind the apartment building, carrying their travel cases. They had no fear in talking to each other, since no human could hear their telepathic conversation. But the vibrations they could cause by running into a garbage can would be noise to human ears. It made for scary going.

"What are you going to do?" Sissi asked, pleading again.

They were in the darkest shadows of one of the open-ended garages that lined both sides of the alley. The rear ends of many kinds of vehicles gleamed in the faint light of distant street lamps.

"Borrow one of these," Guss told her.

"Steal it?"

"Borrow it, I said." Guss moved away, looking into the first car, then the second. "Just like Harry borrowed that Cassal when he tried to rescue Lori, remember?"

"I could have gone all night without remembering *that*!"

Harry Borg had gotten himself killed after borrowing the Cassal. And without the magic of the surgeon, Sassan, he would have stayed dead.

"We have to take chances," Guss said.

"You don't know how to operate one!"

"I saw how they do it on their TV," Guss said. "It's easy."

He was three cars away now, out of sight. His thought came to her: "Ah! Here's one!"

"One what?"

"With a key in it!"

She felt the vibration of the motor starting, and her tongue caught the terrible aroma of exhaust gas. Then the rear end of one of the humans' little vehicles backed into the alley. She ran to it as Guss reached across to open a door for her. She scrambled into a seat that already held Guss's travel case; her own case, along with her belted sidearms, left almost no room for herself. But she managed somehow, driven to the impossible by an almost petrifying fear of being discovered.

"Can you run this cursed thing?" she panted.

The machine was ridiculous. Besides having no room inside, the front and back sloped sharply down. The engine, behind them, vibrated in a flimsy, sputtery way.

"Nothing to it." Guss's tone was smug.

"Then run it out of here!"

Guss had a little difficulty in finding that he had to depress a pedal before he could get the lever into a position that would make the car go forward—it went backward first, knocking over a garbage can, which caused a light to go on in a ground floor apartment—but he finally managed, and they went puttering out of the alley.

"Watch it!" Sissi squealed as he made a wide turn.

"Stop yelling!" Guss said. "You make me nervous!"

"*I* make *you* nervous?"

She was sitting on top of his case, her head crammed against the roof, trying to see past her own case in her lap, trying to hold on while they gathered speed.

Neither of them saw the young man who came running out of the alley after them, almost naked, waving his arms and yelling. They didn't hear him, either, of course.

"Hasn't this thing got lights?"

"I think so. Here, someplace." Guss found the light switch. "There! I can see!"

He saw they were driving down the middle of a dark

residential street. They were in a 1970 Volkswagen Beetle, though he didn't know it. What he did know was that he was absolutely delighted with himself and his achievements. "Shows you how far ahead of humans we essans really are."

"What does?"

"This: I can drive one of their machines without training."

"If you call this driving—watch it!"

Guss, in making another turn, had gone wide again, running up on a sidewalk. He ran along it a way, then turned back onto the street, jolting down over a high curb.

"Does take some getting used to," he admitted.

"I'd rather walk."

"Stop worrying! I can drive it!"

And he did better for a while.

"May I ask where you are driving *to*?"

"To Hoboken! Where else?"

"D'you know the way?"

"Certainly. Harry's apartment is in Reseda, California. He told me that. And California is on the west coast of America, Harry's country. Hoboken is on the east coast. So I drive from west to east. What is so difficult about that?"

"I—I can't *begin* to tell you!" Sissi wailed.

CHAPTER 5

As midnight passed into the morning of Friday, April 4, the dark waterfront warehouse in Hoboken, New Jersey, was still, save for an occasional hoot of a tugboat. During the day, it had been the scene of quiet but desperate activity. Jessica Jones had driven the lean, scragglybearded, bespectacled Hale Benedict into a fury of work all through the daylight hours and, not incidentally, into a condition of insanity almost matching her own. Now, with the help of Nembutal, he was sleeping.

Tomorrow, she would drive him again.

They were both deranged.

While his madness was a hernia that had exploded out of the field of electronic engineering, and hers out of the field of social science, they had both gone so far out of control, so far away from sensible thinking, that they were no longer intelligent beings. And they were sharing what is probably the most common symptom of those who are thus afflicted: They didn't know they were crazy.

On the contrary, they were utterly convinced that they, alone, were sane and that the rest of the community of men, poor souls, were in need of guidance. Guidance they, alone, had been mandated to provide.

Jessica Jones was a lank, storklike, blond-haired woman in her late thirties, born of wealthy parents who had died before she was eighteen. Her lankness was carried into her face—long nose and receding chin—and the steel-rimmed glasses she wore did little to improve her appearance.

She was a woman who had always been, ever since childhood, given to positive opinions. She was one of those for whom other conclusions, other results, other solutions, if they differed from her own, were patently false and unacceptable. If time proved others to be correct and her in error, then her reaction had always been one of bitter resentment. The correct answer, the correct statement, then became to her a monstrous deception put forth by a faceless clique of enormously rich and villainous scoundrels who were bent on controlling the entire world. And that would mean, in her words, "Slavery for the Common Man."

That she herself was rich did not enter into her thinking. The money left her by her parents lay untouched, even hated, in the bank.

For the past ten years, she had been devoting herself to her cause—saving the Common Man from that faceless clique—with a notable lack of success. Oh, there had been a few small triumphs—kidnapping of people in Italy and Beirut by organizations of which she had been able to become a part; bombings of embassies, airports, railroad stations, markets, and the like; and the odd assassinations of political figures here and there. While all these had served a purpose, there had been nothing of serious consequence, nothing that could be said would strike a

blow that would change the course of mankind in any
serious way.

Until now.

Now the opportunity of a lifetime was in her hands.

A short, rotund man with wispy blond hair, china blue
eyes, and a high voice had come to tell her that her life
and activities had been researched and documented and
that she had been selected to perform a mission that would,
indeed, change the course of mankind.

Mission! That word had a glorious ring to it.

She would be provided, the man had told her, with the
parts of a device that would enable her to perform her
mission, and with a man able to assemble that device—
she had come to think of it as "the Hand of God"—and
that all she need do was to find a place in which the
assembly could be done, a few good men to help, and to
deliver the device to the proper place at the proper time.

It would be necessary for her to maintain a low profile,
she was told, which was to say she was to maintain her
usual life-style—scruffy clothes, junk food, infrequent
bathing—and work in great secrecy.

Would she accept the mission?

Would she, indeed!

This was her opportunity to "... strike a blow for the
Common Man that would ring through the halls of history
with that same glorious resonance heard when the flames
consumed Joan of Arc..." The words were hers, voiced
silently, as she lay on the mattress that was her bed in
the warehouse on the Hoboken waterfront, her long face
aglow, her long teeth bared in a grin of ecstasy.

The parts of the device had come as promised, and it
had not been for her to ask whence they came or how
they had been obtained. Her task had been to find the
warehouse, to provide the help—Manuel and Ali, two
tried and trusted soldiers in the Struggle—and guidance

for Hale Benedict, the thin intellectual who could work feverishly for long hours at a stretch but who was inclined, at times, to come to a halt and stand staring at nothing in what seemed a catatonic state from which he could be recalled only by harsh berating.

That berating she could provide. And she had provided it many times in the past two weeks.

Now, looking up at the old iron beams of the high ceiling in the reflected light of distant lamps, listening to the night sounds of the busy harbor, she felt again an exultation. After so many years, so many failures, she was going to make her statement. She was going to write her page of history.

She would not fail.

CHAPTER 6

Chad Harrison was waiting, unmindful of the wind and rain, in the deep shadows beside the south wall of Castle Gonagh, the counterfeit, but substantial and massive, medieval castle Ahmed Hassad had built on the east coast of Ireland. He was a young man, only nineteen, but a magnificent example of what a young American could be: six feet tall and still growing, wide of shoulder, lean of hip and thigh. Beneath a close-fitting knit watch cap, his hair was cotton-white, and in better light and better times it stood in marked contrast to a deeply tanned face and gray eyes. He was wearing an expression of quiet alertness, and quiet amusement, too. His clothes, carefully "civilian" in appearance—slacks, turtleneck sweater, jacket—were "action-wear" in the truest sense, permitting unlimited motion and hiding without a trace the weapons he was carrying. A line, scarcely visible, led up the stone wall beside him to a grapple already secured to the battlement above.

"Quarterback?"

The thought-transmission came through to him clearly, undisturbed by the gusts of rain, the howling wind. The sender was Homer, somewhere on the far side of the castle.

"Read you," Chad answered.

"I'm at the back door," Homer said. "I can blow it on order."

"Right. Hang in."

Homer Benson was twenty, though he looked much older, a lanky, bony six-footer from the ranch country east of Bakersfield, California. "Shoulders as wide as a farm gate, hands as big shovels" was the way sports-writers had described him. "A center to warm the heart of any coach lucky enough to recruit him." A very firm young man, quiet; a rock of dependability.

He was standing quietly, waiting in shadows, beside a huge oaken gateway on the castle side of a moat. He, along with Chad Harrison and the others, had been kidnapped by the Jassans—a long time ago, it seemed now—and had been brought back from that strange, other-dimensional world by Harry Borg. Their certain college and professional football careers had been put aside for more exciting careers as Harry Borg's cadre.

After Jassa, all was new.

After Jassa, nothing of the old would serve.

"Careful, short-stuff." That was Eddie, chiding Arnie somewhere in the rain and the dark. "There be dragons in those waters."

"I thought moats went outa style!" That was Arnie's good-natured grumbling.

"Some folks just don't keep up."

Listening to that telepathic exchange, Chad smiled. Those two—a pair of the finest. As a quarterback, he knew whereof he spoke. Eddie Cole, the lean black, a graceful mover, a graceful leaper, a wide end who could catch anything a man could throw and then outrun anything on two legs. An electronic whiz, too. He had saved Harry's butt in Jassa, and you could take that to the bank! It was more than right that Eddie and Arnie had teamed as a pair. Arnie, the fighter, the charger, who wouldn't admit defeat. Ever. A running back who could carry a ball beyond a brick wall some darned how or other—over it, around it, under it, or, head down and plowing straight ahead, through it, if that was the only way to go.

"Sam?" Chad called silently.

"Ho!" That was Sam Barnstable's quiet response. A lumbering behemoth, as young as the rest of them but big enough to play tackle for the L.A. Raiders, he was placid until aroused, a tank in motion when started. He was a button-nosed, big-jawed kid of an overgrown man. Give him a task and he would do it. Period. He was at the front entrance of the castle now, a gum-wrapper-like strip of foil—another product brought from Jassa—already fixed in the crack of the rain-soaked oak door planks, waiting word from Chad to explode it, after which he would roll through, chin on his chest, shoulders bunched, and heaven help the man who got in his way.

But he waited now, as they all waited. Harry Borg had ordered "fifteen or twenty minutes," and it had not yet been ten.

Inside the Castle Gonagh, the reason for the wait had only just begun. The arena was a thirty-foot square of polished stone flagging, an open space cleared beneath the high-arched, beamed ceiling, lighted by simulated torches set on stone walls and by the flaming logs in the enormous stone hearth.

The spectators were gathered at the long table: Ahmed

Hassad, sprawled in his chair, a cigar in one hand, a glass of fine brandy in the other; Soo Toy, the incredibly beautiful French-Cambodian, her perfect features and her almond-shaped dark eyes carefully inscrutable; Lori Borg, the wife of Harry Borg, five months pregnant, clean-faced, her good cheekbones catching the light; and Tippi Calder, Lori's thirteen-year-old daughter, still a child, still growing, but a gamine, whose startling wit and store of grown-up knowledge was ever a delight.

Lori and Tippi were so deeply under the influence of drugs that they were beyond awareness: they were blank-staring automatons.

The combatants in the arena were five:

Four were Ahmed Hassad's bodyguards. The one with the high cheekbones and wide eyes was the one who had sapped Harry repeatedly into unconsciousness while the lean-jawed cowboy-type had held him. The big blue-jawed man of Mediterranean blood, he of the Brooklyn accent, had driven the car that had brought Harry here. And the huge black, stripped to the waist now, great ropelike muscles gleaming under a skin already sweated, had sat with the Oriental in the back seat, twisting Harry's arms cruelly when he had struggled.

The fifth was Harry Borg.

Even after a beating, he was an impressive figure. Incredibly, the magic of the surgeon, Sassan, had continued in the past months, increasing Harry's height by two inches, and his muscle weight accordingly. He now was six-four, two hundred and thirty pounds of perfectly conditioned bone and muscle. He was stripped to the waist, a fierce light gleaming in his dark blue eyes, his teeth showing through his close-cropped beard in a hard grin. The gold band in his left ear lent a piratical note, appropriate at the moment, for he was a man who wanted fresh blood as payment for a debt that had been burgeoning this past day.

This was the debt:

His wife, his unborn child, and his adopted child, Tippi, had been kidnapped, drugged, and worse. He had been assaulted, beaten unconscious, brought here, and promised torture that would not end until he gave, and death if he did not give.

But these comprised only the first paragraph of charges. The rest of the bill—and this was to be collected from the person of Ahmed Hassad himself—lay in a small box in the pocket of the coat he had laid aside moments ago.

It was half of the little finger of Tippi Calder's left hand—bone, joint, and nibbled nail—severed by one of these men before him, on orders from Ahmed Hassad. The child's left hand now wore a bandage, the pain numbed by drugs; but that missing finger was going to cost Ahmed Hassad far more than one of his own fingers before Harry Borg was done with him. Far more.

But Harry was saving Hassad for last.

First there were the four before him.

The huge black—they had chosen to put him forward first, thinking there would be no need for any other of themselves—was circling in a boxer's stance.

Harry Borg let him circle. He wanted his opponent with his back to the other three, and with Ahmed Hassad, who was half sprawled in his chair in the raised dining area, twirling his brandy glass, on his right. And he wanted the correct distance between himself and the black.

The three waiting jeered:

"No guts?"

"Stand still, y'slob!"

"Y'can run but y'can't hide!"

A glance showed Harry that Hassad, like the others,

had read Harry's moves the way Harry wanted them read, and a fierce glee burned inside him.

"Sorry you can't see this!" he silently called to the young men waiting outside the castle.

An instant chorus of telepathic replies came through— eager, anxious, disappointed, worried, depending on the individual.

Chad's sharp "At ease!" brought sudden silence.

Then he asked, "Sir! What have you got?"

"A turkey shoot," Harry answered. "Four turkeys— and then the gobbler himself."

"You've got three minutes, sir."

"I asked for fifteen."

"Three minutes, sir!"

"You don't take orders anymore?"

"Not when I don't know what they've done to you, sir!"

"Good lad." Harry's tone was serious. "I'll try to get the work done in three minutes—"

That last communication was chopped, for the right moment came just then. The black was three meters away, his back to his confederates—perfect, like pins in an alley—and Harry moved with the sudden, blinding speed of an attacking jaguar.

A flashing stride, a leap, and the heel of his heavy brogue caught the astonished black—he had been expecting a left-hand lead or a haymaker right—squarely on the bridge of his nose. Bone and cartilage gave way. His face was all but destroyed. His eyes were blinded. His blood was spurting. And he was unconscious before he even began to fall.

But he did not really fall. As if struck by an artillery shell, he was blown backward into his confederates, who themselves were knocked down under him or sent stumbling off balance.

Harry, after striking the blow, dropped to his feet, cat-like, in perfect balance. But he did not pause. His movement was continuous from the moment he had left his feet in the face-shattering kick, and it carried him on.

The cowboy-type never knew how his arms had been caught, first one, then the other, to be swept up behind him and broken at the shoulder, to leave him screaming and writhing on the polished stone floor.

Nor did the beefy, blue-jawed man truly see the slashing, hard-edged hand that came his way like a driven sword and caught him just under the ear. He fell to the stone floor unconscious. Though he was never to know it, his neck had been broken.

And that left only the man with the wide-spaced eyes and the high cheekbones, the one who had enjoyed clubbing a man whose hands were held, beating him more than was needed.

That one found his throat caught by a single hand, in a viselike grip he could not dislodge, no matter how he clawed, writhed, struggled. And the grip tightened, slowly but inexorably. And as it tightened, he was forced to stare at the face of the man he had clubbed so unmercifully, at the dark blue eyes that held cold fire, and the line of hard, white teeth showing through the red-brown beard.

And then he, too, was beaten; not with a club, but with a swinging, hard-palmed, open hand that cracked him on his high cheekbone. The hand was a cement-palmed plank, and when it struck, bone broke. On the second blow, an eye popped loose. But the victim didn't know what had happened, for he had lost consciousness with the first blow, his windpipe crushed.

"Go!" Chad ordered. He had climbed to the top of the wall of the Castle Gonagh before giving the command.

Now the front and back gates of the castle gave before the power of explosives. Homer at the rear and Sam at the front, both armed with machine pistols, moved in through the smoking wreckage.

On opposite sides of the castle, Arnie and Eddie, also with machine pistols, dropped down from the walls and ran to stairways leading down into the interior.

Chad took a shorter way, racing in the darkness. The smooth stutter-burst from a machine pistol took him to a rail, and he saw, below, Sam standing wide-legged, slightly bent, watching two palace guards, weapons spewing fire wildly, harmlessly, as they spun and fell. Homer appeared across the inner courtyard, lifted a hand to Sam, who answered, and they both moved on.

"All secure?" Chad asked telepathically.

"No problem."

"Can't find nobody!" Arnie complained.

"Keep movin'!" Eddie said.

Chad raced on. He burst into the huge main room, paused only a moment to catch the scene and place the opposition, and with the quick, instant reflex of the fine quarterback that he was, he threw a burst of fire that caught the man aiming a pistol at Harry's back. The man dropped in his tracks, his weapon unfired.

Then Chad ran to leap up Harry's back.

"Enough!" he yelled.

Harry, consumed with cold rage, was still taking vengeance from the man who had clubbed him, who may well have been the one who, on Hassad's order, had severed Tippi's finger. Another strike with that cement-palmed hand had been on the way, when Chad's clamping arms stopped him in midswing.

The two of them struggled before Chad's voice got the message through. "He's dead, sir!"

In a daze, for the briefest moment, Harry stared at the

broken face of the man who had had cheekbones, and then he dropped him, turning for the last man. Ahmed Hassad.

But Hassad's chair was empty!

And so was Lori's!

Tippi was at the table, her eyes still blank. Soo Toy was at the table, her beautiful face still, her dark-almond eyes shining as she watched Harry discover that Hassad had vanished, taking Lori with him.

"Where are they?" Harry roared.

"Who?" Chad asked.

"Hassad! Lori! They were both at the table minutes ago!"

"I didn't see them," Chad said. He turned to the others —Homer, Sam, Ernie, and Arnie—who had appeared only moments after he had. "Any of you?"

They replied in the negative, their faces cut by sharp concern and by the fear that they had somehow failed.

Harry strode to Soo Toy, caught her shining black hair in strong fingers, and drew her up.

"Where is he?" His demand was fierce, his face an inch from hers.

"He left," she answered. She was not in the least afraid of him. Her voice was calm; her eyes met his without wavering. She read his next question before he asked it and gave him his answer.

"After you had disposed of the first three, he thought it best not to challenge you himself at this time. While you were occupied with beating the last one to death, he took the woman through that door, there." She indicated a door no more than a long stride from the table.

"Chad," Harry said. "Go!"

"No," Soo Toy said. "Listen!"

Chad, in midstride, and the others, in like positions,

stopped and listened. They heard the beat of a helicopter.
The sound grew louder, rising.

"He always has an escape route," Soo Toy said.

The sound lifted, then faded.

CHAPTER 7

They had not driven far. The street that had led them away from Harry Borg's building had suddenly veered left, then left again, until Sissy was absolutely sure that they were going back the way they had come.

But Guss stubbornly insisted otherwise. "This direction is toward the east! I can feel it!"

"Osis preserve us!" Sissi said.

Admittedly, it was hard to be absolutely sure. The overhanging trees obscured the sky, and one street looked very like another. Watching the trees and intersections go by, Sissi became sure they were on the original street, but going the other way.

"Will you stop squirming?" Guss asked.

"Who's squirming? I'm trying to see!"

She had to shift the travel case she was holding in front of her from side to side in order to see out, and sometimes it did slide over in front of Guss's face, blocking his view and causing him to drive erratically, scraping one side of the street and then the other. But what was she to do? Their very lives might depend on her shrieking a warning before Guss took the vehicle on a course that would end with a crash against a tree. Or another vehicle. Or an abode. "They are getting bigger," she said.

"What are?"

"The abodes," she said. "The places where I suppose the humans live. And farther apart. With open space around them. And trees."

"Means we're getting out of the city."

"Or going in circles."

"There's another one," Guss said, fretting.

"One what?"

"The lights. Sometimes they're red, and sometimes they're green."

"Why is that?"

"I don't know why that is!"

"They must mean something."

"Of course they mean something!"

To say that his nerves were becoming frazzled would be to put it mildly—that Guss would admit. The humans had so many systems, and ways of doing things, and machines, and electronics that made absolutely no sense at all to a reasonable mind—a Jassan mind, at any rate— he couldn't believe it. But he did believe that the task he'd chosen for himself was bigger than he had realized when he'd first accepted it. Say, a hass bigger. Perhaps even two hasses.

The zatty streets didn't go in one direction for more than lurss at a time!

The street he was on ended suddenly. He had to go back a short distance the way he'd come, then turn again. Now was he going east? Or north? He'd forgotten the last direction. If that had been more south than east, and he'd

turned to his right, he'd been going more west than—
triple zat!

He didn't put the curse into thought. Sissi would know,
then, that he was lost, disoriented. And she was hard
enough to get along with now.

The last turn had brought him into a rather fine residential street. The homes were set back behind walls and
hedges or were fronted by wide lawns. The homes were
all dark, for it was not yet two o'clock in the morning.

And it was here the Volkswagen ran out of gas.

At first Guss didn't know what had caused the machine
to fizzle to a stop. But it didn't take him long to figure it
out. He knew even before Sissi did.

"You're out of fuel, you turkey!" she said disgustedly.
She'd picked up a lot of slang from the young humans.

"Tell me about it!" Guss said. He'd picked up human
slang, too.

But she didn't tell him about it. This was no time for
churlishness, for nagging, for recriminations. They were
in a difficult situation that could cost them—cost them
what? She wasn't about to list the possibilities. When you
had to start with "losing your life," what purpose was
there in sorting out all the lesser fates?

Guss twisted the key hopefully. There were grinding
vibrations, but nothing useful. He fiddled with knobs and
gadgets. The lights went out, came on. A small device
began busily scrubbing the windshield. Still nothing. He
shook his head. "Won't run," he said.

"Really?" How much sarcasm could a small female get
into one word?

"I had to try, didn't I?"

"You tried. You failed. And now what?"

"Now I've got to think a minute."

She fumbled and managed to get the door on her side
open, and she and the travel case spilled out on the curb.

She came erect, straightened her weapons belt, then leaned back into the car. "Are you done thinking?"

"Sissi, I—"

"Guss, listen." She wasn't picking on him now. She was being very serious; she was trying to help. "We can't stay here. It will be daylight before long, and we've got to be out of sight."

"Out of sight, sure. But where?"

She straightened and looked around.

They were near a driveway that led through a hedge to a rather large home set well back on a lawn. The house was dark, like all the others on the street, peaceful-looking, quiet.

"Why not here?"

Guss got out of the car and stood on the street, looking. She had been thinking straight again, while he, though he wasn't going to admit it, had lapsed into confusion again. They had to get under cover—absolutely. And as she had said, why not here?

"As good a place as any."

He got his case out of the Volkswagen and joined Sissi on the curb. In the faint light of a street lamp, her lovely face was pale but determined; her large, golden eyes, the vertical pupils opened wide in the darkness, showed only a little fear; her forked tongue fluttered toward him, testing, questioning, hoping. But the short muzzle, the faint scales, the eyes, the tongue, and the many-fingered hands—an appearance that was, Guss knew full well, more what Harry Borg called "reptile" than human— would frighten humans.

And he would be even more frightening.

There was more of him. A very handsome Jassan, yes. Refined, extraordinarily gifted in creating fragrances. Admired, even revered, in Jassa. And of a peaceable, gentle, kind nature. But here—here he was a monster! He cringed inwardly. But what else could humans think? A nearly two meter tall lizard—that's what he would be to them, despite the fact that he was dressed in the finest, most expensive clothes Jassa could provide to an affluent celebrity.

Thank Osis, he had chosen not to wear the battle-dress of the Red Flame Brigade, such as the uniform that Sissi was now wearing. That would have, as Harry would say, really scared the wallop out of them.

Yiss! The thought was a mental wail.

He wasn't going to be able to *communicate* with the humans! They would be deathly afraid of him, and, like all creatures fearing imminent death, they would strike back—or strike first—with deadly force.

Naturally!

"Are we going in?" Sissi asked, growing desperately anxious.

"We're going in. We've got to go in."

"Well, then—come on!"

But still he held back.

"What's the matter now?"

"Sissi, listen. They'll try to kill us!"

"We won't let them."

"That won't be easy." He knelt, opening his travel case. "You know we can't hurt them, Sissi."

"Even—to save our own lives?"

"Even that."

He rummaged through the contents of the travel case, finding a number of the things Los Ross had provided and stowing them in his pockets. He finished finally, holding a yellow tube that was a little longer than his hand. He snapped the case shut, stood erect.

"Is that a—mind-blanker?" Sissi asked, a little shocked.

"It is," Guss said. He was trying to see the calibrations

on the fore end of the tube in the faint light, muttering profanity. "Los Ross said it was, anyway. Zat!"

"What's wrong?"

"It will mind-blank a bassoe, so I suppose it will mind-blank a human. But he didn't tell me where to set it! Too little will just make them dizzy. Too much will kill them!"

His hands were shaking again.

"Set it in the middle, you turkey!"

That made him angry. "Sissi! Stop it!"

"Stop what?"

"Calling me a turkey!"

"Whatever that is."

Human slang, that's what it was, and he didn't need it.

He held the yellow tube up and set the calibration in the middle—just as she had said. And then, to be sure, so he shouldn't do any human serious harm, he moved it back a quarter of the way toward zero.

"All right," he said. He picked up his case. "Let's go."

Sissi adjusted her camouflage uniform, set her weapons belt correctly—short sword on her left hip, esso on her right hip, her overseas cap at the right-looking tilt—and then picked up her case to follow him.

"You are, you know."

"I are what?"

They communicated in telepathic whispers, trying to be stealthy as they moved up the fifty meters of tarmac that approached the house. They knew very well that humans could not hear telepathic communications; it was just that whispering was reassuringly secretive. And they needed to be secretive.

"A turkey," Sissi said.

"Come from a long line of them," Guss answered.

Since Sissi was only trying not to panic now, he couldn't

resent being kidded about anything. He was trying not to panic, too.

"Whatever they are," she said.

The driveway curved in front of the house and returned to the street again. But there was a juncture that led to garages beside the house, and to a gate that opened on a patio, and a swimming pool. The gate was secured by a lock, a hoop through holes and a lump of metal—a padlock, though Guss didn't know what they called it.

"Now we'll find out," Gus said, trying not to reveal his nervousness as he went through his pockets, searching.

"Find out what?"

"If Ross knew what he was talking about."

He had to go through three pockets, one of them twice, before he found the small metal tube that was supposed to produce the flame that "would cut through anything."

"He did!" Guss said, relieved, almost exultant.

"What?"

"Know what he was talking about."

The briefest touch of the tiny flame had turned the padlock liquid in an instant.

"Lossly for him!" Sissi said, not joking really.

The gate opened easily, and they went through quickly. The house was dark, silent. The pool shimmered like a sheet of silver in the faint light. Recliners, chairs, and cushions were strewn about. A gas barbecue stood near a metal table sheltered by a huge striped umbrella that was canted at an unlikely angle. A couple of beach towels lay wadded, forgotten. Two containers of thin metal, the tops torn, lay near the towel.

All this was scanned by Guss and Sissi and searched for possible dangers. Sissi picked up one of the thin metal containers and ran her forked tongue through the hole in the top.

"Sissi!"

Guiltily, she put the container down. "Good, whatever it is."

Guss was looking for a way into the house. The sliding glass doors seemed promising. He approached them with Sissi right at his heels. He was a moment or two discovering that the doors did slide—fortunately for him, the owners relied on the questionable security of the lock on the gate—and he very carefully slid the door wide enough for admittance.

"That was easy."

Easy or not, he paused. There was nothing threatening about the interior, except that it was strange and darker than outside, and that was enough to give him plenty of pause. Sissi's hand, pushing gently on his back, persuaded him to take the first step.

"Don't push!" he said.

"I'm helping, not pushing."

"I don't need help!"

"Liar," Sissi said. "We both need help."

They were in a family room, though they wouldn't have known what that meant if they had known the name. A wide and comfortable family room. In the center sat a pool table. There were gun cabinets on one wall, ship models on another, a trophy case on a third. The walls were paneled, the furniture leather. An archway across the room seemed to beckon, and Guss and Sissi moved that way furtively.

Sissi was impressed by what she had seen. "Harry should have something like this."

"Like what?"

"Like this to live in. His hovel is not fit for a tarsis."

"It's the same everywhere."

"What is?"

"The rich live better, dummy!"

"Don't call me a dummy!"

"Turkey?"

"Wise-ass!"

Human slang could be expressive.

Beyond the archway, a hallway offered several choices. A stairway led upward on the right. Across the hall, another archway revealed another wide room with comfortable furniture, and down the hall, they could see tile and equipment that Guss recognized as a cooking area. He stood looking at the stairway. Small night-lights fixed into the wall gave a gentle glow that illuminated the stairway and an upper hallway.

"The humans must be sleeping."

"Up there somewhere!" Sissi's tone was firm, leaving no room for dispute or even discussion, if Guss felt so inclined. He didn't feel inclined. He felt an enormous reluctance to confront the unknown. The gentle push of her hand impelled him onward.

Toward the stairs.

In the master bedroom, George Bushby was lying flat on his back, staring at the ceiling, engaged in what had become, in recent weeks, his principal occupation. Especially in these cheerless hours between two and three in the morning.

He was worrying.

And even the most determined optimist, he was sure, would concede that he had something to worry about. He was broke, for one thing. No, he was worse than broke; he was so far in debt, he couldn't remember what black ink looked like anymore.

Bushby Data, Inc., was bankrupt.

George Bushby was just past forty, a tall, lean man, graying at the temples; a quiet man who looked like an intellectual when wearing his horn-rimmed spectacles, and who was one, in fact, with or without the spectacles. Which was not to say that was *all* he was. Or had been. A three-year hitch in Vietnam, three Purple Hearts, and a Bronze Star said he was more. Or had been more.

Now he was broke.

But that was not all of it, or even the worst of it.

His wife, Sara, that lovely, loyal woman sleeping quietly beside him, was going to divorce him—that was the very damned worst of it. No way was he going to stop her. And it was not because he was broke. Not on your life. Sara would hang in if they had to live in a tent and eat Alpo. Broke was not the problem. She was going to leave him because he wouldn't dump Bushby Data, Inc., into the ashcan.

"You're killing yourself," she kept saying. "Your blood pressure has gone through the roof. I know you're getting chest pains, and you just won't tell me. Call me a coward, if you want to. Call me a quitter. But I'm not going to stand by and watch you go down the tube just because you're too stubborn to admit you're licked. I'll leave you first. So make a choice, George. Me and the kids, or that stupid company. This week!"

Stupid company! That hurt. That stupid company had grossed three mil plus in its second year! It had bought all this—a half-mil house and two cars in the garage, money put away for the kids' college, a trip to Europe. All companies should be so stupid.

All right, he hadn't seen it coming. The crash of videogames. One week hotter than designer jeans, the next gone like beer can openers. Or hula hoops. Or pet rocks.

Videogames, a passing fancy? Who would have believed it?

He took a moment to remember those good days. *The Snapper!* He'd written that program in his spare time, evenings, after a full day's work writing computer programs for VisaCom. An overnight smash hit, wall-to-wall money. Like *Pac-man*, the kids couldn't get enough of it. And after *Snapper*, *Klaxton*, then *Torpedo*. Two good years and enough money to begin Bushby Data, Inc. A dream come true, Bushby Data. Not just videogames. Graphics. And hardware—disk drives, circuit boards, smart modems. But all that took time. And money. And if you were overextended, as they say, and the bottom dropped out of your main market—woweee! Even faster down than up!

But he couldn't just walk away, could he? With all those people depending on him? All those obligations to meet? How would he face them? How would he face himself? A man couldn't, for God's sake! A little high blood pressure, a few chest pains—that could be no worse than the Cong shooting him up, and he'd survived that, hadn't he? 'Nam had left him with a hitch in his stride, a plate in his head, the night sweats—if he could survive all that, he could survive anything.

All he needed was a little more time.

But how was he going to use it?

He couldn't walk out on his company.

He couldn't keep his wife.

It was what he had to call a helluva fix.

Beside him, that lovely, faithful, sleeping woman, Sara, was not sleeping. She had been awake as long as he had, pretending to be asleep, and she knew exactly what was going through his mind. The stubborn jackass! Of course he owed something to the people who depended on him for their jobs. All right, he owed them a lot. And he owed his debtors a lot, too. But did he owe them his life?

Fiercely, to herself, she said, "Hell, no!"

'Nam had been enough.

She was a short woman, gone round with the years, a woman whose brown hair was worn trim, whose profile was still that of a young girl, though her face was round, in keeping with the rest of her. She had brown, caring eyes, a firm mouth, and a very stiff backbone when she needed it.

And she needed it now. Because he wouldn't quit, wouldn't holler uncle, wouldn't say, "I'm licked!"

Unless—that was her gamble. That was her all-or-nothing bet.

"Me and the kids," she had said, "or that stupid company."

She had to make him quit somehow, before a heart attack or a stroke took him away. And since he was not a man who would listen to reason, and since her means were limited, she had taken the only way left. "You quit, or I leave!"

They went back a long time. They'd met and fallen in love in sixty-five, before Vietnam. No "Dear John" for her. They had mated for life before he'd gone, though he hadn't known it. And when he'd been shipped back, a physical disaster, they had legally married while he'd still been in the V.A. hospital—so he'd know, so he'd have something to get well for. And he had known, and he had gotten well. Finally.

They had been married six years before she had missed a period—what a joyful realization that had been! How can you love throwing up? She had—oh, yes, she had! Jackie was on his way. Nine years old now. Then Jillie, a sweet little girl, six years old now. George loved them. He loved them as he loved her. And how much was that?

She was going to find out this week. "Me and the kids, or that stupid company!" She meant it!

* * *

In one of the other upstairs bedrooms, Jackie Bushby was sleeping. But he had been awake earlier, when his mother and father had thought he had been asleep. And he had heard them. Again. His mom had told his dad she was leaving. She had said he was killing himself. She had said she wasn't going to stand by and watch him die. She said she was going to take him and Jillie and get a condominium.

And his dad had said, "You're pickin' a fine time to leave me, Sara." Like it was a song, or something. "Four hungry kids and crops in the field."

"It's no use, George."

"I think I can save the house."

"That's not what the bank said."

"They were threatening, that's all."

"Threatening on the square, and you know it. But that's not the trouble. I'll live anywhere. You—you're the trouble. You won't last to save the house. You'll be gone."

"I'm not so sure."

"George. I talked to Ralph. I know."

"Doctors!"

"A blood pressure two-twenty over one-twenty and climbing?"

"I've survived worse."

"George! Hear me, George! It's no use trying to talk to you. I give up! You've got a week to decide. Me and the kids or that stupid company—and that's final!"

In a second bedroom, Jill Bushby was sleeping quietly. She was a chubby little thing, big dark eyes—her mother's eyes—and soft brown curls. Her face was serene, her breathing quiet. Her dreams must have been of fairies, or angels, or gentle little animals, for her lips moved in smiles when they moved at all.

Little children are a joy. Sleeping...

CHAPTER 8

*"Softly in the morning
Pussy willows kissed with dew
Sway gently while they're singing
A lullaby for you..."*

Lori Borg, lying on a huge, canopied bed in the hacienda called Mesa Grande, was singing silently to her unborn child. The song was one she had composed herself, the music, like the lyrics, intended to soothe the child within her into a restful and peaceful slumber.

And, presently, the child slept.

Lori knew the child was sleeping, not because the child had not kicked her for several moments—and the child had not—but because she had learned to recognize the low, almost indiscernible humming sound that came through her telepathic receptor as the brain waves of the child's sleep cycle.

The unborn child's name was Charlie. Not knowing if

the child was a boy or girl, she had decided on Charlie,
because Charlie could be the diminutive of either Charles
or Charlene as the gender required. And she needed a
name, because she talked to the child.

The Jassan surgeon, Sassan, had done a great deal
for her—he had saved Harry Borg's life while she was
still Lori Calder, prisoner of Sos Vissir, in that other-
dimensional world of Essa—but nothing he had done had
given her greater pleasure than being able to communicate
telepathically with her unborn child.

Admittedly, there was room to argue: Was she *really*
able to contact Charlie? Or was that just wishful thinking?

She had tried for weeks before she had been able to
detect any evidence that Charlie was hearing her. Of
course, he could not respond with any messages of his
own; the only evidence she had was a change in the low
hum, which she had decided must be Charlie's mind react-
ing to her telepathy. Sometimes, she was sure the child
was at peace, for the humming was almost like the soft
purr of a kitten; at other times, she was sure the erratic
hum was a result of fear, a silent crying.

And that hurt. Terribly.

The erratic hum came, she knew, when she herself was
afraid. And, most particularly, when she was angry. She
had been both afraid and angry almost constantly these
past three days. Had it been that long since the men of
Ahmed Hassad had first kidnapped her and Tippi? It must
have been, though she could not be sure. She remembered
all too clearly the needle plunging into her arm that evening in the hotel in Belfast, but her mind was muddled
about the interval between then and now, when she had
awakened in this giant bedroom even more luxurious than
the one in Sos Vissir's castle in Jassa.

It was hard not to be angry and afraid.

"Oh, rats!" she said now. "It's impossible!"

It was even difficult to think straight.

She got up from the bed and went to stare out the huge window that filled almost one entire wall of the bedroom. The window was locked, of course, but it gave an almost unlimited view of what she had been told was Arizona desert. The view was from very high up, because the huge hacienda was built atop a towering mesa, accessible only by a very long and winding road or, more easily, by helicopter. A place of staggering beauty, if one liked the desert scene, and built, she was sure, at a staggering cost.

Who but Ahmed Hassad could afford it?

And he was leaving it. Moving out.

The evidence of the moving had been everywhere in the hacienda. Huge helicopters capable of carrying enormous loads had been freighting away containers, filling the day and the night with the steady racket of their rotors.

Moving out, why? Going where?

Occasional distant, yelling voices told of haste.

She stood at the window, a rather tall woman, but one of lean beauty marred not at all by the swelling of pregnancy. She had been, and still was, extremely fit at thirty-three, quite strong, and able to move with grace and speed. Her light brown, sunburned hair, shoulder-length, was brushed back from a wide forehead. Dark brows were a strong line above eyes that were wide, dark-lashed, and cool gray. Her mouth was generous in width, made for loving and smiling, but it could be thin and firm when the mood was on her.

And the mood was on her now, darkly.

As she remembered . . .

"Mrs. Calder," Ahmed Hassad had said when he found her sufficiently recovered from the drug to be aware. "Am I correct in using that name?"

"Borg," she answered, still having difficulty focusing. "Mrs. Harry Borg, you bastard!"

When had that been? Eighteen, twenty hours ago?

Hassad was untroubled by the curse. "There is no record of your marriage. At least none my people could find."

"Screw your people," she said. "Screw you."

She couldn't remember ever seeing a more handsome man, Harry Borg excepted, than Ahmed Hassad. He had glossy black hair, perfectly barbered, a movie idol's profile, a cleft chin, and perfect teeth. His eyes were dark brown to black, large and expressive under thick, dark brows. And he was huge: His expensive sport shirt and slacks, fitting him perfectly, had to have been specially tailored. The file folder in his perfectly manicured hands seemed notepad-size as he leafed through it.

"We haven't time for recriminations, Mrs. Borg," he said.

"I have time," she said. "Give me a weapon and I'll recriminate the hell out of you."

With forced patience he said, "You were sedated for your own good, Mrs. Borg. A struggle could have harmed you and the child you're carrying."

"What about my daughter, Tippi? And her finger you had cut off? How about that? Necessary, too, you bastard?"

"It was an effort to save you both from worse."

"Where is Tippi now?"

"In Harry Borg's care. We left her. I have had reports she is well and unharmed."

"Except for that finger you cut off!"

"Except for the finger," he agreed without emotion.

They were in an office-library, a huge room in a residence of huge rooms. Men were at work, carrying out things of the most obvious value—paintings, sculptures, antique furniture, first editions and the like—while she faced Hassad from a chair where she had been placed, moments before, by two muscular women, one black, one Oriental. The women were still close by, she knew, though out of sight behind her.

"Why?" she asked suddenly, her voice full of fury. "Harry went to you with a legitimate business deal. All you needed to do to get Vec-Power was pay for it! You're rich, aren't you? They say you're the richest man in the world. Well? Is it true?"

His black eyes held a glittery shine as he looked at her. "It's true."

"And you're a thief! Rich or not, you're a thief!"

"Only when I have to be," Hassad said. "I offered your husband more wealth than he could imagine if he would accept my terms. But he refused."

"Your terms!" She spat the words. "Slavery! Some terms!"

"Not slavery. A life of luxury. But listen!" His voice held sharp impatience now, and the deep anger of a man unused to being denied. "There is no time for argument. There is only time for reason. I want you to reason with your husband."

"Reason? You're asking me to *reason* with Harry?"

"His life. Your life. And the lives of your two children, the born and unborn, surely depend upon it, Mrs. Borg. Believe me. If you want to stay in good health, to have lives full of more luxury than you could ever hope for, then you must persuade him to come with me."

She laughed, not quite hysterically. "Come with you! I don't have to persuade him. He's hunting you now. I can guarantee you that! And you won't like it when he finds you. You won't live long enough to even hate it!"

"Mrs. Borg!" Hassad was losing patience; the glitter in his black eyes had become a gloss of fury, and his face was tense. "Listen to what I have to say. For the sake of the child you're carrying, listen!"

That sobered her. In a moment, she caught his eyes, held them. "I'm listening."

He leafed through the file in his hands, apparently wanting to control his own rage, his impatience. "My people are very good, very thorough," he said finally. "Even though they've had little time, they have learned a good deal about you, about the man who is now your husband. And about the five young men who lived in your neighborhood in Reseda, California."

Lori felt her heart drop.

"There is an absence which is unexplained," Hassad went on. "You were reported missing. The five young men were reported missing. And an aging alcoholic, whose name was Harry Borg, was also missing for an extended period of time. All of you returned at about the same time. The man I know as Harry Borg is anything but an aging alcoholic. And in addition, the young man Chadwick Harrison returned with a young lady, presumably his wife. She lives with his parents when he is away, closely guarded by his father, a retired colonel of the Air Corps." He hesitated. "The neighbors describe her as unusual in appearance." He frowned. "She seems to be covered with—fur?"

He looked at Lori. "Fur. Is that correct?"

"On a lady? Like a mink coat?"

"On her body," Hassad said, checking the file. "Like a cat."

"You mean that?"

"I have it in the file."

"Cat fur on a lady? That I'd like to see!"

"You know nothing of such a person?"

"Of course not!"

Lori was lying. The young lady in question was Illia.

Chad had saved her from being used as food by the Jassans, and her body was covered with soft, gray fur, as were the bodies of all bassoes, the Jassan equivalent of humans. Chad had brought her to Earth as his wife, and, as Hassad had said, when he was away, she lived in the loving and fiercely protective care of his parents. "Finest daughter-in-law a man ever had!" was the way Colonel Jack Harrison described her.

"Fur," Hassad said. "Humph." There was enough doubt in his mind, at least, to let the matter rest until a further check could be made. He turned a page.

"The explanations given for the absence of all of you were accepted. But to me they sounded manufactured. And the explanation for the change in Harry Borg—that he had been in a detoxification hospital—is ridiculous."

He lifted his eyes from the file. "Where were you, Mrs. Borg."

"Visiting friends, like it says."

"And where did Harry Borg get Vec-Power?"

"He invented it."

"And how was he transformed from an aging alcoholic into a young athlete of incredible physical abilities?"

"He was de-toxed."

Ahmed Hassad got to his feet. He was still in control of himself, but only just barely—that was clear. "Mrs. Borg, I want the answers to those questions. And I'm going to have them, one way or another. Within three days. Mark that—three days!"

"Lots of luck."

"I can extract the answers from you. But it would cost you your life, and certainly the life of your unborn child. I'd rather use a more civilized means: persuasion. The offer of unlimited wealth for all of you who disappeared and reappeared. Come with me, all of you, and you will be safe. Refuse, and you will all die."

Her eyes were gray ice as she returned his stare. "You can kill me, but you won't live to tell about it."

He walked away. He watched two men take down a painting and carry it out of the room. Then he turned to look at her.

"You could persuade your husband," he said. "If you explained to him the alternatives, and told him you believed it best if he joined with me, I think he would come."

"I don't."

"I can see that he gets your message, if you will send it."

"No way."

"You will all die if you don't send it."

"I'm not so sure."

"You have a little time to think about it, to change your mind, but not much. A day, possibly less."

"A week. A month. Who cares?"

"One of your guardians will contact me the instant you change your mind."

"Don't hold your breath."

He continued to look at her a long moment. And then the faintest of smiles touched his lips.

"I like your courage," he said. "You might do to take along."

With that, he turned again and walked out of the room.

That had been hours ago. Now, standing at the window, her arms crossed under her breasts, elbows cupped in her palms, she felt a stir in her womb, a kick, and she dropped her hand to cover the spot.

"You awake, Charlie?" she asked telepathically.

The soft hum changed tone. Or at least she thought it did. It seemed to her the tone had become more alert, if only just slightly.

"Call me a nut, but I think you're listening."

If not, then why the kick at just that moment?

"Right on, honey!" She even said that aloud.

Another kick.

"Mama's got problems," she said. "But don't you worry none."

She was trying for a light tone, hoping to reduce the possibility that her fear would communicate to the unborn child. But it was a faint hope. She was very afraid.

The sweat that broke out all over her body now was proof of that. A light sweat, a faint prickly feeling on her skin, a sinking, lost sensation in the pit of her stomach.

Hassad had meant every word he had said. She never doubted it.

She remembered her own weak attempts at defiance. Smart-ass repartee? Whistling past a graveyard? God, she must have sounded silly. But what else could she have done? Given that bastard the satisfaction of seeing her crawl? Not by a damn sight!

What the hell was he up to? Why the big rush? Why the moving out?

She hugged her arms beneath her breasts.

"What's happening?" she asked.

Chapter 9

There was light at the head of the stairs. A dim glow radiating from some low source marked the top of the stairs and the floor of the upper hall, leaving the rest of the upstairs in darkness. A forbidding darkness that might be holding unimagined dangers for an uninvited stranger.

And Guss Rassan knew he was certainly that. Worse, he was a lizard-looking uninvited stranger. They were two lizard-looking strangers, he and Sissi.

Guss had stopped on the stairs with his head just level with the upper floor. Sissi was two steps down, her hand on his hips to maintain contact, waiting.

"What's wrong now?" she asked.

Her telepathic voice had been a conspiratorial whisper. Deep-pile carpet on the stair muffled any vibration Guss could translate as sound, the kind humans could hear.

"I'm testing," he answered.

He was reaching out with his tongue, the forked tips curling, fluttering, sampling scents. There were so many!

He had, of course, in knowing Harry Borg and his young humans, learned the many odors of the human bodies. And there were very many, indeed. They covered themselves with many fragrances in their efforts to conceal their natural body odors! What foolishness! Not that their natural smell was what any Jassan could call pleasant. Far from it! But as long as it was natural, why be ashamed of it!

"Well?"

"All right!" Guss said. "I've got to be careful!"

"How many are there?"

"Two adults down that way. And two young ones—a male, a female—this way."

"You sure?"

"No."

"Zat!"

"Curses won't help."

"Guss, you've got to do something! You can't go on standing here!"

"They're going to be afraid, Sissi!"

"*They're* going to be afraid! I'm frightened to death now!"

"I'm not. I tremble like this all the time."

A feeble joke.

The truth was, he had never been more frightened in his life. It was not enough that he was in a strange world; he was prowling in a human habitation in the dark, liable to meet many mortal dangers he didn't even know about, had never heard of, couldn't imagine, and couldn't hope to be prepared for. While he couldn't harm the humans, they could certainly harm him and Sissi. And probably, out of fear, they would try. They would think they had to preserve their lives.

He couldn't *tell* them he and Sissi meant them no harm. He couldn't *tell* them he and Sissi were here to save them, to save their entire world from extinction. He couldn't even say, "Greetings. I'm from Jassa and I'm a friendly monster."

"Rass Osis! What a liss!"

He was sweating.

The mind-blanker, the small yellow tube he was clutching in his eight-fingered hand, seemed very inadequate. Even useless. What if it didn't work? He only had Ross's word that it would. He should have tested it.

"Give me that thing," Sissi said. "I'll do it!"

"No, it's my task."

Her demand, and her hand pushing on his hip, and the fact he had to do something, even if it was wrong, got him moving again. He climbed the last few stairs and stepped out into the hallway. Sissi was close behind him. Her tongue, like his, was a blur, flickering in and out, sampling the airs; her golden eyes, like his, gleamed like the eyes of a cat when the slightest light caught them. She followed him as he moved slowly, cautiously, toward the first door on the right.

There, against the wall, stood a small table.

Guss could see it in the soft glow of a distant wall-receptacle night-light, but Sissi, behind him, could not. She stumbled into the table, driving it against the wall. And that caused distinct vibrations they both felt clearly.

It was noise, they knew, for humans. They both froze, too frightened to move.

In the dark bedroom, Sara Bushby lifted her head from the pillow. "What was that?"

"I thought you were asleep," George said.

"I was."

"Liar," he said gently.

"Well, what was it?"

He was not unduly concerned. "Jackie, probably. Walking in his sleep again."

"Are you sure?"

"What else?" And then, quietly, "Don't call. We're supposed to wake him slowly, remember?"

"Of course I remember!" she said impatiently.

He pushed back the covers, swung his feet to the floor, and sat up on the edge of the bed. Sara reached out and turned her bedside lamp on low.

"I wish we could do something about it," she said.

"About what?"

"His sleepwalking."

"He'll grow out of it."

"You keep saying that."

"Well, I ought to know. I was one. And a bed wetter, too."

"But he might get hurt, fall down the stairs, or something."

"I used to climb out upstairs windows." He fumbled around for his bedroom slippers. "There's a special angel that looks after sleepwalking small boys." He found his slippers. "And drunks."

"That helps!" she said, as if it didn't at all.

He was standing now, a tall, lean man in baggy pajamas. Prematurely gray, uncombed hair, a thoughtful face: he looked more like an academician than a war hero, though he was both. He scratched. He sighed. Reaching for a robe, he stopped to listen.

The house was silent.

"Guess he went back to bed."

They both listened.

In the dark hallway, Guss and Sissi were still frozen. They had felt the vibrations of the human voices, knew the humans were awake. But Guss and Sissi didn't know what to expect.

"Did we wake them up?" Sissi asked telepathically.

"Of course! They don't communicate in their sleep!"

"So?"

"The male will come out first. I'll blank him."

Guss got a firm grip on the yellow tube, his thumb on the button.

In the bedroom, Sara said, "George. Go see—please?"

"I'm going," George said tiredly.

He walked to the door. There was a light switch by the door that turned the hall lights on, and he touched that switch out of habit as he went through the doorway.

The sudden, unexpected light startled Guss. He almost dropped the yellow tube.

George Bushby, expecting no one, or at the most his son, Jackie, was equally startled. At best, he would have needed a second or two before being able to act. On seeing what he saw, he was held even longer. A prowler!

Wearing a lizard mask?

Two prowlers, wearing lizard masks?

Hastily, Guss leveled the tube at George. He tried to push the button that would release the ray. His thumb had slipped, or the tube had turned—there was no ray!

"Guss!" Sissi's cry was frightened.

The human was lunging straight at Guss, who finally found the button and got the ray to flash. Barely in time, for the human, though suddenly mindless, kept coming and stumbled into Guss, knocking him back against Sissi, who bumped into the table again, knocking it over, causing very considerable vibrations.

"George!" It was Sara. "What happened?"

Her anxious cry was followed by the thud of her feet.

Guss had his arms full of George. Sissi snatched the yellow tube from his hand, and when Sara Bushby appeared in the doorway, Sissi caught her with the ray almost instantly. The woman, her mind blanked, stopped. And remained stopped, eyes empty, staring.

Sissi looked at the yellow tube. "Amazing."

Guss was trying to steady the mindless George against the wall. "What is?"

"This mind-blanker—the way it works. Ziss! They're gone."

"Come on! Help me!"

Together, they managed to lead the two humans back into their bedroom and back to the bed, and got them to lie down. Guss suddenly sat down in a chair.

"What's wrong?"

"Look at me!" He held out shaking hands. "And my legs!"

"Oh, for Osis oss! At a time like this?"

"Just give me a minute."

"There may be others!"

"I know there are—the children."

The encounter of the past moments, the fear, the effort, had drained him. He wasn't the one for this kind of endeavor—that was clear. Almost plaintively, he took time to think, What am I *doing* here? I'm an artist! Not an assassin! Sneaking around in the dark! Blanking humans! Great Essnia!

Sissi was waiting anxiously.

"So I whimper," he said. He forced himself to his feet and tested his legs. They held him, though not very well, and he led the way back into the hall. His tongue flickering, forked tips curling, found the odor of the male child, and he followed it to another door. Moving very carefully, Guss reached in and found the now-familiar light switch, flipped it on, and moved quickly into the room, the mind-blanker aimed.

The bed was empty. Newly slept in, rumpled, but empty.

"He's gone!" Guss said.

"I can see that," Sissi said at his elbow.

Her tongue had been searching. "Guss—" She pointed to a closet door. "He's in there—they are *both* in there."

Guss's tongue had confirmed it. And there was another odor that worried him. Sharp, pungent. A strange odor— lubricant! Lubricant meant metal, and metal meant weapon. Could the child be armed?

"I could turn the blanker up," he said nervously. "I could blank him through the door. If it will go through the door."

"You don't know?"

"No, I don't know!"

"It might go through and kill him. Turned up, I mean."

"So I can't do it."

Guss took a moment, gathering strength, then charged across the room and jerked the door open.

A flash of light! A sharp concussion!

Guss had seen two human children the instant he opened the door, crouched on the floor. One, the male, had been holding a weapon—if a single-shot .410-gauge shotgun, a present from his father on the occasion of his ninth birthday, could be called a weapon—and he had discharged the weapon the moment the door had opened.

The small wad of shot, quite lethal at that distance, had gone by Guss's head, barely a miss, scaring what was left to scare clean out of him. But he had managed to fire the mind-blanker, pinning the children in the yellow spot. Then he staggered back to collapse on the bed.

Sissi moved to the closet door. "Oh, Guss! Look at this!"

"You look," Guss said helplessly.

Sissi was all but overcome with what she had found. The small male child had gotten the smaller female child, and they'd hidden in this little room where all the clothing was hanging—and he'd been protecting her!

"Isn't that the bravest thing?"

"He tried to *kill* me!"

"But of course!"

"Doesn't it matter to you?"

"You know it does."

"A little sympathy, then."

"You're grown. This is a brave little child!"

"Who needs brave children?" he asked plaintively.

The children had not moved after the yellow ray had touched them. Their eyes were blank, unafraid, even unknowing. But their positions told their story. The little female was crouched behind the slightly larger male, and the male was still clutching the black metal tube that had emitted the flash and concussion.

"She's so pretty!" Sissi said. "Come see, Guss."

Guss was lying on his back on the bed, eyes still on the ceiling. His tongue was hanging limply from his jaw; the gray film was across his golden eyes. Before lying back, he had looked at a little window on the yellow tube that held an indicator.

"We've got to tie them up," he said without moving.

Sissi was leading the children from the closet.

"Don't be ridiculous! Tie these little things?"

She had fallen in love with both children. Especially the little female child, sleep-tousled, wearing pajamas, big brown eyes, brown curls, and the softest skin. And the little male! Though his eyes were blank, his young face still wore traces of a look she would have to call defiance.

"We've got to tie those little things," Guss said. "And the big things, too."

"But why?"

He sighed heavily. "The mind-blanker's empty."

CHAPTER 10

It was full daylight when George Bushby returned to knowing. The transformation was gradual, a matter of a few minutes, of moving from a state of nothingness to complete awareness. The crack in the ceiling plaster, a memento of a past quake he'd been meaning to repair for months, was his first reassurance that he was alive and lying on his own bed. And a turn of his head revealed Sara beside him, sleeping.

Sleeping? With her eyes open?

"Sara!"

She didn't answer.

He was awash with sudden panic. Trying to reach her, he found he was tied. Tied at the wrists and at the ankles. A quick convulsive heave, and he managed to roll enough so he could lift his head and look at her face. Her eyes were open, but they were blank, untroubled, staring at nothing. Her color was normal; she was breathing easily. She was unharmed—save for the blankness.

Another concern hit him. "Jackie!" he roared. "Jackie! Where are you?"

Lying stiffly, head lifted, he listened.

No answer.

He fought his bonds in a sudden fury, struggling to break them, to tear his hands free. It was no use. He collapsed, panting hard. His mind was a seething caldron of fear—fear for the children.

The prowlers in the lizard masks! Had they hurt the children? Visions of brutal, senseless murders of children he had read of just recently in the newspapers flashed in his mind. And again he fought the bonds, sweating, panting, roaring the names of the children.

He didn't hear the running feet in the hall. And he didn't see Sissi come caroming into the bedroom, didn't know she was there until she leaned over him. And because she was doing it telepathically, he didn't know she was yelling frantically.

"Guss! It's the male! The adult! He's awake!"

Guss, who had been exploring in the family room, responded with a panic of his own. "He's still tied, isn't he?"

"Yes, but he's turned savage!"

"Don't get too close to him. I'm coming!"

George Bushby's furious, almost insane struggle began to slow as his mind began to assimilate what his eyes were reporting. That—that wasn't a lizard mask this prowler was wearing. It couldn't be. It was too real. That long, forked tongue flickering like a little red flame—that was too real. It *was* real! It couldn't be real. Impossible! But how could it not be? And those large, golden eyes—*vertical pupils*! My God, *it's a reptile*! A reptile wearing clothes—wearing weapons? A sword, a holstered gun. Battle fatigues, for God's sake, GI from the word go. Even an emblem! A red flame! There was no such outfit.

All that crashed into George's awareness in an explosion of realizations that came in as an incoherent jumble. Jumble or not, it had a powerful impact. His utter astonishment washed the immediate fears away; he could only stare, trying to comprehend, to believe.

And Guss came running in to find Sissi worried out of her mind, standing away from the male human, watching him fearfully.

"He's still tied?"

"Yes. But he's fighting to get loose—or was."

And George was thinking, Well, for Christ's sake! as he stared at Guss and Sissi with bewildered, unbelieving eyes. There's two of them! A male and a female, sure as hell! Good God a'mighty, can you believe this? Then, crashing in on him again: What've they done to the kids? The thought set him twisting at his bonds in another fury.

"Where's my kids? What've you done to them?"

Neither Guss nor Sissi could make anything of the percussive vibrations of his voice, but Sissi, perhaps because she was female, was quick to guess the cause. "He's worried about the children!"

And she wheeled away from the bed and ran out of the room, to return in a moment, leading Jackie and Jillie by the hands.

"You untied them!" Guss said.

"Had to, didn't I? To bring them?"

She led the children toward the bed. Their minds were blank, their eyes unseeing, but clearly they had not been physically harmed. She brought the two close to the bed so George Bushby could see them.

"We didn't hurt them! See?" She lifted Jillie's arm to show it functioned. "She's just been blanked. She'll be all right."

But of course George couldn't hear her.

"He doesn't know what you're saying," Guss said.

"He can see, can't he?"

Sissi then went on with pantomime, petting the children, trying her best to make reassuring motions to persuade the adult human that his offspring had not been harmed.

She was no great pantomimist, but Guss had to admit she made a little progress. As he watched, the male human quieted down, his eyes, moving from her to the children, found no blood, no broken skin, no bruises, and that seemed to reassure him. But then the blank look in their eyes, the wide-eyed unconsciousness, penetrated. He lurched to look at the adult female beside him, saw she was afflicted in the same way, and turned a hot, demanding stare on Guss.

"What've you done to them?"

"I think he wants to know what's wrong with them," Guss said to Sissi.

"That's it."

"Tell him they were mind-blanked, like he was. They'll be all right when it wears off."

"I don't know how! He can't hear me!"

"You were doing all right with the pantomime."

"How do you pantomime a mind-blanker, for Osis sake?"

Watching them, George Bushby realized they were communicating with each other. Silently. They had to be, the way they looked at each other and reacted to each other. Signals of some kind? What signals? He couldn't see any. Telepathy? Come on! There was no such thing! No way, a—*telepathy*? Really?

It pretty near *had* to be.

And there was something else: The way they were interacting, the way they were looking at each other— they were worried! There was no other possible translation. They were both worried to a point of desperation.

The male was throwing his head about, waving his hands—
eight fingers!

There were eight fingers on his hands. Good Lord
almighty, George thought. I'm losing my mind. He's a
creature from outer space in my bedroom? Get outa here!
It's not possible. From outer space, a creature? Like UFOs
and all that?

"Who are you?" he yelled suddenly. "Where'd you
come from?"

His sudden change of expression, his sudden intensity,
the jarring percussion of what had to be a demanding
question was not hard to interpret.

"He wants to know about us," Guss said.

"You're right."

"Sissi, we've got to tell him—who we are, where we're
from, why we're here. He won't help us if we don't. He
thinks we're monsters now. He'll kill us if he gets loose!"

"Don't say that!"

"It's true! He's got weapons. All kinds of weapons.
And pictures of soldiers. *He* was a soldier."

"Osis help us!"

"You've got to tell him."

"*I've* got to tell him? *You* tell him!"

"Oh, zat!"

George, who had watched this exchange with sharp
attention, knew they were arguing. But about what, he
couldn't know. Now the male impatiently pushed the
female aside and came to the edge of the bed. He was a
moment, thinking, preparing himself, obviously, and then
he began pantomiming. Watching, George realized it was
a "Me Tarzan, you Jane" routine, so clumsy, so inept, it
would have been laughable under other circumstances.
The creature could not find a way to tell him who or what
Tarzan was. And then, realizing he was only making himself look ridiculous, the creature gave up in disgust.

"It's no use—I can't do it.".

"That's a help!"

The female child chose that moment to awaken with a wail.

"Daddy!"

She broke away from Sissi, ran and climbed up on the bed, throwing her arms around her father's neck. In that moment, the indication of normality was cause for triumph to Sissi.

"See? See? She's all right!"

The child was a moment discovering her father was tied, then her mother, and, squalling loudly, wanted to know why, and who, and all the rest. Her father tried to comfort her. "Shush, shush, shush."

"Waaaah, Daddy!"

"All right! It's all right! You're a big girl! Stop it!"

She stopped it. After all, she was six.

Her round brown eyes looked, and saw Sissi and Guss clearly for the first time. Her eyes got bigger and rounder.

"They're not *people*!" She turned to her father, eyes huge.

"No, honey. They're—they're visitors. They won't hurt us!"

Keerist, he thought. I hope they won't!

"They look funny!"

"They're different is all. Remember *Star Wars*? Those creatures? Nothing to scare you. They're friendly."

Anything to quiet her fears. And he might even be right! Outer-space creatures? *For real?*

He was beginning to accept it.

"They're going to untie us in a minute," he told Jillie. "As soon as we get better acquainted. Mommy's all right— just sleeping."

Through all this, Guss and Sissi were standing by help-lessly. They were trying to look and act friendly, to show they were harmless. When the little female looked at her, Sissi made patting gestures in the air, bowed, and curtsied. Guss tried to copy her and managed a clumsy success.

"It's working," Guss told her. "Keep it up."

"They're really just like bassoes," Sissi said, encouraged.

"Don't you believe it! That big male is lethal!"

But it did seem they were making progress.

Then the male child awakened. And he was something else. Afterward, Guss was sure the child had awakened moments before and had been pretending he was still blank. Sharp little devil. Whatever, he moved suddenly without any prior clue, ducked under Guss's arm, and ran for the bedroom door.

"Watch him!" Guss yelled at Sissi.

They both ran for the boy.

Once in the hall, Jackie got his head down and ran hard. At nine years old, he was fast at any time; scared, he was greased lighting. What he wanted was the .357 Magnum revolver his father kept atop his gun cabinet, and though he had been forbidden to touch it, even though it was unloaded and the shells kept in a drawer below, it seemed to him this was an emergency that would allow breaking the rules. They were being invaded by outer-space creatures—his dad had said so! Goshamighty! He'd even been tied up!

So he'd missed with the .410. Give him another chance and he wouldn't miss!

"That .357's enough gun to take hunting elephants," his dad had said. "Blow a hole in a tank."

Mostly to keep him from fooling with it, Jackie knew. But it was powerful, that was for sure. And the thought was in his head as he went flying down the stairs that if he could grab the gun, snatch the shells out of the bottom drawer, and get outside where he'd have room to maneuver and load up, he'd show those creatures how to suck eggs.

That's what his granddad used to say: "How to suck eggs."

Jackie was fast, but Guss was faster, his legs longer. Guss leaped down the stairs and almost caught the boy at the entrance to the family room. Guss knew there were weapons in the gun cabinet, even though he didn't know what kind or how they worked. And he knew the big glass door was a means of escape. His intentions were only to prevent the young male's getting a weapon or getting away.

"Sissi!" he was yelling telepathically. "Come help!"

"I'm here, I'm here!" She had come into the family room almost on his heels, and she had presence of mind enough to race to the glass door to block the little human's escape. "Don't hurt him!"

"He's after a weapon!"

"Don't let him get one!"

After his first lunge at the gun cabinet, Jackie had veered away, not wanting to reveal the presence of the .357 revolver and knowing he lacked the time to get a shotgun or a rifle. He wanted to get out of the house now but found the monsters had the way blocked.

"You dirty lizards!"

They were closing in on him. He lunged to the pool table that stood in the middle of the room, grabbed two pool balls, threw them, and missed. Grabbed two more and hit the biggest monster in the chest.

"Frass!" Guss swore. "That hurt!"

"Don't be a whisser! Catch him!"

They ran at Jackie from either side of the table. He dropped and skidded under the table, seeming to disappear. As they searched frantically, he squirted out the far side, making for the inner door. Guss managed to get there first and block the way. Jackie turned at once, ran, and jumped up to stand atop the pool table, where he began throwing pool balls again. He hit targets and they hurt.

"Leave me alone!" Jackie yelled.

"Oh, stop it," Sissi pleaded. "We won't hurt you."

"Get out of here!" Jackie yelled.

"Hold still, you little riss!"

"I'll kill yuh! I'll kill yuh both!"

The boy couldn't hear them, and they couldn't hear the boy, but it didn't make any difference to either side. They had to say something, however they said it, because intense effort requires expletives to achieve any success at all. Profanity or threats—what difference?

"Got him!" Guss had lunged and clamped an eight-fingered hand around Jackie's ankle, only to find he had hold of a raging, scratching, hitting, biting fury. He hung on, suffering the abuse, until Sissi could help him, and together they were able to pin Jackie down on the green felt of the pool table.

"I'll hold him," Guss said after strengthening his grip. "Get something to tie him again."

When Jackie felt his wrists tied, he stopped struggling. No use wasting his strength, he knew. They had him—for now. But he still knew where the .357 was and where the shells were, and he would get to them sooner or later. All he had to do was fool them into thinking he was their turkey.

"There now." Sissi was pleased at his apparent surrender. "He was just excited." They had Jackie standing. She straightened his pajamas and patted his hair down. "He's going to be all right."

Guss was nursing a bite on his hand. "Isn't he the bravest thing?" he said with great sarcasm.

"Well, he is!" Sissi said defiantly.

They took him upstairs, where Sissi ushered him in for his father's inspection.

"Jackie!" George was straining at his bonds. "You all right?"

"Yeah, Dad." Jackie was sorry. "I tried to get the—you know what? On top of the you know?—but I didn't have time."

"Good Lord, son!"

"It's still there! They don't know about it."

"But you shouldn't have—" He sank back. "Good kid for trying!"

He was looking anxiously at the two lizard-type invaders for their reactions, to see if they knew what Jackie had been talking about—apparently not. They were still doing their pantomime routines. The female was even pushing Jackie toward his father.

"C'mere, Jackie," George said. "Get up on the bed."

The boy obeyed, hindered only a little by his bound wrists. "What's the matter with Mom?"

"In a faint of some kind," George told him. "I think we all fainted. We came out of it, and I'm sure she will." He was watching the lizard-people. "We've got to be careful, Jackie. Very careful. I don't know what these creatures are. Where they came from, why they're here, how many more there are—anything."

"They're lizards!" Jillie said.

"They seem to be."

"George! George!" It was Sara, returning to awareness.

"Jillie! Cover her eyes—until I can tell her—"

Jillie moved quickly to obey. Sara began struggling, becoming alarmed, then frightened.

"George! What *is* this?"

"Sara! Sara! Listen to me!"

George Bushby had a few difficult moments blocking Sara's panic, persuading her there was no immediate danger from—and how do you explain something like this:

creatures from outer space in your bedroom at eight o'clock in the morning? He managed—Sara was a real gutsy gal—but she didn't believe a damn word of it.

"It's some kind of a joke. A very bad joke."

"No, Sara. It's for real."

While George had been trying to stabilize his family, Guss and Sissi were suffering an emotional wring-out equal to or exceeding that of the humans. Their situation was even more perilous. If they couldn't make friends with these humans, if they couldn't make contact, they were dead. Dead, any way they looked at it. And, for that matter, so were these people—when the nuclear bomb went off.

"He's telling them we're friends," Sissi said.

"I don't know about that."

"But he is, Guss! See, the adult female has quieted down."

"Sissi, for Osis sake! Wouldn't you? I mean, wouldn't you *pretend* you were friendly, if you were in their predicament? Until you could get loose, get a weapon?"

"Oh, liss." She could see he had a point. "But we've got to trust them, to make them trust us."

"But let's keep them tied until we're sure."

George said to Sara, "They're talking to each other, hon. Can you see that? I don't know how they do it. Telepathy, I think. Must be."

"I didn't hear anything."

Sara was watching the two strangers now. There'd been a moment of sheer terror when she'd first seen them, but the terror had passed, perhaps drowned in utter astonishment at the uniqueness of the situation.

"George, have they hurt any of us?"

"No. Not really. And that's something. They've been trying to act friendly."

"Can we trust them?"

"Hell, no!"

"What can we do?"

"Try to fool them into thinking we're harmless, until I can get to a telephone—or get my hands on a gun." He lifted his head to look at the children. "Got that. You, too, Jackie! Leave the fighting to me."

"Dad, I almost—"

"You did fine! But no more—that's an order!"

"Yeah, Dad." A disappointed agreement.

Guss and Sissi could see that the adult male human was establishing dominance and control over his brood: they were relaxing, in a sense drawing behind him. But there was no arguing that he had become less dangerous. He was just more controlled.

"We've got to be very, very careful," Guss said to Sissi.

She was looking at them thoughtfully. "We've got to feed them, Guss."

"I suppose so."

"And they've got to go—you know—missie."

"Oy!" Guss said in helpless despair.

CHAPTER 11

Knowing humans—and in knowing Harry Borg and the young men of Harry's cadre, Guss knew humans well enough—Guss knew that "going missie" at frequent intervals was a necessity if human well-being and peace of mind were to be considered. But the subject was so lacking in delicacy, so coarse, he wanted nothing to do with it. And yet, he was later forced to admit, dealing with the problem would prove to be perhaps the single most helpful step toward establishing a rapport with the Bushby family on this their first morning with them, the morning of Saturday, April 5.

Rapport was so important!

Put in the simplest terms. it was a matter of life and death: for the Bushby family, for the world in which the Bushby family lived, for the lives of him and Sissi.

Time was so short! After this day, only four remained until the nuclear device would be detonated!

The device was on the east coast of this continent.

Guss and Sissi and the Bushby family were on the west coast. Harry Borg, who was the one who would be most likely able to prevent the bomb from being detonated, was nowhere to be found. All of which meant that if the civilization of the humans—and Guss used the description with reservations—were to be saved from extinction, he, Guss Rassan, was going to have to do it.

And he, Guss Rassan, was going to need help. He admitted that now.

He would need the help of at least one capable human—more, if he could get them, to be sure; but one, to start with, was essential. His choices were limited. There were these humans he had tied up on the sleeping pad, and that was about it. Fortunately, the memorabilia on display in the room below—weapons, photographs in uniform, medals—suggested that the male human had been a warrior of some skill and bravery. But without being able to speak the language, and appearing to them to be some kind of a monster, how was he to win the male's support? Clearly, it was impossible.

Until the matter of "going missie" arose.

Sissi—Osis bless her!—was inordinately concerned about the need, and she insisted it be attended to before anything else was done. With that in mind, she chose the adult female as her first subject, feeling that if the parent were shown that they, Sissi and Guss, were truly only concerned about the good health and peace of mind of the humans, the parent would persuade the others. Sissi untied the female and, with rather more coaxing than threatening, ushered her into the room where the facilities made her purpose obvious.

When she returned from the bathroom, Sara had a glass of water, George's blood-pressure pills, and his glasses. She was all smiles. "She just wanted me to go to the bathroom!"

George accepted the pills, swallowed them with water from the glass she held, and let her set his glasses on his nose.

"That's all?" George had been puzzled, even frightened, when the female had taken Sara away. He certainly hadn't expected this. "Just wanted you to take a—"

"That's all!" Sara said hurriedly. "And she was, well, actually sweet about it. She turned her head away. Wasn't that thoughtful?"

"I'll be darned!"

Sissi was pantomiming again.

After reading it, Sara was even more pleased. "Now she wants the children to go!"

George read the pantomime the same way.

"You're next, Jillie."

Jillie, round like her mother, her big brown eyes bright, said, "And do I have to go!"

Her mother, seeing she had permission from Sissi, helped the little girl into the bathroom. While they were gone, Jackie, the freckled-faced gladiator, began to get heroic ideas again.

"Dad, if I get a chance, can't I—"

"I said no!"

"Okay, okay! You don't have to bite my head off."

"The rest of us are hostages!"

"Yessir."

"And besides, I'm thinking."

George's lean scholar's face had, in fact, grown thoughtful.

Guss had been watching anxiously—though the expression in his yellow, slitted eyes was read by the humans as mean and threatening—and when Sara and Jillie returned, again smiling, he voiced his relief to Sissi. "By Sarsiss! I believe you have it!"

"Have what?" she asked.

"Their trust."

"The females', maybe." Sissi was eyeing George and Jackie. "But I'm not so sure about the males. They may be just waiting."

"What about them? I mean, going—in there—"

"They're males," Sissi pointed out.

"You're right," Guss said resignedly.

He took his esso from his pocket. All he had in mind was a pantomime of aiming and shooting to demonstrate what could happen if the males tried to overpower him. But the weapon scared the wallop out of the young male.

"He's going to shoot us!"

"Idiot!" Sissi screamed at Guss. "Put that away!"

George, alarmed, said, "Hey! What the hell?—"

To Sissi, Guss complained, "I just wanted to show them—"

"You showed them, all right! The little one thought you were going to kill them!"

"How could he? I just—"

"And I had them trusting us!"

She had more to say. The exchange was carried on at almost the top of Sissi's mental powers. When Sissi was upset, and she was very upset now, she was inclined to scream. Her screams were telepathic, of course, but they could be heard by another telepath at a considerable distance. In this instance, she was heard by a telepath almost a kilometer away.

Guss finally got a word in edgewise. "Zat!" he said.

He put the esso back in his pocket and then gripped Sissi around the muzzle until he was sure he had her stopped. George was relieved. He had been watching closely, and there had been no way for him to misread what he had seen: The male had angered the female when he had drawn the weapon. She had chewed him out. And he had shut her up by gripping her nose. But she had won.

It figured.

"It's all right, son."

"I gotta go!" Jackie said.

Guss untied the youngster, and with no more than a threat to whack him on the side of the head if he tried anything, took the boy to the bathroom.

"Just do your thing and come back!" his father called.

"I hear you!" Jackie said.

George was next. He behaved perfectly. He was still thinking.

While Guss and George were in the bathroom, Sissi worked hard at pantomiming for Sara, and when the two returned, George found that Sara was quite pleased with the way things were working out.

"She wants me to fix us breakfast!"

"Yeah?" George asked as he was tied again. "In return for what?"

"Nothing. I promised I wouldn't try to run away was all." She paused. "They know about telephones, George. See, she took ours out."

George saw that the bedside phone was gone.

"We can yell out the window," Jackie said.

"No you don't!" his father said.

Guss finished tying George and helped him back on the bed.

"What's going on?" Guss asked Sissi.

"The female is going to prepare food."

"You trust her that much?"

"Have we any choice?"

Guss lifted his hands.

Sara prepared a breakfast of hotcakes, butter, and maple syrup. Sara was a little surprised at herself to find that her fear of the lizard-looking aliens had diminished to almost nothing. They had shown they were concerned about her family's comfort and well-being—and that was

the direct opposite of threatening your life, now, wasn't
it? And they were, well, kind of nice when you got used
to the way they looked. Besides, preparing breakfast was
a soothing occupation in and of itself—a familiar routine,
so to say. She even hummed to herself as she went about
it.

Sissi stood close by to see that the woman did not
violate security—her golden eyes were sharp, her forked
tongue flicked constantly—and she also swallowed a lot.

Sara recognized the symptoms. "You must be hungry!"
She pantomimed the act of eating.

"I could eat an url!" Sissi agreed.

She was, in all truth, half starved, and she knew Guss
was too. The food the human female prepared for her
family looked appetizing, but on testing it with her split-
end tongue, Sissi found it to be overpoweringly sweet.

She shook her head in the universal negative.

And that worried Sara. Being a wife and a mother, she
took pride in her abilities, particularly in her ability as a
hostess who could satisfy the needs of any company in
her house—guests, captors, whatever.

"Don't you worry," she said. "We'll find something."

While her family was eating the breakfast—sitting on
the king-size bed, their feet tied, their hands free—Sara
went through her kitchen cupboards, searching, opening
one can after another, offering them to Sissi to taste and
reject. She finally found a can of something Sissi liked
very much. Sisi served Guss a helping of it before eating
one herself.

Guss was more than pleased. "Marvelous!" he said.
"Put this in the right kind of a container with a nice label,
and I could make a fortune at home!"

The food was Spam, of course.

All this time, George had gone on with his thinking.
After his initial fear for his family and himself had been

allayed by what seemed the desire of the aliens to be friendly, he had accepted the obvious fact that their presence in his house, however they had gotten there, offered opportunities. Golden opportunities.

What he had here was an exclusive!

Any exclusive was an automatic pot of gold in the marketplace, as any jackass knew. And an exclusive of this scope—Aliens from Outer Space, for Lord's sake!—had to be a bathtub of gold, even in the hands of a proven financial incompetent such as himself. There was no telling what might result from an exclusive of this importance—trade agreements, franchises for advanced technologies, markets for products of unimagined varieties and uses—shoot! The possibilities were endless!

But he had to *keep* it an exclusive!

"This is ours!" he told his family.

It was after breakfast, when they were all lined up on the king-size bed again, tied again—but carefully not tight enough to cause any of them any pain or real discomfort—and he had decided to give them the benefit of his thinking.

Guss was in the room, anxiously pacing, trying not to count the hour and minutes. Sissi, who had motioned him to silence, was at the bedside, watching the humans, trying to make some sense out of the vibrations that were coming through to her from their conversation, trying to find clues in their changing expressions.

"We've got to let them talk," she said.

"What if they're planning an attack?"

"Then we'll have to cope with it."

"That might be too late!"

"They'd be frightened if we separated them."

"I'm frightened when they're together."

George was saying, "We've got to *keep* this an exclusive until I can stake out a claim. And that won't be until

I can establish some kind of communication with them. All right?"

"If you say so," they all dutifully responded.

"That means I've got to call in sick," he said. "That's first. If I don't go in to the office on Monday, my secretary will call here. If she doesn't get through, she'll come. Or send someone. Lucky for us, it's Saturday, with today and tomorrow off. But I'll have to call."

"They've disconnected the phones," Sara pointed out.

"That's what I mean," George said. "That's our first problem."

After a moment, looking guilty, Jillie spoke up. "Not mine."

"Not your what?"

"My phone. They didn't disconnect it."

"Why not?"

George looked quickly at Sissi, who was watching intently, head tipped, large yellow eyes sharp, tongue flicking. She was smart, George knew. But how could she know what they were talking about? That was the good part.

Of course, it was the bad part, too.

"How come?" George asked Jillie, lowering his voice in spite of himself.

"It's under the bed," Jillie whispered.

"Go ahead and talk," Jackie said. "They can't hear you."

"Stay out of this," his father said.

Sara's interest was in the possible breach of discipline. "Why is your phone under your bed, young lady?"

"Sometimes I talk to Beth," Jillie confessed, eyes downcast, "after—you know—we're all in bed."

"Really!" Sara said, shocked.

"Hey, c'mon!" George said. "It's the break we need!" He thought for a moment. "But we've got another

problem. They're going to think we want to call for help—
to get somebody to come in and capture them." He half
scowled. "And all we really want to do is keep people
out! How d'you like that?"

"Not much," Jackie said.

"She likes me," Jillie offered. "The lady lizard, I mean."

"So?"

"Maybe I could fool her."

George looked at his small daughter, amazed.

"How old did you say this kid is?" he asked Sara.

"Six," her mother said. "As you very well know!"

"Females," George said wonderingly.

"All sneaky," Jackie agreed. He was beginning to enjoy
all this conspiratorial stuff. "But not you, Mom," he added
hurriedly.

"I should hope not!"

"At ease!" George said.

Sometimes the only way he could get their attention
was to go military. "Now hear this: Jillie's going to make
the call." He gave the child a nod. "I'll leave it to you
how you get it done. And when you get through to Helen,
say these exact words: 'Daddy says he's on hold the rest
of the week.' Those exact words, now, okay?"

"Daddy says he's on hold the rest of the week," Jillie
repeated.

"Code for 'Stall the creditors,'" George told Sara.

"I don't like her telling fibs, a little child!"

"You'll like it if we can save our skins." He smiled.
"Maybe you won't have to leave me, after all."

"I don't know about that," she said.

"Aw, c'mon!"

"Later, George."

"Okay, okay." He turned to include the kids. "Remember now, we're going to be nice to the aliens. Cooperative.
Willing. Most important, we don't want to let anybody

outside know they're here. Tell fibs if you have to, but keep it our secret. All right?"

"All right," they all agreed.

Then they looked at Sissi, smiling their best and most friendly smiles. Sissi, who hadn't a clue as to what they had been talking about, knew that whatever the subject had been, they had all agreed to show an attitude of warm friendship.

"What happened?" Guss asked.

"I don't know," Sissi said. "Whatever they decided, it seems the first step is to be cooperative. Look at them! Soss wouldn't melt in their mouths!"

It was true. They all looked innocent. Very innocent.

"It's a trick," Guss said despairingly. "To throw us off guard."

"It certainly could be," Sissi agreed.

"We've got to watch them every second!"

"And how long can we go on doing that?"

"I don't know. How *would* I know?" He looked at her, his golden eyes wide with what could only be fright. "But it won't be long. We haven't got long!"

"Guss, you're not going to panic?"

"Me? Panic? Don't be ridiculous!"

"You look scared."

"I am scared, but I can stand it—I think."

Sissi was scared, too. "What *are* we going to do?"

"Well," Guss said after thinking a moment, "that's up to you."

"Why me?"

"You're the one," he said. "I mean, you're able to get through to them. You seem to have a way. You—you can tell them why we're here, and all that—that we want to *help* them, not *hurt* them. I know you can do it!"

"You do?"

"Of course I do. You're clever!"

"Thanks a lot!"

"Sissi, I know you can do it!" Guss went on, gaining confidence. "Look at the way you got them to go missie, and prepare food. I'll do the guarding; you do the communicating. That's fair!"

"It is?"

"Isn't it?"

"I don't know."

"Sissi! You wanted to come. You've got to do your share!"

She was looking at him, golden eyes wide.

"Now what's the matter?"

"I think I'm losing my mind," she said.

CHAPTER 12

Oz Tess had been a career officer in the 15th Vessan Guard for fifteen years, and before that a nosser in the ranks, beginning at the very lowest grade; through the hardest kind of work, suffering through the totally degrading years of bowing and scraping to idiots of higher rank, he had worked himself up to Nesso Third. That position, in his view, entitled him to the privilege of spending his remaining years at Plessa, enjoying certain luxuries—lassa, norissa, and unlimited female companionship, to name a few—far away from anything resembling hazardous duty.

He had had his share of that, hadn't he?

He had spent seven years on the Eastern Front, where at any time the Ussirs could have begun a hassan exchange that would have meant almost certain death to thousands, himself included. That they had not, and that the time had been spent largely at exercises—which in themselves were not without risk—did not alter the basic fact that it had been hazardous duty. He had the medals to prove it!

And yet, even after seven years on the Eastern Front, seven years of faithful, unflinching service, who had they selected to lead the noss into the world of intelligent bassoes, charged with capturing Guss Rassan and the female, Sissi, and returning them, dead or alive, to pay for their criminal disobedience in a court of law?

Oz Tess, that's who!

"You stupid kess-ness!" his mate of twenty-three years had screamed at him. "If you had any guts, you'd tell them to take their medals and—"

Kissi was a good mate, but she could be vulgar at times—very vulgar when she was angry with him—and she had been very angry with him when she'd learned of his assignment.

"It's suicide!" she had screamed.

Now, standing in the fore room of the building that for centuries had been the residence of the Rassan family, and where the blundering sissal-player had broken a hole into the world of intelligent bassoes, the world they called Earth, or something, Oz Tess had to admit his mate had probably been right.

That is exactly what it was. Suicide!

If all the inhabitants were like Harry Borg and the other intelligent bassoes who had been in Jassa, it was a world of barbarians. Monsters might even be a better word for them.

Oz Tess, in contrast, knew himself to be finer goods. Rather slender, perhaps, but quite fit, and he knew he wore his green uniform well. Why send an officer of his caliber on a suicide mission?

Madness! That is what it was. Waste! Utter waste!

There were others less important to Jassa, less skilled in military techniques, less refined in appearance, who might be more easily spared. But none of those had been chosen.

He, Oz Tess, had been chosen.

Rasso, that sniveling risser, had pointed a finger at him and said, "You, Tess! You have just volunteered!"

Rasso had not told him how he was to find Guss Rassan after he had gone through the Gateway into the world of the intelligent bassoes. And if Guss Rassan were not just the other side of the Gateway, and if that world proved to be as big as their own—reports said it was identical— where in that world was he to look?

Absolute insanity!

Osis! They had the Gateway open!

Lss. Zass and Lss. Hass, the two nossers chosen from the ranks to accompany him, were both trying to hide the fact that they were almost paralyzed with fear. They were waiting at rigid attention, waiting for his command, yellow eyes bulging, tongues limp.

Assuming what he hoped was an appearance both debonair and stout-hearted, he tucked his liss stick under his arm, said, "Follow me," to his two deputies—his voice gone only a little shrill—and strode through the Gateway.

Into, he was sure, oblivion.

Joe Lansky, the manager of the Bedford Apartments, had known there was something funny going on in apartment 3-A from the very beginning, right from the day the old lush, Harry Borg, had disappeared. After his brother, or the big guy who claimed he was Harry's brother, had showed up and then disappeared, there had been strange noises. Toilets flushing? Water running? Television going? C'mon! There had to be somebody or something in there! Toilets don't flush themselves. Televisions don't go on and off by themselves.

But when he'd knocked on the door and then keyed himself in, there'd never been anybody there.

All right, Harry Borg was paid up. But a manager had responsibilities: he had to know who was using the apartment, and for what. And if he didn't know, he bloody well had to find out.

Joe Lansky never considered himself to be a hero type. He was old for that, past fifty, getting bald, and, sure, he was carrying thirty pounds of blubber. Sat around a lot, was why. Had to, with the way he was short of breath. Asthma. Had to be. The medics said it was just that he was out of condition, but what do doctors know?

He was grumbling like that to himself when he got his old army .45 pistol off the top shelf in the closet, worked the slide to check the load, and went next door and rapped.

"Yeah? Come in!"

Joe Lansky went into Fred Harrow's apartment and found the old bird at his easel, painting another of his messy blobs—the blobs said something to Fred, but nobody else in the world could make a bit of sense out of them—and told Fred he'd heard noises in 3-A again.

"Got to be somebody there this time."

"Flush the toilet?"

"The television. Sounded like Woody Woodpecker."

Fred was sixty, a World War II vet, tall, gray, balding. He had agreed to back Joe Lansky the next time they heard noises in 3-A. Now he put aside his palette, got his .38 police special, and together they went up the stairs to 3-A.

"You stand over there," Joe told Fred. "I'll key 'er open, and we'll go in together."

"Ought to knock first," Fred said.

"We tried that," Joe said. "Let's see if we can catch 'em this time." He slipped the key in quietly, turned it slowly, took a deep breath. "Let's go!"

Joe went in first, head down, .45 in his fist, rolling like a small tank down the short hall and into the living room, Fred right on his heels.

Kee-rist!

It all happened so fast.

Joe and Fred saw three of them. They looked like soldiers, or cops, in their uniforms and could have been from Syria or someplace, until you saw their faces. Like lizards, for Christ's sake! Big yellow eyes, muzzles, and when their mouths flew open, big, long forked tongues! And they were grabbing some kind of guns out of their holsters!

Oz Tess and his deputies had felt the vibrations of the door opening and had turned to see two of the intelligent bassoes come charging at them with weapons in their hands. Osis sake! Savages! Barbarian savages, bent on killing.

"Retreat!" Oz Tess screamed.

Retreat to where? The fools had closed the Gateway. They were trapped!

Oz Tess drew his esso in fumbling haste. Lss. Zass, who had had his esso in his hand from the very first moment they had entered the strange world, saw the shorter barbarian leveling his weapon, and fired in desperate haste.

Joe Lansky saw the purple ray, and then it killed him.

Fred killed Lss. Zass with one shot.

In the next instant, the Gateway opened. Oz Tess caught a hand in Lss. Hass's blouse and jerked him toward the opening, just as Hass fired his esso. The ray dissolved away the weapon and the hand of the tall barbarian. Then both Oz Tess and Lss. Hass fell back through the Gateway to the safety of their own world.

The Gateway closed.

Fred Harrow got a thumb on the artery under his upper

arm to stop the bleeding from the stump where his hand had been. He stared, unbelieving, at the space where the Invaders—what else could they have been?—had disappeared. He stared at the Invader he had killed, lying crumpled on the floor. He stared at Joe Lansky, whom the invaders had killed.

And then he yelled for help.

Among the many practices common to most governments—and those of Jassa and the United States were certainly not exceptions—was the practice of imposing an instant news blackout on every occurrence that might be of major interest to the public. It had first to be decided by those in power whether the occurrence was in fact of major importance, and then whether the public was capable of using the information wisely.

Such was certainly the case with the debacle in Harry Borg's apartment on the night of Saturday, April 5. Fortunately, the squad car that answered the call was driven by Sergeant Oscar Retten, a man with an active interest in UFO lore, a reader of science—and science fiction—publications, who had been a "Trekky" since the age of fourteen. He had no trouble at all in recognizing a real-life, in-the-flesh alien when he found one dead on the floor in Apartment 3-A, Bedford Apartments, Reseda, California.

He'd been expecting one for a long time.

"From Titan," he said, sucking a tooth. And added, for the less well informed, "That's one of Saturn's moons."

Sergeant Retten ordered the area closed and would allow no one to enter or leave. His superiors commended him for his actions and, going even farther, imposed a total news blackout immediately.

NEWS ITEM:

PRIME MINISTER TO ADDRESS
JOINT SESSION AS PLANNED

WASHINGTON—Prime Minister Margaret Thatcher will address a joint session of Congress Wednesday April 9, as reported earlier. The problems of reciprocal trade agreements, tariffs, monetary funds, and world population growth have been suggested as topics she will discuss. It is thought by many, however, that her real purpose for coming here is to explain why American cruise missiles can no longer be permitted on British soil . . .

CHAPTER 13

After leaving Tippi Calder with her aunt, Harry Borg had gone on with scarcely a pause in pursuit of Ahmed Hassad. He had no need of police, even had time allowed it. And he wanted none. This was a task he wanted for himself.

Hassad had left the challenge: "Mesa Grande—if you dare."

A taunt, knowing Harry would not refuse.

And he had not.

Now, he was standing before the desert complex of Ahmed Hassad, the place known as Mesa Grande, at a distance of about three miles. Daylight of Sunday, April 6, had just broken across the desert, and the mesa loomed like a massive column of red stone, thrusting up out of the level desert floor. The colors were vivid, the landscape forbidding.

A road led, arrow-straight, through the cactus and sage to the mesa, then climbed a tortuous way toward the top.

Chad Harrison, the white-haired young warrior—it had become impossible for Harry to think of the young men of his cadre as anything else but warriors—had taken that road a short time before, driving a truck he had "requisitioned" from among the many freighting all manner of equipment and furnishings away from the complex. With him were Sam Barnstable and Arnie Garrett, and all three were heavily armed, their weapons perfectly concealed.

Chad would call when they were in place.

For himself and his two men, Homer Benson and Eddie Cole, Harry had requisitioned a helicopter. It had been no trouble to approach one at the badly lighted unloading zone at the railroad depot, overpower the crew, and fly it away. The crews of the other helicopters had been too occupied with their own tasks to question who might be flying which craft.

They waited, then: Harry Borg, big, powerful, red-bearded, a giant seething with cold and murderous rage; Homer Benson, the young, wide-shouldered farm boy grown suddenly to a calm adult, lethally capable; and Eddie Cole, the slender, graceful-moving black, a jaguar when a swift stroke was needed.

Homer and Eddie were filled with the same fury that burned in Harry. In taking Harry's pregnant wife, a woman they held dear, even loved, Ahmed Hassad had earned himself the beating of his life. But in mutilating Tippi, a child, Hassad had earned himself something worse than a beating, far worse.

The chance was slim he'd live to tell about it.

The distance was too great for telepathic communication, but in a few moments the radio in Harry Borg's hand came alive with Chad Harrison's voice, quiet and controlled. "Do you read me, sir?"

"Loud and clear," Harry answered immediately.

"We're on top," Chad said. "In the complex."

"Contact with Lori?"

"Negative."

"She'll be drugged," Homer said at Harry's elbow.

"Very likely," Harry agreed, his jaw tight.

Holding Lori, Hassad held control—Hassad knew that. And Harry knew that. And Harry knew, too, that even beyond this, and bearing heavily upon this, there was something of enormous importance going on, something that was clearly outlined by Hassad's unreasonable need for haste, his folding of tents both in Ireland and here, but something that had not yet been described in enough detail for him to understand. He did know that neither he nor Lori was going to be safe until he had discovered what Hassad was about, and he knew that he was not going to stop driving after Hassad until he knew it all.

"What have you got up there?" he asked Chad.

"A madhouse," came the answer. "They're sacking the place, moving out."

"Security?"

"Six armed guards in sight. Expect more in the buildings."

"Take positions and wait. We're coming in."

"Take positions and wait—sir!"

If there was anything more frustrating than working with electronic circuitry that had lain in a museum storeroom for over a thousand years, Los Ross could not imagine what it would be. However well protected by vacuum and tissal covering, the micro imprints found ways to disintegrate. Not to a marked degree, to be sure, nothing one could see at a glance or find in an hour's search. It had to be something so minute, so well hidden, one had to search hours to discover what it was—and why the LX-10 was indicating a negative mossless, when common

sense said it had to be positive, or at the very worst
neutral. In this case it had proved to be a break in a circuit
he'd had to magnify ten thousand diameters to trace.

Then he had to find a replacement part. The LX-10
had not been used since the Tesso Rule!

Without the LX-10 and its speed-of-light search ability,
the hunt for a means to break the Sessor Code would
require months, when even hours would be too long. There
wasn't time!

Even though his assistant, Dosis, was doing her level
best to find the part, and though he was able to complete
certain functions while he was waiting, there was no real
hope of final success unless the LX-10 could be brought
back on line.

And the hours were clicking by relentlessly.

Los Ross had spent the last two days in unrelenting
work in this circular cell thirty meters in diameter. Half
the walls were covered floor to ceiling with various mon-
itor screens, glowing now with displays of mathematical
problems in various stages of solution, with graphs indicating progress, with lines undulating to hidden rhythms—
all the results of the workings of the computer that used
the remaining wall space, a computer Los Ross had fab-
ricated, for the most part, out of museum parts.

There was one significant benefit of being almost the
only one in Jassa who could understand how this particular computer worked and what it was working at. If the
people in Foss—President Moss, in particular—knew
what he was trying so desperately to do, he would be
most probably ossed out of existence where he sat.

Los Ross had grown so thin and bent from overwork
and lack of sleep that he looked ill. His large, yellow eyes
behind his spectacles were red-shot, his lightly scaled skin
mottled. His eight-fingered hands, as they moved over
the keyboards, trembled at times to the point of useless-

ness. Even his smock was dirty, and to Los Ross, a neat person, that was the surest sign of near exhaustion.

But he couldn't stop. There wasn't time!

Those fools who called themselves the Vessan Guard had gone through the Gateway in pursuit of Guss Rassan. They had botched the assignment horribly, killing one, possibly two, of the intelligent bassoes. Worst of all, they had left one of their own behind!

Word of this had just reached Los Ross.

"The stupid hasses!" he had screamed.

Now the humans must know there was another civilization, another race of creatures, of beings, somewhere close by! Before, only Harry Borg and his people had known. Now, as surely as the Tass rose each morning, their TV—wasn't that the name of it?—would broadcast the word to the ends of their Earth. What would happen then? Panic? Would the military gather? Would millions of the race run screaming into the night?

Only Osis knew!

What Los Ross knew was that Guss Rassan and Sissi were in desperate trouble, and he, Los Ross, was responsible. He had sent them to Earth on what he realized now had been an impossible errand. That nuclear device was going to be exploded within four days, and there was nothing Guss and Sissi could do to prevent it. The world of the intelligent bassoes—the Homo sapiens—was going to suffer total devastation.

But Guss and Sissi would never live to see it. As soon as the panic set in, the Earthlings would instantly kill all creatures who walked on two legs and looked even faintly reptilian, and that would mean Guss and Sissi would be the first to go.

Unless he, Los Ross, could break the Sessor Code!

If he could break the Sessor Code, he could establish Points of Proximity—providing, of course, the authorities in Foss didn't arrest and execute him first—and then there would be some hope for Guss and Sissi. Some hope. Not a lot. Some.

But he needed the LX-10!

And where was Dosis and the spare issis?

Tippi Calder was feeling less pain in the stump of the little finger of her left hand now. The surgeon in Dublin to whom Harry Borg had taken her after that terrible business in Hassad's castle had decided almost at once that there was no hope of grafting the severed part back where it belonged; he had cleansed and sutured the stump, given her painkillers, patted her head, and told her hardly anyone would notice when she grew up.

Some surgeon!

The surgeon in Jassa, who'd put Harry back together when he'd been blown almost to bits, would give her another little finger, she was sure. And she was sure she'd be going back there one day—Harry would see to it; he had promised.

But it would have to be later. First, Harry had to get her mother. Imagine anyone kidnapping a pregnant woman!

A beast, that's what Ahmed Hassad was. Or worse. Using her mom to try to make Harry give him Vec-Power. What kind of a start was it for a baby that wasn't even born yet? But that was Hassad—if he could cut off a person's finger to make someone do what he wanted them to do, he was liable to do just about anything. To anyone. Even to an unborn baby.

These were the thoughts of Tippi Calder as she walked through the neighborhood near her aunt's home in the suburban district called Hidden Road, a district of fine homes close to the community of Reseda, California.

Harry had left her with her aunt Edith the night they

had returned to the States from Ireland. She would be safer there than at home in the apartment, he had said. But even though her aunt's home was very big and very comfortable, and even though Aunt Edith was the very soul of kindness, her worry about her mother and Charlie, the pain in her finger, the anger at having had it cut off, had made it impossible for her to sit still. After making a solemn promise to stay in the area, she had been allowed to walk for as long as she needed to tire herself out.

Walking and thinking.

And maybe she was still a little woozy, a little mixed up from the dope Hassad's people had shot into her. It seemed like she was hearing things. Sometimes she thought she could even hear Sissi scolding Guss Rassan. How about that?

Out of sight! Because to hear Sissi would mean she was getting telepathic messages through her receptor, and that was impossible.

Wasn't it? Sissi was in Jassa. In another world. In another dimension!

So it had to be her imagination. Something to do with the dope, or too much excitement. Still, it seemed so *real*! And fooling around with the idea gave her something to do and something to think about while she was trying to walk off her anxieties. So, as she walked along the street where the fine homes stood back from the street on fine lawns, she had begun listening hard, hoping to hear Sissi. And then, every once in a while she had begun to stop and cup her hands around her temples—the way she would cup her hands around her mouth if she was going to yell in the normal way—and scream silently.

"Sissi! Sissi! Where are you?"

The mental scream was loud enough to carry a block or two, but it was not a scream an ordinary person could hear. Ordinary people passing by did wonder, however, why the pretty girl with the bandaged hand would stop, put her hands up like Mickey Mouse ears, strain silently, then walk on.

They couldn't know she was silently screaming.

"Sissi! Can you read me?"

And a little later, a little farther on, she would scream again.

"Tippi calling! Come in, Sissi!"

It didn't matter that she got no answer. It kept her mind away from other things, like a worry for her mother that approached terror.

Jessica Jones did not know exactly the moment when the realization had come to her. It may have been growing in the back of her mind for some time, unnoticed, festering, causing a deep-seated unease that set her pacing in the dark hours when she needed rest. When it did leap into being suddenly, fully formed, fully realized, it was frightening.

She was not in control!

The mission for which she had been working all her adult life—or so it seemed to her—her chance to truly strike a blow that "would change the course of all mankind!" that "would save the Common Man from a life of subservience, even slavery!" could be taken away from her. Whoever that man or those people were who had assigned the Mission to her could take it away from her at their whim.

My God! She had overlooked the most vital step. She had not *secured* her Mission.

From the police, from the government forces, yes. She had been most careful in selecting the people she needed: they were as dedicated, as selfless, as she. But she had left exposed the most vulnerable flank. If the person or persons who had supplied the working parts of the device—the Hand of God—with which she was going to make her single, gigantic statement decided *not* to continue through to the final moment, she was helpless to prevent them from stopping her.

And she had done so well up to this point!

It was just after midnight April 4. She was lying again on her sleeping pad in the warehouse on the waterfront of Hoboken, New Jersey, when this dreadful realization had come to her, frightening her so severely that she broke into a shivering cold sweat.

A tugboat in the harbor began a series of short hoots, and they came through to her as jeering laughter. What a fool she had been! She should have realized her vulnerability, the vulnerability of her Mission, long before.

Encased shroudlike in her sleeping bag, she lay staring at the old iron beams of the high ceiling. Hale Benedict's shrill, drug-induced snoring coming from the dark corner where he lay in his sleeping bag seemed to echo the jeering laughter of the tugboat. Manuel and Ali, her men, slept silently the sleep of men fixed in their purpose, safe in their belief in her and her Mission.

Hale Benedict had said he needed only this coming day to complete the assembly—that it would be done two days ahead of schedule was due only to the fact that she had driven him so relentlessly—and that was progress totally unexpected by the rotund, wispy-haired man with the china blue eyes who was their connection to that unknown person who had made the Mission possible.

There was still time, she saw now.

She could secure her Mission. It was within her power to make absolutely certain that no power on earth would

be able to prevent her—to prevent the Hand of God—
from making the most important statement the world had
ever heard.

All she needed to do was move.

CHAPTER 14

Looking back on the night just past, the night that had begun on Saturday, April 5, and had ended on the morning of this day, Sunday, April 6, Guss and Sissi were each to call it one of the worst nights of their lives: a night of tedium, fright, and despair.

Guss spent the night trying to stay awake in the half-light of the bedroom where the two adults were sleeping. And trying not to count the days, the hours, the minutes that were left—three days, seventy-two hours, or a mere four thousand three hundred minutes, give or take a few. And trying not to admit how hopeless it all was.

He was on the west coast of a continent populated by monsters who considered him to be the monster and themselves the norm, while the bomb that would destroy them all was on the east coast, three thousand of their miles away.

His only hope of preventing the bomb from being detonated lay in the tall, thin, sickly—his mate was always insisting on him taking some medication or other, wasn't she?—male human who was sleeping on the bed. That human may have been a warrior of some skill and bravery in times past, if you were to believe the medals, but he was proving to be so mentally dense that there seemed little or no hope of ever communicating with him.

And in the final analysis, he might prove to be *not* a potential ally, but instead a determined foe who was concealing himself behind an outward pretense of friendship.

Osis, how those hours dragged by!

He sat in the half-light, listening to them snore. He dared not relax, lest one of them overpower him. He dared not even let the soft gray membrane draw across his large, golden, wide-slitted eyes too long, lest he fall asleep. He had to remain rigidly awake, constantly testing the odors with the flickering, curling tips of his tongue—and some of those odors were quite repulsive, even nasty, to a person of his refined sensibilities; wasn't he a maestro of symphonic fragrances? He sat with all sixteen fingers clenched with an intentionally painful force.

How did one fall into such an idiotic predicament? How could he be an idolized personage one moment and a forgotten outcast bent on a hopeless mission in a strange land the next? The gods were cruel!

The night for Sissi was no better. She spent it sitting in a bedroom with the children. The light from small buttons of radiance in the walls, and from the glowing numbers of an electrical timepiece, revealed their young faces as they slept quietly, innocently: the young male with his red hair and strangely spotted face, his stubborn bravery; the young female, so enchanting with her round little body and her enormous brown eyes. Sissi, too, tried not to count the hours and minutes, tried not to realize the hopelessness of it all and to wonder why she was doing this, why she was here.

All she had ever wanted was Guss. From that glorious night her parents had taken her to the Concert of Fragrances in Larissa, where she had seen him on stage, playing the sissal, where he had created the most heavenly fragrances ever imagined—a young female could lose her mind when such delicate, entrancing odors bathed the tender tips of her tongue—she had had but one goal, one purpose in life: to mate with him. Forever.

And she had managed that.

Not easily, to be sure. He hadn't known the mating was the start of a forever thing; malelike, he'd thought it only a moment's dalliance. Her success had come only after years of relentless pursuit, of being willing, even at the risk of going to prison until she reached the age of maturity as punishment for breaking the strict Copulation Laws, and at the risk of causing him to go to prison for much longer for breaking the same laws with a juvenile. It had meant becoming his mistress—also illegal—because he had been impossibly frightened at matrimony, as so many males were. Wouldn't you know, he had professed his love, his willingness to become her legal mate, only a few moments before they had set out on this impossible journey.

Had the course of love *ever* been so difficult?

And oh, the problems facing them now! Of them all, only the little female among the humans was her trusted friend. The little one's hand came so easily into her own; the large brown eyes so readily accepted her appearance as different but perfectly all right. The little one followed her almost everywhere, her face tipped up, her mouth emitting vibrations that had to be questions, questions, questions. Questions she could not understand or answer.

The male child with his engaging grimace—smile?—was a constant worry. He was unsuppressible. Push him down one place, he would pop up in another, happy, mischievous-eyed, grimacing. What was he going to do next? Set her on fire? Steal her sword?

The adult female seemed determined to mother everything and everyone almost to extinction—how could you not love one like that? And how could you, really, trust her?

The adult male had become so outwardly willing to do anything and everything that was asked of him that he had to be the most suspect of all. He was *too* willing. And more, that he was so *dense*! However hard she tried, however ingenious her pantomime, she had been unable to make him understand that they—he, his family, his civilization—were going to be exterminated *in three days* unless she and Guss, who had come here at extreme peril to themselves, were able to save them.

Or was she the one who was dense? Could someone more clever penetrate to the brain behind those ridiculous dark-rimmed spectacles, behind that gentle, agreeable, good-humored, silly-smiling countenance? Surely there must be intelligence there. Was it hiding, waiting for that moment when their defenses were down, their backs turned, to strike and kill both her and Guss?

A most dreadful thought!

How she wished for Harry Borg! How she wished she could see that enormous, kind, smiling, ferociously effective human, who had come to Jassa by such strange chance and who had changed all their lives in a brief span of months. How she wished she could see him come striding into her life right this minute. He would sweep her up in his great arms, she knew, hug the breath out of her, and, with a roar of laughter, make all her terrors vanish in a moment's time.

But where was he? How was he to be found?

There was Guss, to be sure. No warrior he! One could not question his basic courage—hadn't he come here feeling sure his life would be forfeit, even if he were to suc-

ceed? What greater measure of courage could there be?
But a clever doer of dangerous deeds he was not. He was
too imaginative. He was a creative person, too fragile
mentally for such frightening escapades.

She knew it had become her responsibility somehow
to keep him on course, to direct him to practical ways,
to provide him with means. And wasn't that an irony?
She, a female, quite young, an illegal mistress, had to aim
him, her lord and master, toward whatever success could
be found, and had to somehow fire him in that general
direction?

And thus her night passed, sitting in the dark beside
the bed that held the children.

In the morning, breakfast was served. Whether out of
a sense that whatever was going to happen would happen,
or whether the adult male, with his assurances and good
humor, had been persuasive enough, the family was permitted to eat together at the table in the room where the
female had prepared the food.

There were good vibrations emitting from all of them;
that was sure. Guss and Sissi, watching, worried and
tensed, could feel the vibrations and could sense no
immediate threat.

"How about this?" George was saying. "Just like
uptown!"

"Pass the eggs, Pop," Jackie said.

"You too, Jillie?"

"I don't like scrambled eggs," Jillie said.

"Eat your eggs," her mother said. "Or I'll give you a
hit."

"Yikkkk!" Jillie said, and stuck her tongue out. But
she accepted a helping of eggs and even nibbled at them.

George smiled at Guss and Sissi. "Y'see?" he said to
his family. "I've got 'em coming my way."

"Or you're going theirs," Sara said.

"A meeting of minds, all right?" George said. "Any

way you slice it, I'm going to end up with some of the most lucrative franchises the world has ever known!"

"What's a franchise, Mom?" Jillie asked.

"Like McDonald's—that's a franchise."

"Pop's going to own a McDonald's?"

"No, dummy!" Jackie said. "He's gonna get a lizard franchise here."

"To make lizard-burgers?" Jillie was shocked.

"Oh, boy!" Jackie said.

"Eat your eggs," her mother said.

George grinned at his wife. "Well, they're not scared. That's a help."

"I'm still scared," she said.

"So am I," he said. "What I'm saying is we're making progress."

She frowned worriedly. "Yes, but toward what?"

"Come on, let's look at the brighter side!"

During that exchange, Guss was speaking to Sissi. "Well, what d'you think? Are they making plans to cut our throats?"

"Stop talking like that!" Sissi said. "They're being nice!"

"I wish I had your trust."

"You give me a choice, and I'll take the other one."

"All right!"

"Anyway, I've got an idea that might work."

"Don't tell me about it—I *like* going mad!"

"You're so unpleasant!"

Guss was immediately contrite: "I don't mean to be, love."

Then she was contrite. "We're both worried ragged. But—what I think I'll do, since my pantomime doesn't work, I'll draw pictures. The little female has some color sticks she uses. I'll borrow them and something to draw on, and maybe I can get through to one of them. They ought to be able to understand pictures, don't you think?"

"Yeah, I'd think so."

"But what will I draw?"

"I'll leave that to you."

"You're so generous."

"It's just my nature," Guss said. He patted her shoulder. "But don't get me wrong. I think it's a great idea. I don't know why I didn't think of it myself."

"Maybe because you can't draw."

"Don't get smart! You can't play a sissal!"

But they hugged each other. Because things were beginning to look a little better. If they could get their message across, there might be a small chance of living another twenty-four hours or so.

When the humans had finished their meal and the empty containers had been put away, they all resumed their places at the table as Guss and Sissi indicated they should with gentle pushes, gestures, and pats of reassurance.

"What's going on?" Jackie asked.

"Beats me," his father said. "But it doesn't look dangerous."

Guss stood by at a little distance and tried to look friendly, though stern, while Sissi went for the smallest child's color sticks and some material on which to draw. She was back in a moment.

"I have it!" Sissi told Guss.

"Hey! She's going to draw pictures!" Jackie said.

"Good show!" his father said.

"Those are my crayons and my sketch pad," Jillie said proudly.

"I do hope we'll get answers," Sara said. "I have bridge today."

George smiled at her. "Atta girl."

"What do you have?" Guss asked.

"The thing to draw," Sissi told him. "I'm going to draw

a dass, if I can. That should make them understand how serious it all is."

"Would *our* poison symbol mean anything to them?"

"Maybe not. But if it frightens us, maybe some of our fear will communicate to them."

She began to draw, her long, forked tongue thrust through the side of her mouth, her brow scarred with the effort. She was not a capable draftsperson, or even a pretty good one—she was about as good as Jillie would have been doing the same thing—but she was trying hard.

"Lucky our poison symbol is a picture of an Oss," she said.

"That helps," Guss agreed.

"Poisons kill everybody; Osses kill everybody."

"That doesn't look right," Guss said as her drawing began to take shape. "An Oss has five sides, all the same length!"

"Zat!" Sissi said.

She tore the page off, crumpled it, and started again.

"Don't swear in front of the children," Guss said.

"The lady can't draw as well as you, Jillie," George said.

"I could draw it for her—if I knew what to draw."

"Hoo, boy!" Jackie said.

"She only wants to help!" his mother said.

George, watching Sissi draw, became thoughtful.

"Now you're getting it," Guss said.

Sissi had done better with this effort. The universally recognized poison symbol—universally recognized by the Jassans, to be sure—had begun to take a recognizable shape.

"They know a lot about us," George said soberly.

"Why do you say that?"

"She's drawing the Pentagon."

"What's a pentagon?" Jillie asked.

"It's where our generals are, isn't that right, Dad?"

"That's right, son. Headquarters of our armed forces."

Sissi, after much effort, had completed half of the poison symbol. She had, even though clumsily, added the dimensional lines to give it a three-dimensional appearance.

"Very good!" Guss complimented her.

She paused to rest.

The humans were all looking at her, she found. Their faces were wearing looks of what seemed to be worried expectancy. She couldn't hear George say, "Come on, everybody, smile!" but she did see that the smiles that returned were different from the ones she had seen before. Strained? False? She couldn't be sure. She could only go on.

She drew the connecting bar.

"Maybe it's not the Pentagon," Sara said.

"Maybe not," George admitted, somewhat relieved.

It could be, he admitted to himself, that he was still very apprehensive, subconsciously, and that the apprehension was leaking out at even the slightest opportunity. He had to admit, however, that there was reason for apprehension. He was watching an alien female—lizard in appearance, wearing battle-dress, complete with short sword and sidearm, large golden, vertically slitted eyes intent, forked tongue protruding, an eight-fingered hand gripping one of Jillie's crayons—trying to draw pentagons, and that was anything but an afternoon at the ballpark watching the Dodgers. Which was not to say he had lost track of the main chance. No way! He was still going to make a bundle out of this freak happening some damned how or another.

"Keep smiling, look happy!" he told his family.

"My mouth is starting to hurt," Jillie complained.

"Think of Disneyland," Jackie told her.

"Way to go!" his father said.

"Something scared them," Guss said to Sissi. "I can feel it. I can see it."

"That's what a poison symbol is supposed to do, isn't it?"

"But *our* symbol?"

"Guss, please!"

Guss relented. "Sorry."

Sissi went on drawing. She finished the connecting bar and then drew the second pentagon. And she wasn't at all disappointed with the effort. It was now two pentagons connected by a bar—roughly, a dumbell shape—the symbol that in Jassa had come to mean: "This container holds deadly poison!"

"You sure got their attention," Guss said.

George was staring at her drawing. Quietly, he said, "They know our Pentagon means our military headquarters. She's showing us they have a military headquarters, too—another Pentagon."

"Are you sure?" Sara asked.

"What else?"

"Cripes!" Jackie said. "They're talking war!"

"I don't believe it!" Sara said. "They're nice people."

Sissi saw she had not only not achieved understanding; she had instilled a worry of some kind, a deep concern—even fear.

"Oh, liss!" she said. "What do I do now?"

"Smile!" George told his family. "Come on!"

"They're trying to look happy," Guss said. "So you'd better keep trying."

"But how? Doing what?"

"I know. Show them what the poison symbol means. Show them a bomb going off, people dying. Like that. Show them we're afraid they're going to get killed."

"Well, all right."

Sissi gripped her forked tongue in the side of her mouth again, gripped the crayon, and tried once more. The drawing she made was again very crude—her figures were a child's stick figures—but the subject was not one that needed accuracy of draftsmanship to be fully understood. The mushroom-shaped cloud was easily recognizable, and the prone stick figures told a story of their own.

"What does it mean, George?" Sara whispered.

"The way I read it now," George said, "she's telling us their armed forces are going to attack our armed forces, using nuclear bombs."

"Oh, my God!"

Sissi, looking at the humans, hoping for understanding, saw that their faces held not only fear now but shock as well.

"Sarsiss, help me!" she said. "What have I done?"

"They've turned white!" Guss said.

"Are they *that* afraid?"

"But all you did was—"

Jackie, at that moment, found that Sissi was looking at Guss and that her holstered sidearm was within easy reaching distance. He made a lunge for it, knocking over his chair, grabbing at her weapon.

"Watch the child!" Guss yelled.

The esso was locked in its holster, but Jackie didn't know that. He grabbed it and tried to wrestle it free. When Sissi felt the boy's hands, she squirmed and began fighting him.

Sara screamed.

George yelled, "Jackie!" and tried to get up to help. He was momentarily trapped between table and chair.

Jillie screamed.

Guss, rattled by the sudden activity, drew the esso he'd been gripping in his pocket. He couldn't aim it at any living thing, so it was by chance that he was holding it high over George's head when he pulled the trigger. The silent, purple beam drilled a hole the size of a baseball through the wall, cut a few small limbs off a tree outside, and vanished into the sky. It frightened Guss as much as it frightened George.

Sissi screamed at Guss. "No! No! No!"

She was still wrestling with Jackie. But her first concern was for Guss and the fact he was shooting holes in walls.

George, unhurt but awestruck, reached out to grab Jackie away from Sissi. He finally forced the panting lad back in a chair. "Stay there, dammit!"

"But Dad, I—"

"You damn near got me killed!" his father said. And then, on seeing his son's stricken face, his tone softened. "Look at that hole in the wall."

Jackie looked. "Geeze!" he said.

Sara had the sobbing Jillie in her arms. "Shush, shush— it's going to be all right, hon. No one's hurt."

They, the Bushby family, had drawn away from Guss and Sissi, back against the wall of the breakfast room, their faces pale, full of stress and fear. And yet they were full of courage, too—they were more like captive animals than possible allies now, captive animals willing to fight as long as they could to save their lives.

"Look what you've done!" Sissi wailed.

"I didn't mean to!" Guss said. "The cursed thing just went off!"

"You pulled the trigger!"

"I swear, I didn't!"

"Look at that hole! Look at them!"

"But it was an accident. The way the child grabbed at you!"

"He couldn't get my esso!"

"How did I know that?"

"How do you know anything, you stupid kess-ness! If you—"

Sissi, very upset again, had been screaming at Guss at the top of her mental powers. But now she had stopped as if struck on the head. She stood dazed, unbelieving, staring at Guss, not seeing him at all. And he was staring at her in the same way. What they were both doing was listening.

They both had heard a telepathic scream not their own, a distant, wildly excited scream.

"Sissi! Sissi! Is that you? Sissi!"

"Is it possible?" Sissi said, unbelieving.

"Sounds like Tippi!" Guss said, growing excited.

"Sissi! Sissi! Answer me! Come in, Sissi!"

"It is!" Sissi screamed. "It's Tippi!"

She began jumping up and down, waving her arms. "Tippi! Tippi!"

The scream from Tippi became joyous. "I knew it! I knew it!"

"Where are you?" Guss asked.

Tippi's scream became even happier. "Guss! Are you here, *too*?"

"I'm here. Where are you?"

"I'm on—on—oh, gosh, I can't think straight. I'm on Tisson Avenue, between, ah, Marsh, I think, and Meadow."

"Wherever *that* is!"

"Never mind. Where are *you*?"

"In a big habitation where humans live," Sissi told her.

Out in the street, Tippi was going out of her mind. She was whirling around, looking in every direction, trying to get the clearest mental signal possible. While the voices of Sissi and Guss were distant, they were not too distant— two blocks away at the most, she thought.

"You're in a house!" she said. "Can you describe it?"

"You tell her, Guss," Sissi said.

"Me tell her! Great Essnia, it was dark!"

"There aren't too many houses along here," Tippi said.

She had begun running in the direction that made the telepathic voices stronger. A passing gardener in a pickup truck, seeing the young jeans-clad girl running, braked to offer help. He saw her stop suddenly and cup her hands to her temples. When she saw him, she waved him furiously away.

Hurt, the gardener said, "Kids!" and drove on.

"That would be a hedge," Tippi was saying. "Three houses along here with hedges on the sidewalk. Approach? You mean driveway. Okay, I'm looking, I'm looking! A curving driveway."

In the house, Sissi had already lost her mind, but it had been to a giddy sense of relief so overpowering that it was making her legs weak.

"You're getting nearer," Guss said. "I can hear you better."

He had taken charge now, becoming once again cool and efficient. Help was close by, needing only to be guided in. He could do that as well as anyone. "A building that houses their transport is on the right," he said.

"Garage on the right, curving driveway. I read you." Tippi's mental voice reflected her physical exertion, but there was no letup in her excitement, her eagerness.

Sara Bushby was watching Sissi and Guss. "George, what happened? What are they doing?"

"They're talking," George said carefully. "Telepathically."

"Oh, dear! I wish they wouldn't do that."

"So do I!" George said fervently.

"Dad? Who're they talking *to*?" That was Jackie—right to the heart of it, like a terrier.

"One of their own, who else?"

"Geeze. You mean we're going to have a bunch more in here?"

"Calm down!" his father said, trying to seem stern but unafraid. "We don't know. All we can do is wait and see."

"I always hate 'wait-and-sees,'" Jillie said.

"You may like this one, hon," her mother said. "They can't be all bad." She put a protective arm around her daughter.

Outside, Tippi was yelling telepathically. "Got it! Hedge, curving drive, garage—hey! And there's the gate!" A brief moment, then: "And the lock's been burned out." Her voice was quite clear. "Shall I come through?"

"Oh, yes, Tippi!"

"You go and meet her," Guss said. "I'll keep an eye on these."

But Sissi had already gone, running, and she met Tippi as the girl came through the sliding glass door into the family room. The two rushed into each other's arms, Sissi so desperately glad that she was crying, Tippi overjoyed at finding her friend from Jassa—she had *not* been imagining strange voices after all!

"What are you *doing* here?" Tippi asked when she could.

"Come, come! Tell these humans we're not enemies!" She all but dragged Tippi into the kitchen.

When Tippi saw Guss, she broke free and ran to him. She jumped, flung her arms around Guss's neck, and hugged him. And he hugged her. Seeing this human child was the best of all possible things to happen.

"You're a lifesaver!" he told her.

"Why? How come? What're you two doing here?"

"Tell these humans we're friends!"

Tippi looked at the Bushby family. She saw a man, his wife, and two children, staring back at her, scared to death. Their faces were as white as sheets, their eyes wide and wary.

"It's all right!" Tippi said to them. "They're friends!"

"You can *talk* to them?" Sara said incredulously.

"Yes! Yes!" Tippi told her. "I have this thing in my head. I can talk to them. And I can hear them. So I know it's all right. My name's Tippi Calder. What's yours?"

"Bushby," Sara said. She indicated the others. "My husband, George. Our children, Jackie and Jillie."

"How nice!" Tippi said. "This is Guss Rassan—he's a very famous sissal-player. And this is Sissi, his—his companion."

Sara was looking questioningly at her husband. And her husband was looking steadily at Tippi. His face was stone-hard, his eyes darkly watchful. And that gave Sara Bushby new cause to worry.

"What is it, George?"

"She's a ringer," George said.

"Ringer? What's a ringer?" Jackie asked.

"A fake," his father said. "She's one of *them*."

CHAPTER 15

Earlier on that same morning, Sunday, April 6, Harry Borg lifted the helicopter from the desert floor as the white, burning disk of the sun broke above the distant rim of the desert and began the climb into the blue and cloudless Arizona sky. He did not take the craft high, preferring to skim just above the scattered mesquite and sagebrush clumps. An occasional jackrabbit bounced off beneath them. A small herd of antelope, white rump patches flaring their alarm, kept pace for a kilometer before turning away. A hawk, poised above some prey on the ground, wings beating, was almost overrun.

"How do they make it out there?" Eddie yelled in Homer's ear. "What's there to eat?"

"Sagebrush and bunch grass, if you're vegetarian," Homer yelled back. "Each other, if you're a carnivore."

Harry Borg grinned. These two, just twenty—one a handsome son of the farm country, the other the product of an inner city—could wonder about such things as they were being flown into what they knew would surely be a firefight.

The barren land raced beneath them.

The motor clattered.

In the distance, Mesa Grande thrust up from the almost flat desert floor like a huge broken-off column of stone, brick red in the early sun. There was other flat land at almost the same level as the mesa top, but at a distance, leaving this one to stand alone, like an island in a sea gone dry in ages past, a thing of awesome beauty.

The road that serviced the mesa led around to the far side, where it climbed a tortuous, twisting route to the top, and now two eighteen-wheel silver-sided moving vans appeared as they reached the flat land, and the drivers looked at the low-flying chopper with no more than a passing curiosity. One of them flashed a thumb up, which Harry returned.

"Moving day, for sure," Homer said.

"Damn it, why?" Harry asked. His dark brows above his dark blue eyes wore a scowl, and the strong chin under the close-cropped, red-brown beard showed an angry forward thrust.

From the west, the approaching file of three helicopters spaced widely apart indicated the landing pattern, and Harry went that way to rise swiftly and take his place in line. Now that he was near, telepathic communication again became possible. "Chad, do you read me?"

"Loud and clear, sir."

"How are you placed?"

"Sam at the truck depot. Arnie at the main house. I'm at the security office. Three armed here, sir—sergeant in charge, two patrolmen. It's the communication center. And sir?"

"Yes?"

"Closed-circuit TV monitors everywhere."

"Copy. Stand by."

He glanced at Homer and Eddie. "You read that?"

They said they had.

The landing pattern took them once around the mesa before they could land in their turn. Below them the complex that was known as Mesa Grande told how unlimited wealth could be spent on whim and caprice.

"Can you believe it?"

"No way."

"All it takes is money."

The centerpiece was the oasis. A shimmering sheet of water, acres in extent, sky blue in color, was surrounded by date palms and white sand, none of it native, all brought in. The tent of a Bedouin prince, a sheik of great wealth, covered almost an acre, a gently billowing sea of striped nylon held on guyed steel poles, carpeted, one could be sure, by fine Persian rugs, cushioned with silken pillows. There were even camels standing in the care of a small figure.

"What'll you bet that kid's the real thing?" Homer asked.

"Got the turban and the dhoti."

"From Egypt, Persia someplace."

"You can bet on it."

The main residence, la Casa Grande, was U-shaped, with a red tile roof, and embraced in its arms an extensive garden-patio complete with exotic shrubbery, sparkling fountains, and tiled walks. There were shaded walks behind pillared arches along the inner walls, and on the outer walls, patios and balconies overlooked the deep desert floor.

Supporting the main residence, and at a distant edge of the mesa, were the service buildings, and they were of a number suggesting a village. The truck depot, the warehouse, was at the head of the road that had climbed its twisting way to the top. The security office had to be the blocklike building at the edge of the helicopter landing area.

"Chad," Harry said telepathically. "We're next to land."

"Have you in view, sir."

"Homer and Eddie will go to la Casa. You and I will take the security. Sam, can you hold the depot?"

"No problem," Sam responded easily.

"All copy?"

"Copy, sir."

"After I touch down and cut the rotor. On the count of two."

"On two—sir!"

Chad Harrison, his white hair covered by a worn baseball cap, his lean and powerful frame covered by the dusty, oil-stained coveralls of a working man, had stationed himself, as if by chance, beside the security office. He leaned there, watching the helicopter flown by Harry Borg as it came in toward a landing very close to the glass doors of the office. Only a hand search would have revealed the weapons hidden in Chad's soiled coveralls; only hand contact would have revealed that the young athlete was as ready to go as a cocked rifle.

He saw the helicopter touch down, heard the motor cut. The heavy glass doors of the security office squeaked open.

"What the hell's the matter with you?" one of the security guards demanded angrily. "Can't you fly that damn thing?"

Chad eased around the corner. The security guard, a big, ruddy-faced man in a too-tight uniform whose belly bulged over a shiny cartridge belt, was standing two meters from the sliding glass door, bent, waiting for the rotors to stop. In the helicopter, Harry had cracked the door on the side near the guard, and on the other side Homer and Eddie were already on the ground.

"Let's keep them all alive," Harry told his men silently.

"Copy," they all responded.

"The count is one—two!"

Chad saw the door of the helicopter swing wide, saw Harry emerge, a smooth-flowing powerhouse, gathering speed, and he left the potbellied guard to his certain fate, going behind the guard to enter the security office.

"What the hell?" The sergeant, a hard-looking Mexican-American, stroked a general-alarm button, drew his service pistol, and tried to kill Chad. Left no choice, Chad shot the sergeant through the shoulder, knocking him back over his chair. The guard's gun went flying away. Chad swung his own gun to cover the man, once a guard, now a frightened youngster, at the communications bank.

"Freeze!"

"Damn!" It was Harry at Chad's shoulder. He had crumpled the pot-bellied guard and stepped over the motionless figure. His curse was for the bad luck that had caused the sergeant to be shot, that had sounded the general alarm, now wailing throughout the mesa. "Hold this!" he said to Chad.

"Sir!"

Harry was halfway to the entrance of la Casa Grande when he heard the general alarm sigh into quiet and knew that Chad had the security office under control. But the rest of the security force had gone battle-ready. The wicked slap of a rifle shot went close by Harry's head as he ran; the muzzle blast came an instant later from the direction of the garden-patio. He saw Eddie, the lithe black panther, flash through the shrubbery, heard yells of pain and fear.

There were no more rifle shots.

"Sorry about that." It was Arnie, talking telepathically to Eddie.

"You got more?" Eddie asked.

"Two inside."

"Where's the lady?"

"Dunno."

Harry joined them at the huge mahogany doors, which now were standing wide. "Let's go in and find her."

They burst into the wide foyer, running, and split up: Eddie ran to the right, down a long corridor; Arnie, the stocky but swift fist-faced running back, good for three yards against any defense, went straight on toward the back; and Harry Borg went up the wide stairway toward the upper floor three steps at a time.

Two guards converged on Harry Borg as he neared the top of the stairway. Strangely, they made no effort to draw or fire weapons. Harry accepted that fact as ground rules, left his own weapon holstered, and welcomed the guards with open arms. He took them both in a bear hug, though they were by no means small men, and fell backward, deliberately, in a crashing, bouncing fall that took them clear to the foyer below.

"That is one fierce-fighting man," Ahmed Hassad said to Lori Calder with admiration that was not at all grudging. "He may be as close to indestructible as any man I've ever seen."

"Oh, he can be hurt," Lori answered. She did not add that she had seen one of his arms and one of his legs blown away, had seen his blood gushing, had watched the blaze go out of those dark blue eyes, and that she had held him as he died in her arms. And she didn't add that in Jassa there was a surgeon named Sassan who could restore life and limbs to a human so badly destroyed— that was information, she knew, for which Ahmed Hassad would pay the ransom of a king.

No, damn him! She would tell him nothing.

They were in an underground city. She had seen enough of it, as they had brought her in, to so describe it. She had seen the far reaches of enormous caverns, lighted streets that disappeared into the distance, buildings that soared, traffic that moved, people who walked—all deep beneath a range of mountains somewhere in the western United States. They had brought her finally to a black glass building, and then to a luxurious apartment, and, after a time to this very comfortable room where she and Ahmed Hassad were watching, on a wall-size movie screen, what he had said was a live broadcast of Harry Borg and his young men in the act of storming Mesa Grande in search of her.

Damn Hassad! Damn him! Damn him!

Hassad was sitting beside her on a wide divan, perfectly relaxed. His long legs, clad in carefully tailored slacks, extended before him; his fingers steepled before his wide, silk-shirted chest where a gold chain and medal gleamed in black chest hair only faintly touched with gray; a smile of interest and appreciation on his darkly handsome face.

"This should prove interesting," Hassad had told her earlier as he had brought her into this room, his large dark eyes teasing. "My people have orders not to kill him, but short of that, they are at liberty to go as far as they like."

"You laid a trap for him?"

"He's a willing victim."

Hassad had made her comfortable and together they had watched dawn break at Mesa Grande, and the first of Harry's young men arrive and disperse to await Harry's arrival. And they had seen Harry's helicopter lift from the desert floor and come in, finally, to land before the security building at Mesa Grande.

"I challenged him to come," Hassad had said, smiling.

"You knew he would!"

"I want that man," Hassad said now, as he watched the spill of bodies as they rolled down the stairs at la Casa Grande. He turned his beautiful dark eyes on Lori. "I want Vec-Power," he said. "I want all the things you people know and won't tell me, but I want that man as much as the other. Allah! He is a genetic warehouse! He could father a race of giants."

"You won't like it," she said, her lips pressed thin.

"Won't like what?" He had only half heard her, his attention caught by the action on the screen.

"When he gets his hands on you."

Lori was watching the screen, too. Her good, high cheekbones were flushed with anger and excitement, her gray eyes wide. She was wearing her wheat-colored hair drawn back scalp-tight to a thick, single braid—her fighting coiffure, she'd called it, because the first chance she got, she was going to kill this SOB sitting beside her—and her simple peasant dress covered a rounding figure that was tense, jerking in an effort to help her husband as he fell.

The big, stupid idiot was going to break his neck!

The spill of bodies, arms and legs flailing, ended in a heap on the terrazzo floor. Harry rose easily, a big hand gripping the neck of each of his assailants, both of whom were limp.

"Had enough?" she heard him ask pleasantly.

"Godawmighty, yes!" one said, scrubbing blood from his mouth. The other could only nod pleadingly.

Harry threws them aside, turned, and raced up the stairs again. But he stopped halfway, for he saw, at the top, an elderly white-haired man in butler's dress, waiting. The man bent a head and spoke in a quiet, formal tone. "Mr. Borg, I assume?"

"You got it!"

"There is no need for more violence, Mr. Borg. If you'll come this way..."

Neither the butler nor Lori and Ahmed Hassad, who were listening, heard Harry check with his men telepathically before he moved. They all reported no more trouble. All opposition had folded as if by some hidden order.

"Come to la Casa," he told them. "Upstairs."

"On the double," Chad told him.

Lori and Ahmed Hassad watched Harry climb the stairs and follow the butler into another room. A different camera picked them up as the butler made an indication toward what Lori suddenly realized was another huge television screen, on which they were visible to Harry.

Harry's first reaction was sudden, obvious relief. "Lori! You all right?"

"Harry! My God, you almost killed yourself! You—"

But Harry's eyes, hot with fury, had shifted to Hassad. "You bastard!"

"Hello, Borg," Hassad said, quietly amused.

"Where are you?"

"All in good time," Hassad answered. "First, your wife. As you see, she is enjoying perfect health—for the moment."

"Hassad, you can't hide. I'll find you—if I have to crawl the last mile on my hands and knees!"

"No need of that," Hassad said. "I've sent transport."

"When?"

"It should be there now."

And as if on exact cue, Harry heard the distant, growing sound of a powerful aircraft. It passed directly overhead to hang, thundering, over the helipad.

"Check that," Harry said to Ernie, telepathically.

Ernie turned and ran, and a moment later reported back: "A jet-chopper, sir. A big one."

Harry nodded, and his eyes went back to Hassad. "You think I won't take you up on that?"

"I'm sure you will."

"You're damn right I will. And I won't come alone."

"Bring as many as you like," Hassad said agreeably. "I especially admire the young men you have with you now."

He reached forward and touched a button, and the screen went blank.

CHAPTER 16

George Bushby wanted to believe the little ringer. As a matter of fact, he had never wanted anything as much before in his entire life. If what she had been telling them was true, it would mean he had almost within his grasp not only the answer to all his financial problems but the answer to his marital difficulties as well. Being the first man in on a business relationship with aliens from another world could only mean, literally, billions without half trying. And if he were once again financially secure, he would be free from the worry and stress that were causing his life-threatening high blood pressure—if they were indeed the cause of it, as his doctor and Sara claimed—and then Sara would no longer have her reason for leaving him.

Of one thing, however, he was absolutely certain: He was not going to let *anyone* in on the fact that aliens were here—not the police, not the government, not the news media, not a friend, not a business associate, not a single damned anybody—until he was sure he had a lock on it.

And he hadn't a lock on it yet.

Were they friendlies? Were they enemies? Or were they just passersby, stranded here by some quirk of chance, wanting nothing but to go on unmolested?

He was no longer afraid of them, not really. At six-two and a hundred and ninety pounds, a man who stayed in shape, he was more than a match, physically, for both the aliens together. And while the weapons they carried were bloody lethal, he had weapons of his own—not including his hands—with which he could blow them away. And, when it came to that, he'd had three hard years in 'Nam learning to kill. He could go on acting the friendly, confused, even stupid professor, smiling, nodding, until he knew exactly who and what they were and what exactly they wanted.

This little ringer—if that's what she was—was damned good.

Tippi Calder, she'd said her name was. She'd had no trouble winning Sara over. Or Jillie. Both had accepted the child almost from the instant they had seen her. But not Jackie. Jackie, like himself, had a hard head. They both knew that if the aliens could come here from a distant planet, the task of creating a clever image of a human and programming it with a lot of data to give it authenticity would be no great problem.

And this little ringer had the data. Street addresses, descriptions of neighborhoods, high schools, Rose Parades, baseball teams and players were all at the tip of her tongue. She could be the real McCoy—a human who'd been in their world and had an implant that enabled her to talk with them—and she could be a ringer, an android. There was time to make damned sure, one way or the other.

"Make no mistakes," he'd told himself. "Get it right!"

And he was still hanging in, though it was no way easy.

His credulity had been stretched to the breaking point.

Get this: the aliens had come here, she had told him, to
save the world from a nuclear holocaust. How about that?
The holocaust was scheduled to begin in three days, she
had said, with the detonation of a nuclear bomb somewhere in the east, and the aliens wanted *him* to help *them*
prevent some terrorists or other from detonating the bomb.

Ever hear a wilder tale?

Pretty selfless aliens, coming all that way, going to all
that trouble to help a race of creatures they didn't even
know very well.

What was in it for *them*?

Nothing he'd been able to discover. The little ringer
was saying they wanted to save the human race from total
destruction as a kind of a public service. Hey, come on!
These two aliens were here alone—just these two—risk-
ing their lives to save the human race?

All right, it could be true.

On the other hand, it could be a pack of lies.

But there was still time to be very very damned sure.
So he sat, smiling, looking friendly, waiting.

Across the room, the little ringer was looking frustrated. "I can't understand it!" she was saying.

She had taken a time-out from her fight to make the
stubbornly doubting Mister Bushby see the light, and had
persuaded the family to assemble in the living room. The
two children were lying on the floor before the television
set, watching a rerun, and the two adults were sitting on
a divan, holding hands and watching her and Guss and
Sissi.

"He thinks I'm an android!" She was talking to Guss
and Sissi, who had taken chairs across the room, though
she didn't appear to be doing anything but sitting collapsed in a chair, looking at the Bushbys with total frus-
tration. Telepathy had its useful aspects, not the least of
which was the ability to hold a private conversation while

in the company of others without being overheard.

"Me? An android? That's an insult! I think they've been watching too much Saturday television, or reading too many comic books, or something."

"I suppose we *are* hard to believe," Sissi said.

"What's so hard about it? I mean, there you are! In the flesh, as any dunce can plainly see!"

"It's *why* we're here," Guss said. "I think that bothers him most. To think we'd go to all this trouble to help creatures in another dimension, total strangers—that *is* hard to swallow." And, after a moment's thought, he added, "I can hardly swallow it myself."

"Swallow it, lisser!" Sissi said. "You're here!"

"We haven't got forever," Tippi said. "Y'know what time it is?"

"The day's about gone."

"And that stubborn jackass keeps asking the same questions over and over. Just when I'm sure he believes me, he starts all over again. Who's on first, and all that silly nonsense."

"Is he so afraid of us?" Sissi asked.

"Not that much anymore."

"He's just overly cautious."

"He'll cautious the whole world right over the brink!"

"The mother seems ready to believe us."

"And the little girl."

"But not the boy."

"He's imitating his father."

"Figures."

Tippi drew a deep breath, gathering her forces. "Mr. Bushby," she said aloud. "What in the world can I do to make you understand that—that we can't go on wasting time? There isn't any time to waste!"

George Bushby, perhaps caught by the sincerity in her plea, got to his feet. Standing, he seemed to take on another appearance; he seemed leaner, harder. The brown eyes behind the horn-rimmed glasses had a sharper, more intense look. The gentle smile gone, his mouth had become flat, his jaw hard.

"I'm about ready to believe you, little lady," he said. "I want to believe you. All I need is a little more proof to bring me around."

"A little more. Okay. What?" Tippi asked, relieved.

"Have them give me their weapons."

"Oh, my gosh!" Tippi said. Her distress was obvious to Guss and Sissi.

"Now what?" Guss asked telepathically.

"He says he will believe us, and I suppose help us, if you'll give him your weapons."

"Our weapons!" Guss said. "For Osis sake, why?"

"Why?" Tippi asked George.

"To prove to me they are friendly."

"He says to prove you're friendly," Tippi told Guss.

"How do we know *he's* friendly?" Guss asked.

"Oh, good heavens!" Tippi said, both aloud and telepathically. "You two could go on like this till the end of time!"

"I can wait," George Bushby said quietly.

"You *can't* wait!" Tippi was ready to scream. "You've got to—"

"Hey, look at this!" Jackie, on the floor before the television set, pushed up with excitement and concern, pointing at the television screen. "There's a dead one!"

"A dead what?"

"Lizard-man! A dead lizard-man! It's a bulletin! Just came on!"

And there was, indeed, a picture of a dead Jassan on the television screen. It was Lss. Zass, who had been killed in Harry Borg's apartment. The news blackout finally had been broken.

"... invasion by aliens," the anchorman was saying, "of unknown numbers in Reseda, California. One American citizen is known dead. One wounded. The body of the dead alien, of an unknown race, from an unknown planet, is under intense scrutiny by scientists. Two other aliens are said to have escaped, though by what means and to what destination is not known. The sole witness, Fred Harrow, age sixty-eight, of Reseda, suffered the loss of a hand in an alleged gunfight with the aliens. He has been unable to make a coherent statement, authorities say, because of injuries and shock."

There was more, much more.

"They came after us!" Guss said to Sissi.

"You knew they would," Sissi answered.

"Who?" Tippi asked.

"The Vessan Guard—that's their uniform."

"Who're they?"

"Government police," Sissi said. "The Gateway was officially closed, guarded by Bissi. The penalty for going through was death—and they, the Guard, came after us."

"Oh, wow!"

"They got caught and ran back!" Guss said, half in disgust and half in fear. "Now everybody knows about us!"

"They killed a human!"

Sissi was terrified. She backed away from the television set, her eight-fingered hand going to the holstered esso. Guss, seeing her movement, realizing with her what the reaction of the male human would be, drew his weapon.

"No! Guss! Sissi!" Tippi screamed.

She saw that George Bushby had become, almost instantly, a very sinister man. He had shed all pretense of being a harmless academic, and he stood poised, the trained killer he had once been, with the scars of Vietnam to prove it.

"No, Mr. Bushby," Tippi said desperately. "Please listen!"

"Talk," George said. "I'm listening."

"Those were police—*their* police! They were looking for Guss and Sissi because it was against the law for Guss and Sissi to come here to help you! Honest! It was the death penalty for them! See, they got scared, or something! I mean—oh, please believe me!"

"Tell me about it," George said.

There'd been a change in him in the last moment—as if he'd devised a plan, as if he wanted to talk, to use up time. "I'm beginning to see the light," he said. "They were police, you say, looking for these two?"

"The male child!" Sissi screamed. "He's gone!"

While the others had been caught in shock, confronting each other, Jackie had slipped out of the room. Sissi raced to the archway, then into the foyer, the tendrils of her forked tongue holding the scent of the boy, following him. She raced up the stairs to the upper floor and followed the scent to Jillie's bedroom. From the doorway, she saw Jackie's heels protruding from under Jillie's bed.

"Name of Osis!"

She caught Jackie's heels and dragged him out, still clutching the telephone Jillie had left hidden there, still yelling into the mouthpiece.

"We've got lizards here! Two of 'em!"

Sissi tore the telephone from his hands.

"He called out!" she yelled telepathically to Guss.

"Outside?" Guss asked, his mental voice gone shrill.

"Outside, yes!"

Sissi was wrestling with Jackie. She had a hand in his collar, and she was jerking him, dragging him back into the hall.

"The cursed little monster—a communicator hidden under the bed."

She went down the stairs running, dragging Jackie. Right now, furious and frightened, she had the strength of a half dozen boys Jackie's age. Reaching the living room, she threw the lad, stumbling, across the room to his family. They were being held against a far wall by the threat of the esso in Guss's trembling hand.

"I called nine-one-one!" Jackie said. He was scared, triumphant, crying.

"For God's sake!" his father said.

"Told 'em we had lizards—all I had time for!"

"You shouldn't have!" his mother scolded. She had hold of him, checking him for possible arterial bleeding. "They might have killed you."

"It's what Dad would have done!" The boy, squirming in his mother's arms, looked at his father. "Ain't it, Dad?"

His father was swearing furiously but silently—his lock on the alien presence was shot to hell now.

Tippi translated for Guss. "Nine-one-one! It's the emergency number. The police will come!"

"Zat!" Guss said. He didn't know what else to say. He was holding the esso on the adult male. Great Essnia, how that one had changed! Now he could believe that the human had earned those medals he had seen in the case down below. He was another Harry Borg, as dangerous as a cage full of rasses!

"The Guard killed one of them," Sissi said. "They're going to think we're killers, too!"

"But you're not!" Tippi protested. "I'll tell them!"

"They won't believe you!"

"This one didn't believe you! Why would they?"

"But I can't let them kill you!"

"The first thing to do is tie these up!" Sissi said.

"Yes!" Guss agreed. "For Osis sake, hurry!" He centered the weapon in his hand on George Bushby.

Whether Guss intended to shoot or not made no difference to George—that eight-fingered hand was shaking so badly that the damned shooter could let go a purple hole-buster at any minute. He stood stock still and let the female alien tie his wrists again.

Tippi helped. "I'm sorry, I'm sorry," she sobbed as she tied the wrists of Sara and, very lightly, the wrists of Jillie. "It's gonna be all right, honey. Don't worry."

Sissi tied Jackie. Not lightly. "Cursed little monster!"

"They'll kill us," Guss said. "We look different—they'll kill us!"

"Tell your friends it's no use fighting," George said to Tippi.

"They don't want to fight!" Tippi protested. "They want to *help*!"

"Whatever," George said. His mouth wore a thin smile.

"Honest!"

"There'll be a SWAT team here in ten minutes," George said. "If you're real—a human—you know that. If you're not real, I'm telling you now. Our police are tough. They won't let you get away alive. Put a white flag out the window. Give up."

"He's saying you better surrender," Tippi told Guss.

"Tippi!" Guss exclaimed. "For Osis sake! We killed one of the guards! The guards killed one of them! It's war, Tippi!"

At the sound of sirens, Tippi ran to a front window. It was growing dark outside, but she was able to see the first arrivals, two black-and-whites, as they flashed past the driveway. She heard them stop out of sight. More sirens were drawing near from various directions.

"Oh, wow," Tippi wailed.

Gus joined her at the window. Though he couldn't hear sirens, he could certainly see the uniformed figures of two patrolmen as they ran, crouching, guns drawn, to take up positions on either side of the driveway. Tippi's despair was communicated to him, and to him, excitable as he was, it came through as terror.

"I can manage this," he said. He lifted his esso, took careful aim through the window, and sent a purple bolt into the trunk of a fairly large tree standing on the parkway. The purple ray was spectacular in the growing darkness; the crash of the tree falling, its trunk sheared off cleanly, was even more spectacular. The tree fell into the street, causing two approaching squad cars to crash with a great rending of metal and a strangling siren sound.

"No!" Tippi screamed. "Guss, for Jesus' sake! Why?"

"Harry Borg did it," Guss said. "It was very effective."

"You've got a problem now!" George said. "The SWAT team's gonna take that as a warning you'll kill them!"

"He's saying the police are going to think you're killers," Tippi explained to Guss and Sissi. "What a mess now!"

"That's my Guss!" Sissi said. "My hero!"

"They'll think twice before they attack us!" Guss said, defending his actions.

"The third time they think, they'll blast us away!"

Tippi was running back and forth. "Oh, my Lord, my Lord!" She stopped in front of George Bushby. "What're we going to do? You can think of something, can't you? You owe these two something! They're trying to save your lives!"

George had been watching sharply, seeing the obvious fear in the aliens, the shock and despair over the shot the male alien had fired with what must have been a dramatic result outside, and he was becoming persuaded that the girl, Tippi Calder, might be what she said she was. Her reactions were too damned human to be alien!

"Let me talk to the police," he said.

"He wants you to let him talk to the police," Tippi relayed to Guss.

Guss was shocked. "That's a trick!"

"We can't trust him, Tippi!" Sissi said.

"They don't trust you," Tippi said, despairing again.

And then the loud, metallic voice of a bullhorn came through the walls. "This is the police. This is the police. You are in no danger. Repeat, you are in no danger. Do you understand?"

Tippi, her eyes round, translated. "They say you're in no danger—they don't want to hurt you, Guss."

The bullhorn blared again. "The house is surrounded; the streets are sealed off. We have a combat force. We ask you to surrender peaceably."

"They say they've got a SWAT team—police fighters," Tippi explained. "Guss, they don't quit!"

The sudden brilliance of high-power searchlights burst through the front window, frightening those in the living room even more. Guss raced to the window to pull the cords that drew the draperies. Then he peered around the edge, and what he saw made his large golden eyes bulge, made his forked tongue whip. There were lights everywhere out there, like enormous, fierce, malevolent eyes staring back at him.

"Osaris preserve us!" he moaned.

"It's not that bad, Guss!" Sissi said, trying to calm him.

"It's worse!" Guss said.

"Get that gun away from him!" George said to Tippi.

"But he's frightened!"

"I can see he's frightened! So am I! If he starts shooting, we'll all go up in smoke!"

"Put your gun away, Guss!" Tippi pleaded.

"It's all I've got!" Guss said. "I wouldn't last a tiss!"

"We aren't going to last a tiss, anyway," Sissi said.

George turned to Tippi. "You go out and talk to them.

Tell them we're hostages in here—that we need a little time!"

"Can I go out, Guss?" Tippi asked. "I'll tell them you want to talk."

"They won't believe you. They'll take you!"

"And we'd have no one to—"

The front window crashed; a small object blew its way through the draperies, banged against a wall, fell on the floor, and immediately began spewing out a mist.

A voice outside yelled, "Who the hell did that?"

"It just went off—"

"Goddamn! Take him in custody!"

Guss grabbed the tear-gas shell and threw it back through the window. He didn't know what a tear-gas shell was, or how dangerous it was—it could have caused the house to vanish in another moment, for all he knew—and he fired another bolt of purple through the window, high up, hoping to discourage another such attack.

"Guss, no!" Sissi's scream only added to Guss's growing hysteria.

George yelled at his family. "Roll against the wall!"

Jillie was crying. Her mother was trying to comfort her, though she herself was frightened out of her wits. Jackie, his freckles standing out like leopard spots against his pallor, was staring at Guss round-eyed. "Geeze cripes! Geeze cripes!" he said, over and over.

The bullhorn yelled, "Hold your fire!"

Guss was at the draperies again. "They're coming in!"

He had seen three men charge across the lawn, bent over, weapons held before them. There was a sudden burst of vibrations from the rear of the house. "More trucks!" Tippi said. "More SWAT team!"

She was right about that. With cornered aliens shooting purple death rays at them through the windows, there was more than enough reason for the police to issue a riot call of unprecedented proportions. Every agency of city, county, state, and federal government was sending forces. The streets for miles in every direction were already jammed. There was scarcely room in the sky for another helicopter, media or police, as they all jockeyed for a position that would let them focus lights on the house below.

Tippi could hear it. Guss and Sissi could see it on the television screen.

All television channels had been given over, naturally, to a story of this dimension. The armed forces gathering outside the house were shown. But, more important, the utter hopelessness of their own position was made abundantly clear to Guss and Sissi.

"We're finished!" Guss said.

He could see the assault force on the television screen.

"Well, we tried," Sissi said.

And—if it wasn't at that exact moment, it was so close to it that it didn't matter—there was a loud *crack* and *snap*, and right there in the living room a glowing space appeared.

A Gateway!

Then, framed in the Gateway, for Guss, Sissi, Tippi, and all the rest to see, was a figure of a Jassan. He was wearing a dirty smock, his spectacles were askew on his muzzle, and he was carrying a yellow-tubed mind-blanker, just in case. His yellow eyes were worried, searching.

"Guss? You there?" the figure asked.

"Los Ross!" Guss yelled.

"Oh, thank you, Osaris!" Sissi said to the sky.

"Sorry I took so long," Los Ross said. "Dosis couldn't find an issis, and I couldn't—"

Sissi went through the Gateway like a shot.

"I'm coming, too!" Tippi screeched, and followed her.

But not Guss. Guss held back, caught by a thought

that was important to him. And now that an escape and safety were at hand, with a moment or two to spare before the human police crashed in on the scene, he could think clearly again.

"Give me that!" he said.

He took the mind-blanker from Los Ross's unresisting hand, turned, and went back to the humans. He pinned each of the humans in a yellow ray that left them without will, staring senselessly. Then he untied them all, got them to their feet, and guided them toward the Gateway.

"What are you *doing*?" Sissi asked, shocked.

"They didn't believe me," Guss said. "This big liss called me a liar. Nobody calls Guss Rassan a liar! I'm going to show them what I am, and who I am, and that what I said was true!"

"You've got to *show* them?" Tippi asked.

"Oh, for vass sake!" Sissi groaned.

The Gateway closed with them all safely on the far side.

When the police finally stormed into the living room of the Bushby residence, they found the house empty.

CHAPTER 17

Globe One was known to thousands of people in and out of government, and in and out of the media, as an experimental operation, privately owned and financed, engaged in a search for a practical method of producing usable oil from oil shale.

That it was secret was considered necessary and permissible, owing to the intense competition among major oil companies. And since the end result was going to benefit all mankind, the operation had been allowed, even encouraged, to conduct its efforts without the intense government and media scrutiny that a less philanthropical enterprise would routinely suffer. Neither did it hurt that the philanthropist who was spending such enormous amounts of money for such a selfless purpose was Ahmed Hassad, a man who many said was the richest single individual in the world; the very rich enjoy privileges not given to others.

The fact that the operation was taking place in a very

remote area of the Rocky Mountains, accessible only by private railroad and highway, and by air only to a private airport, made secrecy a relatively easy matter. And the complex of buildings that could be seen on the ground outside the entrance to Globe One—warehouses, equipment yards, and office buildings, all behind strong fences— was no more than would be expected of an enterprise of this kind.

Admission was by pass only. The guards who checked the passes were heavily armed; some even carried combat rifles. The locals—the few there were—had learned it was unwise to go near the place. Trespassers, even the curious caught with binoculars at a distance, were not welcome. A number of the latter had left the area after being caught, it was said, and their relatives were still awaiting letters.

Harry Borg and his cadre came in by jet helicopter, arriving midafternoon of the same day on which they had assaulted Mesa Grande—Sunday, April 6—and were met by a squad of heavily armed security guards. The first few moments were tense, since the matter of visitors carrying weapons was a possible point of contention, but the matter was not even brought up. The security guards were big, flint-faced young men, not at all friendly. The coldly polite broken-nosed sergeant said, "This way, please."

And that was about it.

"Close up," Harry said to his men.

They were taken to a buslike conveyance, open-sided and battery-powered, which rolled swiftly and silently on rubber tires along a paved kilometer from helipad to portal.

"Would you look at this!" Arnie Garrett said to Eddie Cole, sitting beside him. "Fort Knox should have such a gate!"

From a distance, the entrance to Globe One seemed not at all unusual—simply a shaft entrance into a mining operation. But close in, passing through it, one saw that two enormous doors, each a meter thick and built of steel and concrete, were capable of sealing the twenty-meter opening airtight.

"Discourage visitors," Chad said. He flipped a large wad of what looked like gum-wrapper foil at the door hinge on the right to show his disdain.

"Keep 'em in, too," Homer said.

He flipped gum-wrapper foil at the door hinge on the other side.

"You take a good burglar," Sam Barnstable said as he turned to watch the gigantic doors close silently behind them. "He always likes to keep a door open somewhere." He dropped a gum wrapper.

"Homer's a burglar?" Arnie asked, pretending surprise.

"Not Homer—Sam," Eddie said.

"I didn't know that!"

They were speaking telepathically, so the security guards were unaware they were saying anything at all. Nor did the guards pay any attention to the gum wrappers the lads continued to discard along the way.

Harry glanced at his cadre and felt cold pride.

He was more than angry now; he was pure mayhem being held on a very short leash. He waited with impatience as the conveyance took them deep into the mountain, his hands flexing, wanting the throat of Ahmed Hassad. The day, the moment, would come—and damned soon.

The corridor ended, revealing to Harry Borg and his cadre an unbelievable scene. An underground city! There were buildings several stories high, there were streets, there was vehicular traffic, there were pedestrians. The actual extent of it all was hard to estimate, but it had the look of going on and on and on.

This was *not* a shale-oil operation. But what was it? And why was it here?

"Reminds me of that command center in Jassa," Chad said telepathically. "Not as big. Not as old."

"But just as bombproof," Harry said.

"What I was thinking, sir."

"Why would a man like Hassad build a bomb shelter?" Sam asked.

"Knows something *we* don't know?" Homer suggested.

"You got it," Eddie Cole whispered softly.

"What I got is my hair going stiff," Arnie said.

"At ease!"

They had stopped before the entrance of a building, and Harry wanted his mind sharp and unencumbered. The building had the look of a headquarters, bigger than the others, stronger, made of finer materials. The security guards motioned them out, formed up around them, and took them inside. Marble halls, softly lighted, echoed with the clicking of their heels. Soft, warm air, lightly scented, blew in their faces. Distant music played.

They were brought, finally, to Ahmed Hassad. He was in a richly carpeted, low-ceilinged room, standing beside a Rodin sculpture. A big man, as big and as powerfully built as Harry, and, Harry saw again, almost unbelievably handsome. When he smiled his pleasant smile of greeting, he showed a row of perfect teeth. "Ah, my determined adversaries."

"Where's Lori?"

The words had come through clenched teeth, harsh, grating, almost a growl, for Harry Borg's anger had seethed to a boil at the sight of Ahmed Hassad.

"She's here, unharmed," Hassad said.

"I want to see her. Now!"

"In good time," Hassad said.

A glance backward showed Harry that the security

guards had gone, leaving himself and his cadre alone with Hassad. He turned back, and without wondering where the guards had gone or why, he lunged to take Hassad's throat in his hands—and found only thin air.

Hassad seemed still to be there. But he was fragmented now, the pieces of him bathing Harry's hands.

"What the hell?" Harry swore.

Hassad's laugh was pleasant and only a little taunting. "A hologram," he explained.

"Whatever the hell that is."

"A picture—a three-dimensional image. It's done with lasers."

"Bloody coward—I should have known!"

Harry had retreated, and the image had formed again.

"I'm many things, but not a coward," the smiling image said. "Now I want other things. Are you done with your aggression? Can you talk sensibly?"

Harry fought himself for a moment, gained control. "I am."

"You won't need your weapons. Leave them with your men."

It took only a moment for Harry to agree. His hot blue eyes held Chad's calm gray ones as he took the short-barreled police special from his belt holster. "You men stand at ease until I get back," he said aloud, for hidden microphones.

Telepathically, he was saying, "I'll be in touch every foot of the way. Look worried, talk among yourselves. Don't let anyone disarm you. Understood?"

"Copy," they all replied.

"I don't like it, sir," Homer said aloud. "One of us ought to go with you. I'm volunteering."

Harry winked. "You do as I say!" he said angrily.

"Sir!" Homer said, apparently chastened.

As Harry left the room, the young men were arguing loudly and convincingly among themselves. Goddamn,

Harry was thinking as he moved down the hall, they still make 'em right back home!

"Copy that." Chad's telepathic voice was soft. "Thank you, sir."

"A straight corridor here!" Harry's mental voice became suddenly harsh. "Twenty paces to an elevator. Up two flights. Opens on a foyer, a wide room. This is the buzzard's nest—unless it's another mirage."

He waited.

Then Ahmed Hassad entered the wide room from the left. All that movement—he had to be in the flesh. Smiling, he crossed to a bar. Harry measured him as a man would measure a bear he was destined to meet in hand-to-hand, to-the-death combat. Hassad was his equal in size. His red silk shirt, open at the throat, rolled back at the sleeves, revealed his chest and arms, covered with dense black hair, a symbol of virility not seen in his too-handsome face. He was all man—make no mistake about it. One heluva tough man.

And Harry Borg was glad of that.

"I'm going to kill you one day," Harry said. "With my hands."

Hassad slanted his head. "I'm sure you'll try."

He had poured wine. "A very good sherry," he said.

He motioned to Harry as he moved away from the bar to sit in a large, almost thronelike chair. Harry accepted what seemed more a challenge than a hospitable gesture. He crossed to the bar—and found not one but two glasses of sherry.

He didn't take either. He turned.

"Harry! Thank God!"

Lori came to him, running, from an entrance across the room. He caught her in his arms, and for that instant all hatred and violence were gone, swept away by a sudden flood of love and relief. She was so warm, so sweet,

so fragrant with the body scent that was just her own—
he hugged her close, kissed her lips, her hair, her cheek,
her lips again. Then he held her away.

"You all right?"

"Yes."

"The baby?"

"Yes, darling. We're both all right." Her gray eyes, so
wide and beautiful beneath her strong eyebrows, were
wet with tears. "We've missed you Harry."

"God! I've missed you!"

He looked at her. Her strong cheekbones were shining,
her light brown hair was drawn back severely, her wide
and kind mouth looked pale; she was wearing a simple
smocklike garment. But in his eyes she was beautiful. He
hugged her again.

"Remarkable," Hassad said. "I envy anyone capable
of that kind of love—or that much."

Harry and Lori turned from each other to face him.

Hassad was sitting in the thronelike straight-backed
chair, one leg crossed over the other, the glass of wine
swirling gently in a big hand, an expression of quiet
amusement on his darkly handsome face.

"Please sit down." He motioned to a divan a little distance before him.

Harry guided Lori to the divan. Because she was pregnant, he wanted her off her feet and resting. But he would
not sit. He stood behind her, a hand resting on her shoulder. "She's going with me when I leave," Harry said.

"That's up to you." Hassad sipped his wine.

"I'm leaving now, then."

Hassad smiled. "Soon. After you've answered a few
questions."

He set his glass aside, rose to get the two glasses Harry
and Lori had left on the bar, served Lori—with a special

smile—then set Harry's on a small table near him.

"You may as well relax," he said. "We're going to be a while."

Lori looked up. "I've told him nothing, Harry," she said telepathically.

"Good girl," he answered in kind.

Hassad took the thronelike chair again. He was very serious, all pretensions dropped. "I know you both want a full and happy life. And I can see to it that you have it." He sipped the wine. "Or that you don't have it."

"Like hell you can!"

"Please, don't challenge me just yet." He looked at them, his long-lashed, dark eyes bright. "I can give you more luxury than you've ever dreamed possible. I can promise you a long life together to raise as many children as you like. I *want* to do these things for you. All I ask is your cooperation."

"You had your chance!" Harry said.

"And you refused to cooperate."

"You didn't want a deal," Harry said. "You wanted it all!"

"There wasn't time—there isn't time—for haggling. I want Vec-Power. Not just an interest in it, not just the right to use it—I want to own it."

"You want more than that!" Harry said.

"You're right. I want to know its secret—how it creates energy."

"And even more—you wanted me."

"Yes, I want you. Very much."

"No Sale! *I'm* the man! You'll find that out when I get my hands on you—when I'm sure you're not just a picture in the air." He looked around the walls. "And when I'm sure you haven't got snipers ready to drill me in the back."

"Your threats bore me," Hassad said impatiently. "There isn't time for such nonsense!"

"What's your damned rush?" Harry asked suddenly. "Moving out of Ireland, moving out of Mesa Grande, moving in here! What is this place, anyway? Shale oil, your ass! I don't believe it."

Hassad's face went cold. "Answer my questions, and you'll get the answer to your questions."

Lori felt Harry's hand stiffen on her shoulder. She caught the hand in one of her own and tipped her head to look up at him.

"Harry, please. Take a little time, listen. Talk to him."

The short red-brown beard on Harry's face moved as the muscles in his jaws worked against his rage. He gained control again. "Ask your questions."

Hassad took a moment, testing Harry's control with his eyes before he spoke. "Where were you between August and November of last year?"

"None of your damned business."

"It *is* my business," Hassad said evenly. "I've made it mine."

"Lots of luck!"

"You're life is at risk, Mr. Borg."

"I'm used to that."

"But never have you been in such danger." He lifted the glass of wine in a gesture that stopped Harry's response. "Let me explain my interest in where you were."

"I'm listening," Harry said.

"You were an aged alcoholic when you left," Hassad said. "You returned, younger by thirty years, no longer an alcoholic, an athlete of considerable strength and prowess. My people have documented through fingerprints that you are the same man." He paused to study Harry's reaction. "I know of no detoxification hospital, or procedure, capable of that kind of rejuvenation."

"There's a lot you don't know."

"Obviously. And you're going to fill me in."

"You put me, my wife, and my men back outside and we can talk about it."

"You won't leave here until I have the answers."

"Then we've got a long visit ahead of us."

The soft, golden tone of a bell sounded; Ahmed Hassad rose in answer to its call.

"I'll be back in a moment." He paused. "You are being watched. Be wise, be patient."

He left the room.

"Chad?" Harry said telepathically.

"Sir!" Chad's response was immediate, though distant.

"You secure?"

"All secure."

"I've got a stalemate here."

"Need assistance?"

"Not at the moment. Just—stay loose."

"Loose it is, sir."

Lori had been listening. "Chad and the boys are here?" she asked Harry silently.

"They're here."

Aloud, for the microphones, he said, "Now, don't you worry, hon. We're going to walk out of here. And we'll walk out rich, you'll see."

"Harry, I'm scared. I think he's mad—I mean, insane." Telepathically, she added, "And I'm not kidding."

Harry agreed with her aloud. Also aloud, he blustered and bragged about what he was going to do and not do, what he was going to say and not say, and for how much. But mind-to-mind, he reassured her: "Hang in, hon. The lads are loaded with enough power to whip an army. And I'm loaded. We'll get out of here, no matter what."

She caught his hand, held it against her cheek.

They gave their attention to each other then, yielding

to the desire to make up for the time they had been separated, to heal the wounds suffered at being torn apart. He kissed her gently, she kissed him in return, and they looked at each other, faces close, and drank from each other's eyes.

When Hassad returned a few moments later, he returned with two men carrying a television set. And Hassad was a different man. He was sharper now, more intense, cold. He was almost a different personality. Harry wondered what had happened that could change a man that much.

The men put the television set down, plugged it in, and left. Hassad turned the set on.

"This is a tape," Hassad said. "Made a few moments ago."

The screen cleared.

"Damn!" Harry cursed silently.

"Sir?" Chad asked. Harry's curse had carried telepathically.

"They've got a picture of a dead Jassan on a TV screen here," Harry told him. "A Vessan Guard, by the uniform."

"Where'd they get him?"

"Don't know."

Harry found Hassad's eyes riveted on him.

"Well?" Hassad asked.

Harry pretended ignorance. "What the hell is that—that creature?"

He was not a convincing actor.

"You tell me," Hassad said.

"How would I know?"

"He was killed in your apartment. In Reseda."

"He *was*?"

Impatient anger tensed Hassad's features. "Let's stop the damned nonsense! I want answers! That creature is not of this world. And there were two more in your apartment. They killed the manager, wounded another man, and escaped. You know who and what they are! You know where they've gone and how they got there!"

"Y'think so, eh?"

"You were there!"

Harry was still feeling the shock of seeing the dead Jassan. He was trying to pretend he knew nothing, but pretense was not for him—he was too direct a man. What was showing was the reaction of a hard man who had been kicked in the belly and was trying to pretend it didn't hurt.

Christ! The Jassans had come through the sealed Gateway! The highest government command had said no one could go through, but the damned Vessan Guard had gone through. Why? And they'd killed Joe Lansky, the manager? Damn it to hell!

Lori's cry of sympathy was telepathic. "Poor Mr. Lansky." Harry gripped her hand. "Say nothing, baby."

"These creatures," Hassad said, "they're public knowledge now!"

Harry took a deep breath, forcing himself to adjust. There was no longer a need for secrecy. He had to accept the new parameters. "And you want in?"

"I'm going to get in!" Hassad said. "You're going to tell me what I want to know if I have to tear it out of you with the damndest tortures you can ever imagine—beginning with your wife and that unborn child. Your options are running out, man!"

"We don't scare," Harry said.

"Nor do you reason," Hassad came back.

"Try me again."

"Is it true you were—where these creatures came from?"

"If it is?"

"And is it true they rejuvenated you?"

"And if *that* is?"

"Then all else becomes unimportant, as you damned well know!" Burning with rage, Hassad was up and pacing. "If it *is* true—if there is another planet, another race of beings in contact with us, then—then nothing else matters!"

"You can see the possibilities?"

"Endless possibilities!" Hassad said from across the room. There were two spots of pallor on his cheeks. "Your Vec-Power came from there—I know it did! And there has to be much more. There *is* much more!" He pointed a rigid finger at Harry. "Your rejuvenation—that process alone! It has a value beyond sight!"

"If it exists."

"Damn it, man!"

Harry showed his teeth in a hard grin. "I've got you coming my way now, you bloody bastard!"

Hassad glared at him, then finally gained control. "You only think you have," he said softly.

"I know I have. I'm going to own you!"

"Not possible," Hassad told him. He was thinking hard now, measuring, balancing. His eyes had become keen and shiny again. After further moments of thought, he made a decision. "I'll make you a deal."

"I'm listening," Harry said. He was quiet, cold and wary. Whatever was going to come from Hassad was going to be like nothing he'd heard before—that was sure. Harry knew that from the deadly seriousness of Hassad's manner, from the new glitter in his black eyes. But in a moment Hassad changed, as if he had backed away from something. And what he said then seemed a weak substitute.

"By telling me what I want to know now," Hassad said, "you and your woman can live the rest of your lives in luxury."

"You've said that before."

"I'm saying it again—and meaning it."

"And if I don't tell you what you want to know?"

"There will be much pain—beginning with her."

Harry looked at Lori and found her looking at him, her eyes wide.

"Steady, girl," he told her telepathically. "He's bluffing. I'm going to call his hand."

"We don't scare that easy," he told Hassad.

"You're a fool."

"A fool with a counteroffer."

"And that is?"

"I want a contract for Vec-Power, a bona fide contract that will hold up in a court of law. I want a million in gold up front. When I have that, and we're on the outside—and when I've had a chance at you with my bare hands, man to man—I'll sit down and answer your questions."

"I refuse your offer."

"Think about it, chump. Take a day or two."

Hassad lifted a finger in a signal. Two strong-looking women appeared almost at once and advanced toward Lori.

"No, you don't!" Harry said.

He took one step toward Hassad—and heard the flat *crack*! of a bullet passing close to his ear.

Three of the pictures that decorated different walls of the room had fallen forward to reveal gunports; automatic weapons were covering Harry from three different angles.

"You bastard," he breathed.

But he remained standing motionless as the women took hold of Lori and led her toward the doorway. She looked back at him, eyes very wide, fearful, and protested telepathically:

"Harry, for God's sake!"

"Don't worry!" Harry answered in the same way. "He's bluffing!"

"How do you know?"

"Played a lot of poker."

She was shocked, outraged. "With my life, you're playing poker?"

"It's the only way to go."

She was swearing out loud when the door closed behind her.

CHAPTER 18

Maywood Tucker was a man of no distinction. When remembered at all, and he seldom was, he was remembered as someone who brought the Christmas season to mind. His china blue eyes, his white, wispy hair, his round figure, his gentle benevolent smile, were faintly reminiscent of Santa Claus. To accept him as such a person, however, would be a dreadful mistake. Many of those who had done so were dead now. Maywood Tucker was a very dangerous man.

But he was not dangerous at the moment.

He was blinded by total darkness. Sitting on the floor, his back against the wall, he could see absolutely nothing. He knew he was at the end of a narrow aisle about ten feet from the locked door that closed this space. On either side of him were floor-to-ceiling steel shelves that were packed, he had found by groping in the dark, with office supplies—boxes of paper, boxes of file folders, envelopes, pencils, tablets.

There was no possible way to escape. He had tried everything he could, beating at the door, yelling, but all to no avail. He had spent the past several hours as he was now, wondering where he was and how he had gotten here.

His head ached abysmally.

The pricked point of entry where the needle had gone into his upper arm ached also, but nothing like his head. Whatever the drug the turbaned devil had used, it had been effective. He could remember only a few moments after the injection—the dark face of his assailant, the questioning look in the glittering black eyes, the slow turning wheel of the walls and ceiling of the old warehouse as he fell. And now this.

But he was not helpless. They had missed the small automatic pistol he carried snugged up in the fleshy concealment of his crotch. Whoever opened the door, be it the turbaned devil or any other, was going to die a moment later. And that was a solid promise he had made over and over.

He had gotten the order by telephone: "Cancel!" That was all.

And that was all that had been needed. Certainly a project of this magnitude required one signal—one sharp, immediately recognizable, unarguable signal—that would bring the project to a halt, instantly, at any moment, up to the last split second. No confusion, no delay, no debate. "Cancel!"

And it was done.

Except that when he had gone to the old warehouse on the Hoboken waterfront to relay that command, he had found the warehouse empty. He had thought it abandoned, until he found the tall, very thin, very weary-looking man, who wore a beard and a red silk turban, coming out of the shadows. A Sikh? Very probably, though he spoke perfect English in softly accented tones.

"Jessica Jones?" He had seemed puzzled. "Nay, sahib. I know of no such person."

And the building was empty.

Yesterday the device had been just there, where the light of the dirt-caked windows fell, there by the workbench, now empty, there where a faint impression suggested that a cradle had stood. Yesterday, the thin, smock-clad figure of Hale Benedict, working in a blind, dedicated, cursing fury, had been weaving wires inside the stainless steel interior of the shell. Yesterday, Manuel and Ali, the assassins, had hovered near.

He had moved into the empty building angrily, trying to fight back sudden panic. The responsibility for this project—the assembly of the device, whatever it was—had been his, and if he had lost control of it, he had lost his life.

"They were here!" he said. "Where the hell did they go?"

"They?" The soft question came at his shoulder; the turbaned man had followed him. "I know of no 'they,' sahib. This building has long been vacant. If you are interested in a lease..."

That was all he remembered, but for the sharp prick in his shoulder, the wheeling of the ceiling and walls, and then—this darkened room.

His tongue was growing thick for want of water, and his belly growled with hunger. He had relieved himself, and he did so near the door, and that degrading necessity further infuriated him. When that door opened, someone would die. He guaranteed it.

The small automatic pistol was cocked, ready.

Finally, a small sound alerted him. He shoved himself up. He held the gun before him, waiting, but he got no chance to use it. The sudden light blinded him. He could not see the short barrel of the machine pistol. He did hear the muffled sputter, and perhaps he felt the impact of the bullets—but surely not for long.

"He's dead now," Kolankov said. "Depend on it."

Jessica Jones had waited at a distance in the protective shadow of a printing press. She had come forward to watch as Kolankov, a huge block of a man, backed out of the supply room, dragging the body of the pudgy man with the china blue eyes, leaving a trail of blood. She felt no sympathy for the dead man. She picked up the small automatic pistol Kolankov had tossed out of the store-room and looked at Sri Singh with disgust.

"You disarmed him!" she said.

"I thought I had, memsahib." The turbaned Indian was obsequious, his voice soft, though his black eyes never lost their glitter. "And the drug should have killed him." He moved his thin hands expressively. "The gods wanted it otherwise."

"Gods, your ass," Jessica said. "You screwed up."

She turned to include them all.

She had five with her now, Vladimir Kolankov, Sri Singh, Manuel and Ali, and Sandra Hope. All proven, all trusted. She was proud of her fierce and totally dedicated group. And she was proud of her accomplishments of the past two days. This was what it meant to be in control— you could make things happen.

Jobe's Stationery was an office supply and printing business that had been in Washington for a half century. They were known and respected by everyone; their truck—a very large one, bearing the distinctive logo, a Benjamin Franklin figure and a printing press—was a familiar sight, accepted on any street in the capital. What wasn't known was that the owner had been in such desperate financial straits that he had been willing to accept an enormous amount of cash, take no more than his hat, and vacate the premises at once.

Now the business, and the truck, belonged to Jessica Jones.

By the time anyone got around to looking into the transaction, it would be too late. She was only three days from her moment of glory. She had the Hand of God safely here. Hale Benedict was safely in his Eternal Sleep, and that meant that no one—apart from whoever had sent Maywood Tucker to her with the assignment in the first place, and with Maywood Tucker dead, that mysterious one could never find her, or the Hand of God, in the time remaining—but no one even knew what was going to happen.

Those with her thought it was going to be a simple explosion, something larger than usual, but only an explosion.

But it was going to be so much more than that.

The knowing had been like the Light of Salvation, growing in her, burning. In the moments of darkness, when sleep would not bring her rest, she had been nourished by the visual image of those first moments of her Statement—when the Hand of God would strike.

Thus, it would come to pass:

In that first instant, all within a distance of three miles of ground zero, the point at which she chose to leave the truck containing the Hand of God, would vanish! Steel and concrete and brick and all flesh would simply cease to be. With the blinding light, enormous wind would then blow outward, like a gigantic torch from hell, flinging cars, people, buildings, trees, houses away, flaming missiles, and this scouring of the earth would go on to a distance of five miles. And then, as the enormous mushroom cloud arose, the winds would suck back, gathering even more force, sucking up all that had been burned and scattered.

Beyond the five-mile radius, to a distance of ten miles or more, heat and radiation would melt flesh from bones, or so contaminate flesh that life would cease soon afterward...

A hundred thousand struck down in righteous wrath.

Purged.

Purified.

The mental picture so exhilarated Jessica Jones that she even considered staying near ground zero to witness firsthand her Statement as it was written into the pages of history. But beyond that Moment of Glory, there would still be work to be done, and who would there be left to carry on that work if she were gone?

Responsibilities were a burden.

"Manuel," she said, "you and Ali get rid of this carrion. But before you go, I want all of you to listen."

She told them that their moment of victory was not long away. She told them that after the body of Maywood Tucker had been disposed of, they were to remain here, indoors. Several of them, known to the police to be terrorists, had been under constant surveillance, and since they had disappeared from sight, they would be sought after with warrants for immediate arrest. Most important, she told them, they were to guard the Hand of God with their lives.

"Kill anyone you have to kill. Understood?"

They understood.

CHAPTER 19

George Bushby was brought back to awareness by the sound of a Klaxon sounding an alarm. His conditioned reflex, burned into him during his days as combat soldier in Vietnam, was an intense alertness, built half of cold terror and half of sharp, murderous awareness. Too many times he'd found himself at the point of death only a few moments after the sound; twice he'd been severely wounded. So now, with the jarring honking filling his head, he erupted out of his state of unawareness, to sit stiffly upright, all muscles taut, quivering.

He didn't know where the sound was coming from.

It seemed to be everywhere.

Hell, no! It was inside his head!

He clutched his head in sudden new terror.

Dimly, through the honking, he heard the sound of running feet. His eyes went to the single doorway of the room just as there was a splintering crash, and he saw a purple beam tear away a large portion of the door casing.

He knew the beam.

It was an attack!

His eyes flew around the room. He was in a ward, and there were three other beds—*Holy Christ!* Jackie and Jillie and Sara were in those beds, sleeping. George was out of his sitting position, out of his bed, lunging. He caught up his two children, and with them in his arms continued on, tipping over the bed on which Sara lay, tumbling her out against the wall and then falling on top of her and the children behind the barricade of the bed.

"Bastards!" George cursed.

From the scant shelter of the bed, George saw a second bolt tear out more of the door frame. An instant later, a manlike figure appeared in the shattered doorway, a weapon in his hand. He was there only long enough to search, to send a wildly aimed purple bolt from his weapon hissing across the room to drill a hole in the wall just over George's head, before a third bolt of purple from beyond the door turned the top half of him into a blood blotch.

He dropped where he stood.

Three more manlike figures burst through the doorway then, leaping over the fallen one. The first to enter rushed toward the bed. George had scrambled into a fighting crouch, still with time enough to act only by reflex, and was ready to launch himself into an attack. But the figure turned away at the last moment, and George heard him call out:

"They are safe! No harm done!"

The one who had called was a lizard-man—an alien!

They were all lizard-men—they were *all* aliens! The dead one, not in uniform, these three in uniforms—aliens! Now George fought panic. And confusion. And it was no wonder—in the space of fifteen seconds, on returning from a state of nothingness, so much had happened that he couldn't grasp it all.

The alien before him, in uniform, began a babble of apologies. "I'm sorry, sir. I'm very, very sorry."

He got hold of the bed, pulled it upright. Behind him, coming through the shattered doorway, stepping over or around the corpse which the two remaining aliens were dragging away, were two, three, four smaller aliens—females, obviously, nurses to judge by their uniforms—who hurried to George. They, too, were apologetic; but even more, they were worried frantic.

Since George was standing, they apparently considered him to be unhurt, and they pushed him aside to get at the others. All three were unhurt, but they were still in the state of unawareness, of seeming sleep, that George remembered from his awakening at home to find the aliens holding him and his family hostage.

"Where the hell are we?" he asked.

He was helping an alien nurse get Sara back on the bed. Sara was wearing a silk gown. The children were wearing silk pajamas. He was wearing silk pajamas.

"Siss State. A hospital," the nurse answered.

"Where's my glasses?" he asked.

"There," the nurse said, pointing. His glasses were on a bedside table.

When he got them and put them on, he saw that the alien nurses were still most concerned about the children and Sara. They worked hard but gently, getting them all back into bed, straightening the coverings, checking their vital signs.

George checked his own vital signs. He hadn't been hurt.

Suddenly other aliens rushed into the room. Leading them was an alien George recognized—he was the one who had held them hostage—and right with him was the smaller one, the mate. She was still in combat fatigues, wearing the cute overseas cap, still with the sidearm and the stupid sword. She proved most anxious of all, rushing to Jackie and Jillie, finding them unhurt, and to Sara.

And she was furious.

"How could it happen?" she was saying. "How *could* they get past the guards? What kind of rassiss security do we have here?"

"They shot their way in," her mate was saying. "Killed two."

George, still trying to cope, had a complaint. "That one tried to kill us!" he said. "Me and my family!"

"I know, I know!" It was a desperate apology from the taller alien. "It shouldn't have happened! What can I say? We did manage to stop them in time. No harm done."

He was pushed aside by a burly alien who seemed to be running interference for a smaller one in a white smock. The latter wore glasses crookedly on his muzzle, and he had a worried, puzzled look. He also seemed a man of authority. A nod from him and the aliens, with gentle, caring strength, forced George back to the bed where he'd awakened. Since they seemed to mean him no harm, he did not resist. The questions came back.

"What *is* this? Where is this place?"

The others in the room fell silent.

They saw the sudden shock on his face. George had finally realized he was talking to them.

"I'm talking?" he asked slowly. "You hear me?"

"Yes, yes, of course," the man in the smock said. "The voice part is unnecessary. We can't hear that, just feel the percussion." He had reached out to take hold of George's head and turn it so he could inspect the back of it.

"Any pain?" he asked.

George quickly felt the back of his head, found a small lesion. "No, no pain. You mean you—"

"You're now transmitting and receiving thoughts

directly. You had to become telepathic or we couldn't talk to you. Isn't that true?"

He could talk to them! Good Lord! That little girl, Tippi—the one he thought was a ringer. She must have been telling the truth!

"Yes," he replied slowly.

"Then stop complaining."

"But—I don't know your language! You don't know mine!"

"The conversion is made for you by the implant. And for us." He was checking George's eyes now, and George saw no threat in the large, vertically slitted eyes that were looking at him.

"My name is Sassan. I'm the head of this hospital, a surgeon."

"George Bushby," George said. "My wife, Sara; Jack, Jill, my kids." He had a sudden thought. "You do them, too? I mean, the dingus in the head?"

"Yes. You don't mind?"

"If it doesn't hurt them."

"Not at all." Sassan stood back a little. "You were more of a problem."

"Me? Why?"

"Your blood pressure was very, very high. You were at risk of dying at any moment."

"My God—my pills!"

"Your what?"

"Pills! I'll explode if I don't have Catapres!"

"Medication?" Sassan looked even more puzzled. "That suggests you were in a doctor's care. Why didn't he correct your condition?"

"He did! He was! That's what he was doing with the pills! He was keeping me alive. Stupid, but alive." His alarm grew. "You can't keep me here without Catapres!"

"You don't need Catapres."

"The hell I don't! I can't live without 'em!"

"But you have normal blood pressure now." He seemed a little offhanded about it. "While I was about it, I corrected your condition. A very minor procedure, really. You see, the kassrosis is a central nerve in the—" He caught himself. "Never mind. You're one-forty over eighty now. Will be for the rest of your life."

"Like a high school kid?"

"Whatever that is." The surgeon turned away to the children.

George stared at Sassan's back, stunned by the good news—then reality caught him. He suddenly wanted a lot of answers. "Hold on! Just a damn minute!"

The tall alien who had held them captive before came quickly to put his eight-fingered hands on George's chest. "No, no! Don't get up! I'll answer your questions. Stay right there."

George let himself be pushed back.

This was the one all right, the one who'd held him captive at home. A klutzy character. The little female had been always steering him around trouble. There was something about the expression in those large golden eyes—worried, caring, desperate—you couldn't hate him entirely. He'd shot the hole in the breakfast room, sure, but he hadn't meant to. Scared the hell out of him, George remembered, and it had gotten him chewed out by the female.

"Where the hell are we?" he asked.

"On Essa, my world. In Jassa, my country. I apologize." The alien was waving his hands, trying to explain. "There was so much excitement. Remember? At your home? They—your police—had gathered outside. They were shooting at us. All those bright lights. And when Ross opened that gateway, I—well, I must have lost my head. I thought I should bring you here—to keep you safe, or something. I'm not sure—" He waved his hands. "My name's Guss Rassan. I play the sissal—" He was really upset.

"George Bushby," George said.

"My pleasure." Damned if he didn't offer a hand.

Damned if George didn't take it.

"You shouldn't've done it!" George said. "Snatching us like that. Me and my family. You had no right!"

"I know, I know! It's all I've been hearing! Sissi— that's her there—she's blissin' the zass out of me, and she won't quit."

"She your wife? Mate?"

"In a manner of speaking." He seemed embarrassed.

George changed the subject. "Well? Why'd you do it?"

"You wouldn't believe me!" Guss said. "I told you I was trying to help you, and you wouldn't believe me! That hurt! Even when the little girl told you, you wouldn't believe me."

"The little girl, she all right?"

"She's quite well."

George's mind seemed to be working in fits and starts— he was getting so much, so rapidly, his clutch was slipping, or so it seemed to him. But the memory of the little girl, Tippi Calder, and what she had told him, and what he had refused to believe, came back to him, out of a back room of his memory, like a dreadful monster, stalking. He was almost afraid to face it.

"That—that story about the nuclear holocaust?"

"Yes! Yes! It's true!"

"There's gonna be one?"

"Yes!"

"Really? You sure?"

"I'm sure!"

"How can you be sure?"

"We have instruments. I mean, Los Ross . . ."

Guss pulled a chair up to the bed, sat down, and told George about Los Ross: who the scientist was, how he'd come to know what he knew, how he'd persuaded Guss to make the effort to save the human world, and at what cost.

"I'll be go to hell," George whispered.

Listening to Guss, hearing it all from this vantage point—in the utterly unbelievable world of Jassa—he found he had to believe what this creature was telling him. If that Jassan scientist Los Ross could open a door between the two worlds—well, hell! He could spot a nuclear bomb then, couldn't he?

"When?" he asked. "When's the damn thing go off?"

"In three days."

"Three days?"

"Three days."

"My God! That's no time at all!"

"I tried to tell you. You wouldn't listen."

"Where is this bomb?"

"A place called Hoboken. You know it?"

"Hoboken, New Jersey. On the east coast."

"That's it!" Guss was gratified. "In your home, I thought if you would help me, we could neutralize it, keep the holocaust from starting. But you wouldn't believe me!"

The fact that he hadn't been believed seemed to bother him most.

"Would you?" George asked. "Would you believe a crazy story like that? Somebody from outer space tells you your world is going to go up in smoke. Would you believe it?"

"I'm not from outer space."

"Well, you're different. Maybe not a monster, but different."

"I'm not a monster!"

"Sorry! Sorry, I didn't mean it that way."

"If I could have just found Harry," Guss said despairingly.

"Harry who? Who's Harry?"

And Guss told him, at length, who Harry Borg was.

George listened impatiently but with great interest.

While this was going on, the doctor and his retinue
went away, taking all but one of the nurses. A Jassan with
a bucket and mop cleaned up the blood left by the dead
Jassan. Two more came to take measurements of the dam-
aged door. A Jassan nurse came with help and moved
them all to a new and bigger room where there was no
hole in the outer wall.

The little female in the combat fatigues joined them,
after she had seen Jackie and Jillie and Sara in new beds,
and after George had been gently forced onto a new bed.
Guss was still telling George about this human superman,
Harry Borg, but he paused long enough to introduce the
female.

"This is Sissi."

Remembering all she had done, and knowing why she
had done it, and with what great difficulty, and at such
peril, George found he liked her very much. And admired
her even more.

"You are Guss's wife—in a manner of speaking?" he
asked kindly.

"I'm his mistress," she said.

Guss winced. "And very outspoken," he said. "But
we're going to get married—if we live through this."

"Who says I want to?" Sissi asked belligerently.

"Sissi, please!"

A family quarrel in Jassa? It seemed so.

George found he was still trying to cope, still trying to
catch up. So much had happened in less than fifteen minutes. It was enough to blow a man's mental fuses. A

nuclear bomb was going to start a holocaust *in three days*, and he was stuck in some kind of outer space, talking to weird creatures!

And there were Sara and the kids to think about. Godfrey mighty! Where did a man start? He didn't have answer one!

He had no chance to think, for at that moment Sara and the kids woke up. And then he *really* had his hands and his mind—full of a whole new kettle of fish.

"My bridge club! It was my turn to have them!"

"Holy catfish, Dad! Can I go outside?"

"Daddy! Daddy! Where's Tippi?"

George fought hard to keep his senses together and hold on to his temper, but it was no easy struggle, and he didn't win it entirely.

"Let up, will you?" he finally hollered. "We're in a fix here, and I've got to start thinking straight!"

When he got his family quiet, he spoke to Guss and Sissi. "I'd sure like to meet this Harry Borg. Sounds to me like the man we need."

"We couldn't find him!" Sissi said.

"That place we went to, his place—he wasn't there! And that's were the Vessan Guardsman was killed."

"It's the place to start," George said. "If I go back, I can tell the government—hell, the President! The FBI! The CIA! Everybody! And they'll stop it! Let's go! Get me some clothes. Come on! I mean now!"

Both Guss and Sissi looked ill. The gray film they used to cover their golden eyes when they were very upset closed, and they seemed to have gone away.

"Hey, what the hell? You two. What's with you?"

"We can't go," Sissi said.

Her eyes came back into view, hurt, scared. Then Guss's came back, and he looked no better.

"Why can't we?"

"They'll kill us," Guss said.

"No, they won't! Not when I tell them—"

They were shaking their heads.

"What d'you mean?"

"We're prisoners here," Guss said. "If we try to leave this building, we'll be taken and executed. Not by your people. By ours."

That took a while to explain.

Siss, the hospital, was a sanctuary. All hospitals were sanctuaries. They had been sanctuaries since the law to separate science and government had been passed, twelve hundred and fifty years ago. No police could enter a hospital and arrest a fugitive who had taken refuge there for any reason. It was holy. It was inviolate. Of course, the fugitive could never leave the hospital. Taking sanctuary to avoid arrest was also a capital offense.

"And they'll kill you if you leave?"

"Yes, they will," Guss said.

"They were going to, anyway," Sissi said.

"Anyway?" George asked, his voice getting a little shrill. "Why?"

"Going through to the Gateway to help you," Guss said weakly. "*That* was a capital offense. We killed a couple of Bissi to get there, and that alone—"

"Bissi? What the hell's a Bissi?"

Guss and Sissi exchanged weary glances, each waiting for the other to take up the burden. Guss outwaited Sissi, and she turned to George. "Well, a long time ago—"

"Never mind! Enough!" Then a new thought occurred to him. "What d'you mean, the police can't come in here? They did, didn't they? Tried to kill me in bed! And my family!"

Again, Guss and Sissi looked at each other, waiting for the other to take over.

"They weren't police," Guss said finally.

"They weren't?"

"They were Peacekeepers."

"Peacekeepers?"

George's mental voice had gone shrill with incredulous anger. Sissi and Guss worked together to calm him while opening a whole new can of unbelievable worms. They explained that Peacekeepers were pacifists who had become militant in a century of trying to further their cause of universal peace, and explaining wasn't easy. The whole idea didn't make sense, even to them.

George's final reaction was a kind of stunned stupidity. "How about that?"

Guss shook his head helplessly.

"They tried to kill Harry Borg when he was here," Sissi said. "They'll try to kill all humans, because they think humans are a threat to peace."

"Can't argue with that," George admitted.

"I didn't think, I—" Guss was embarrassed, sorry. "When I brought you with us, I mean. Well, I didn't realize—"

Sissi, impatient, interrupted. "He's trying to tell you the police will execute you, too, if they catch you."

"Why me?"

"A law was passed," she said. "No humans can enter Jassa."

"On pain of death," Guss said weakly.

George stared at him. "And you brought me here? Thanks a lot!"

Guss looked at Sissi helplessly.

She tried to help. "Harry used to say, 'Sorry about that.'"

Chapter 20

The room felt like a barracks, though no military barracks had ever offered the comfort, the divertissements, or the cuisine that was offered here. The beds were severe in appearance but perfectly comfortable; the floors were bare but shining clean; the latrine was antiseptic, gleaming; the food would make Chasen's weep with envy; there was big-screen television; there were games.

There were even windows, and if one could forget that what one saw through the windows was not the great outdoors but only backscreen taped television views being presented to give the illusion of space, one could resist the claustrophobic terrors that go with the knowledge that one is a mile underground. Locked in.

Arnie Garrett, a confessed claustrophobic, had apparently succumbed to the madness. He was attacking Homer Benson. Arnie was a fist-faced nineteen-year-old who would fight a tree if it got in his way, and he had apparently gone bats enough to try to buzz-saw his way through the wide-shouldered, big-handed, even-tempered Homer who was, compared to Arnie at least, a tree in size.

Homer took a hard blow that glanced off his cheek and knocked his head up. He rattled his head to clear it, bunched a shoulder, and swung a maullike fist that sent Arnie sliding on his back across the room.

Eddie had apparently suffered the same dementia. He was trying to strangle Sam Barnstable, the behemoth. Though Eddie was working with savage intensity, he did see Arnie go sliding by, and he took time to pant a word of encouragement. "Hang in, knuckle-nose! He's gettin' weaker!"

Sam tore Eddie loose from his throat, caught him by the waist, and sent him sliding across the floor after Arnie. He couldn't have done better with a bowling ball. Eddie struck Arnie just as the other was trying to get to his feet, and knocked him down again. The two of them ended up in a tangle against the far wall.

Sam dusted his hands and high-fived with Homer.

Eddie and Arnie got up, growling, ready to go again.

"Time!" Chad called.

"C'mon!" Arnie protested. "I can take that big bazoo!"

"Gonna use an ax on Sam," Eddie said. "Chokin' won't kill 'im."

Sam grinned. "Ax won't, either. Takes a cannon."

He had Homer across his shoulders now and was doing deep knee bends with the two-hundred-pounder for a weight. Homer was riding up and down like a kid on a teeter-totter.

"Couple of pipsqueaks," Homer taunted.

Chad, lying on a bunk, his feet stacked, his hands behind his head, was dreaming of his lovely wife, Illia. In the time since he had brought her from Jassa, he could count on the fingers of one hand the weeks he had been able to spend with her. The lovely slopes of her body, soft-covered with gray fur, the gentle touch of her fingers, the love in her enormous brown eyes—how much he loved her, how much he missed her. It was only with great effort that he was able to bring himself back to the tasks at hand. He pulled his head forward so he could see better.

"Garrett! Cole! On your feet!"

They jumped.

"In place!" Chad barked. "Run!"

And Eddie and Arnie, already heavily sweated, began running in place, their breathing whistling through their mouths. Homer and Sam traded places, and now it was Homer laboring under the two-hundred-and-sixty-pound bulk of Sam, trying to do deep knee bends. He had less success than Sam had had, but he groaned away at it.

In a few moments, it would be Chad's turn.

The others would drill *him* until he dropped.

They had been confined to this small complex for two days and a little more, and so as not to lose fitness, and to add to their skills, they had gone at it like this—weight lifting, running in place, judo, boxing, wrestling, dirty fighting, tumbling, walking on hands—until they fell flat from exhaustion, and then got up and did it all over again.

For Harry Borg, it had been the same thing.

But he had to do it alone, because he was confined alone, in a separate small complex, equally clean, equally secure. Now he was doing push-ups on the floor, where he had fallen after doing a marathon—twenty-six miles of running in place. He was drenched in sweat, his breathing hoarse.

But he was not *really* alone.

"Knock it off, sir!" It was Chad's telepathic voice, giving a suggestion, not an order, because the younger man was junior in command. He went on to chide. "You're not a young man anymore—sir."

"Work *your* ass off!" Harry panted.

"That'd be a day!"

Harry let himself collapse, and used a towel to wipe sweat.

"Sam could take you both," Lori put in. She was confined in yet another part of Globe One, and she, too, spent most of her time in the same way the others were spending theirs—exercising the very hell out of herself and Charlie, her unborn child.

Sam agreed. "Betcher life I could take 'em, ma'am. With one hand, easy."

Sam had always been a favorite of Lori's—he was so everlastingly big, so good-humored, so gentle-mannered. She hoped Charlie would be like Sam. Charlie's father, Harry, was so damned ferocious! Here, lately, anyway.

Unknown to Ahmed Hassad and his jailers, all of them had been in constant telepathic communication, and the fact that they could talk to one another had pulled the fangs from Hassad's savage effort to make any of them tell him what they knew about the mysterious aliens.

Harry was supposed to think Lori was being tortured with an infinite slowness—the water torture, water dripping drop by drop on her forehead, or the death of a thousand slices, being slowly whittled to the bone. But instead, being able to talk to her every moment, Harry knew she had not yet been hurt. But let the first hand touch her with violence in mind, and Harry would know it, and an instant later Hassad's gigantic underground complex would start coming apart at the seams.

"Hassad's gotta think I'm the most heartless bastard alive," Harry told Lori. "Here I am, a slob who'd let him torture his wife and unborn baby for two days already, and I still won't tell him my secrets."

"You'd never do a thing like that!"

"Like what?"

"What you just said."

Silence.

"Harry!"

"What, hon?"

"You wouldn't let him torture me, would you?"

"Baby! Need you ask?"

"Harry Borg, when I get out of this, I'm going to kill you! I'm going to beat you to death with a feather pillow!"

"Love you, too."

Harry could not really know, of course, what Hassad was thinking about his refusal to break under the threat of torture to Lori. Hassad had not come near in the two-and-a-half days they had been here.

Harry was willing to say Hassad was *capable* of torturing Lori and himself, but he was gambling that he would not *want* to, now that he had discovered there was a new world close by. It would be far more to his advantage to have Harry and Lori healthy when he finally learned about the new land.

Chad had a fit description of what was going on.

"You know what you're doing, sir?"

"You tell me, son."

"You and Hassad are playing the goddamndest game of chicken I ever heard of."

"You're right," Harry said. "And if there was a way to call it off, I'd be the first to holler. Stakes like these are out of sight. Hell, they're out of mind!"

"We gotta win, sir."

"I'll copy that."

Very early the next morning, Wednesday, April 9, five heavily armed men came to escort Harry back to the large room where he'd last seen Ahmed Hassad. The wide spaces, the deeply carpeted floor, the bar, the divan, the framed pictures that were actually sniper gunports—nothing had changed.

But Hassad seemed different. It was something in his

manner, Harry decided as Hassad brought his eyes to fix on him. A banked fury. He was madder than hell, Harry realized, about something. Angry mad rather than crazy mad. And there was a look of a decision made. A final decision—one he was about to share with Harry.

Hassad took a glass of ice and bourbon from the bar and nodded for Harry to take the one that was left.

Harry grinned pointedly. He was looking at the gunports that were pictures again.

Hassad, understanding, and with an impatient gesture, went back to the bar and poured two new drinks, using the same bottle. He left the choice of glass to Harry, and he took the one Harry left, drank half of it, and moved to the thronelike chair.

"Suspicious bastard," he said.

Harry laughed. "Wouldn't I be? Your own mother couldn't trust you, if she had a dollar you hadn't already stolen."

"I was born an orphan, as far as I know."

"I can help you out there. Your mother lived under a porch and barked at strangers. She never knew your father's name."

"Now that we agree on that," Hassad said, "let's discover if there is something else we can agree on."

"Give it a try," Harry said.

"You can tell me what I want to know and save the human race."

"I can *what*?"

"Save the human race."

"The human race? From what?"

"A nuclear holocaust."

"Oh, for Christ's sake!"

"You don't believe it could happen?"

"*I've* been saying it was going to happen for years. We go on building nukes, and the Russians go on building

nukes, and it's just a matter of time until some madman
pushes the button!"

"My feeling exactly."

"So what else is new?"

"Much else."

Harry laughed. "You're so scared of what might happen, you went and spent billions on this huge bastard of
a bomb shelter? That's what it is, isn't it? A bomb shelter."
He roared his ridicule. "You're a survivalist freak!"

Hassad was rigidly silent.

Harry had never enjoyed a triumph as much as this
one. He'd found that Hassad was a cringing coward! A
paper tiger! He laughed again.

When he stopped, Hassad's tone was ice. "Are you
ready to be sensible now?"

"Give it my best shot," Harry said, still grinning.

"There is *going to be* a nuclear holocaust," Hassad
said.

Harry stared at him.

"You're serious. This *really is* a bomb shelter. How
many people have you got in here?"

"Over three hundred."

"I'll be damned! How long could you last?"

"Indefinitely. We expect the need will be twenty years.
And these people will be the progenitors of the new civilization. You and your people can join us—the decision
is yours."

"Hey! That's real big of you!"

"You don't realize how big."

"One problem," Harry said. "You don't catch me running from a bugaboo, hiding in a hole. Before *I* crawl into
a hole and pull the hole in after me, I've got to know I'm
hiding from more than a threat. I've got to know it's the
real thing—for double-damned sure."

"I feel the same way."

That sharpened Harry's attention. "What d'you mean?"

"I'm double-damned sure."

Harry spoke very carefully. "You *know* there's gonna be a blast?"

"That's right."

"And you know when?"

"Right again."

The cold certainty in Hassad's tone made Harry's skin crawl. "I can't believe what I'm hearing."

"But you're beginning to believe it."

"Good God," Harry whispered. "You can't be serious."

"I am serious," Hassad said. "If I didn't know the exact moment a nuclear holocaust was to begin, I would die with the rest of the human race. If I knew the exact moment, and had prepared for it, I could save myself and the nucleus of a new race. I made sure that I would know the exact moment. There is a bomb in place."

"Mother of God . . ."

The full meaning of what he was hearing was too enormous, too monstrous to be absorbed instantly. Images of infernoes exploding, of flesh falling from bones, of a billion screaming faces, of a rich land consumed in flame, turning to ash, the atmosphere gone black with smoke, sudden dark, endless winter, all animal life gone, emptiness for centuries—all this caused by one man, *deliberately*?

"You can't mean it!"

"I do mean it."

"*You're* going to push the button?"

"Not exactly."

"What the hell does that mean?"

"The button is no longer in my control. The bomb has been stolen by the people who constructed it. I've spent the past two days directing over a hundred of my personnel in a search for it, but we couldn't find it. And we've run out of time. The bomb will be detonated."

"When?"

"Today. At about three o'clock this afternoon."

"Three *this* afternoon?" Harry was incredulous.

"Yes."

"Where?"

"Washington, D.C."

"Washington! Three o'clock!" he stared as his brain whirled. "The joint session—Margaret Thatcher—Reagan—the Joint Chiefs—"

"Yes."

"Jesus Christ!"

Harry headed for the door.

"Stop! There's something *you* can do!" Hassad said sharply. Harry came to a skidding halt.

"I'm gonna stop that damned bomb!"

"You can't. You *can* contain it."

"Contain it? What d'you mean, contain it?"

"You can limit the damage. You *can't* stop the bomb being detonated, but you *can* prevent a *total* holocaust."

"Make some sense!"

"When this bomb explodes, our defenses will call it a first strike by the Russians. They—our defenses—will send a counterstrike of nuclear warheads at the Russians, which the Russians will think is a first strike against them."

"And that will be the bloody end!"

"I can prevent our defenses sending that first strike."

"How?"

"I arranged for it to be sent. I can stop it."

"Then stop it!"

"Tell me what I want to know!"

"There's no time, dammit!"

"Time enough to stop the major damage. And I'll stop it, if you can prove to me there is another race, another civilization, another world close by. I would give *them* priority."

"The Jassans are there—here."

"I want proof. Sit down. Tell me!"

"There isn't time! I've got to find that bomb!"

"My men couldn't find it—*you* can't find it!"

"The hell I can't!"

Harry turned to the door again, to discover it blocked by a squad of Hassad's security police. He came to a grinding halt, turned to see the picture-gunports open again and three automatic weapons trained on him. Hassad, standing near the bar, was cold-faced, determined.

"The outer portal is sealed," he said.

"You bastard!"

"You can't leave," Hassad said. "Not now. Not ever."

"I'm leaving," Harry said. "Like it or not."

"Put him back in his cell," Hassad said.

The guards clamped hands on Harry.

He did not resist. And they took him away.

It was five o'clock Wednesday morning.

CHAPTER 21

At five o'clock Wednesday morning, Guss, Sissi, and George Bushby were sitting on the floor in a windowless room. They were at the end of a journey that had begun on Monday night, two days earlier.

Guss couldn't remember when he'd last had a real night's sleep.

Fits of dozing while sitting up, a few moments here and there, and that was about it.

He was sure he'd lost weight. Looking in a mirror, he found proof of it. His large golden eyes seemed sunken. The usually narrow slits of his pupils had widened to circular dark holes that gave him a haunted look. The fine flecking of his scales stood out against sickly gray skin. He extended his tongue, curled the forked tips. Just as he had thought—coated. Even his fingers, so supple, so graceful on the keyboard of a sissal, had the look of sixteen fragile, bony sticks. He was wasting away.

And why?

My Osis! he thought to himself. What a stupid question.

He was a prisoner here!

If ever he left the confines of the hospital, he would be immediately arrested, given a quick trial—because he was now a national celebrity, the most renowned composer of fragrances now playing the sissal—and then he would be taken to the Converter and turned into fertilizer.

Could you really call a person in a position like that alive?

Hardly.

There was not even a decent sissal in the hospital. And even if there were, what possible use would there be in composing symphonies of fragrances if there were no audience to appreciate them? No use at all. It would be like talking to yourself. Or crassing your sister. Sterile. Meaningless.

He waved his arms.

Then he cracked himself with both hands at once on the sides of his head, realizing how selfish, how thoughtless, he was being. He was nothing but a whimpering whiss! Moaning and groaning over the prospect of spending the rest of his life in a luxurious prison!

What about Harry Borg and Lori!

What about those fine young males?

What about their whole, entire human race?

What about their world?

In—what was it now—two-and-a-half days, they were going to be seared! Seared! Turned to ashes! All of them. And their beautiful land along with them!

For a thousand years—nothing but emptiness. Osis! There was a prospect!

And he had failed them. He, Guss Rassan, had had the foreknowledge and the time! If he had been half the person he should have been, he could have saved them and their world. But he had botched it!

Harry had been right. He was a klutz!

And he had to live with that for however long he would be able to endure life as a captive in a hospital sanctuary. Now, looking around the rather luxurious apartment, he saw it as reward for failure, a monument to disgrace. A perfect place for a whimpering whiss like himself to end his days.

No! he decided. None of this for him!

He was going to walk out of here. He was going to walk right up to the first Vessan Guard he saw and say, "Arrest me! It's just what I deserve!"

The thought was a dreadful one. He could feel the tears on his cheeks.

Behind him a voice said, "You, too?"

Sissi! Guss rubbed at the tears before he turned.

"Me too, what?"

"Can't sleep?"

She was standing in the doorway, and she was not wearing that idiot combat garment. She was wearing a light silk sleeping gown, and she was beautiful. Small, even for an essan female, but mighty! Those large golden eyes could be cold, even frightening, when she was threatened, when the pupils became black strokes of ink; her lovely eight-fingered hands could fire an esso with deadly purpose—he was alive now only because this was so.

But she was not being mighty now. She crossed the room to him, unaware that the light behind her, shining through her gown, silhouetted a lithe and most desirable figure, her hands held out to him with anxious, loving concern. He took her in his arms, accepted the warmth of her curling tongue against his own.

After a moment, she reached up to touch the moisture on his cheeks. "Guss—Guss, why?"

"They've only got two days, Sissi."

"I know."

"Two days, and that enormous searing agony will start.
I can see the flesh melting from their faces—I can see
their mouths screaming—I can see their buildings turning
to ashes—I can see their trees burning, their skies going
black—"

"Guss, stop it!"

He stopped and stood, shaking. Then his shoulders
dropped. "I failed them, Sissi."

"No, darling!"

"Yes, I did! Failed! Failed! Failed!"

"No! You attempted the impossible! That's not failure!"

"It's failure if you don't achieve—whatever it is."

"Not if you tried your best. And you did! You were
ready to give your life, and that's as hard as anyone can
try."

"Someone better could have done it. Harry could have
done it!"

"Guss, you can't go on comparing yourself to Harry.
You're good at what you do. You're the best! He's dif-
ferent, the hero kind. But there are all kinds of heroes!
And you're another kind, believe me."

"Oh, sure! I'm another kind of hero." He waved his
hands at the room. "And this is my reward, my medal!
A prison for the rest of my life!"

"It's not too bad. Maybe someday—"

"I'm not going to wait for someday, Sissi. I'm going
out."

"Guss, no!"

"Sissi, I can't face a life in here. I simply can't!"

She backed away from him then, though her eyes went
on holding his. She sat down slowly on a straight chair.
"I feel the same way," she said.

"Sissi! *You* can't leave!"

"I mean about the humans—and failing."

"But you didn't fail! I did!"

"We both did, then."

He went to her this time, and he knelt beside her. "Don't feel that way. You were great. You saved my life, for whatever that's worth—"

She put a hand up to stop him. "We both failed. Like you, I see the same things—their world dying under a great ball of fire, their skies going dark. A thing that terrible can't be allowed to happen, not if there is even the most remote chance of preventing it."

"There's no chance. None."

"Maybe there is."

"Sissi!"

"Would you—would you be willing to try again?"

"Would I—" He stared at her. "Of course I would!"

She twisted her fingers together, looked down at them, then at him again. "Do you think they've changed the key to the Gateway?"

"I couldn't say." He was becoming sharp, intent. "But I wouldn't think so. Cost a fortune, and you know how the government is."

"Do you still know it? The combination?"

"Yes. Yes, sure! But what're you saying?"

"Sassan feels the same way. About the human race, or any race, being incinerated out of existence. He said it would be easy to steal his personal craft, if it were to be used to save the humans."

Guss's mouth was open, his forked tongue flying. "He's got a Triss-nass! Flies higher and faster than anything this side of a kliss and carries five!"

"He would make it easy—to steal it."

Guss shoved to his feet and paced away, shaking his head. "No! No! Sissi! It's insanity! We wouldn't have a chance in the world of getting through the Gateway. Wouldn't be Bissi guarding it now, it'd be Elite Vessan Guard—depend on it!"

"Maybe not. We could try."

"Name of Osis! You're talking suicide!"

"The alternative?" Sissi asked.

"Well..." His voice dropped; he stared at her.

"You just told me you were going out and let them kill you," she said.

"But Sissi! Even if we *could* get through the Gateway—and the chances are a hundred to one against it—we'd still have the same problems that beat us last time. We can't talk—"

He left that hanging, staring at Sissi. Then he whispered, "Mr. Bushby."

"Mr. Bushby," she agreed.

"Do you think he'd go with us?"

"They're *his* people; it's *his* world."

"That's right."

"We could ask him."

Guss was sorely tempted but still unable to decide.

"Do you want to end with a whimper, Guss?" Sissi asked quietly. "Or do you want to end with a shout?"

Guss took another moment to stare at Sissi. Then he lunged forward and caught her slim shoulders in his hands. "I want to shout!"

"So do I!"

"Come on, then! Let's talk to Mr. Bushby!"

When they awakened George Bushby, he thought he was being attacked again, and for a moment he fought them. Then he recognized the mental voice as that of the lizard-man he knew as Guss Rassan.

"Quiet, quiet."

George became still, staring, listening.

He heard them tell him they wanted to come away

from his family, out into the hall. And there, in the hall,
his back against the wall, he listened to Guss and Sissi
outline a plan that was sheer insanity. Suicidal! They
admitted it was. They said there was a chance they could
break back into his world before the final holocaust began
and, with his help this time, stop it—but only a very slim
chance.

"Do you want to go?"

"For Christ's sake, yes! If I can get through, I can
contact the FBI, and *they* can stop it!"

"What's an FBI?" Guss asked.

"Our federal police."

"Would they believe you?" Sissi asked. "You wouldn't
believe Tippi."

"You got a point," George agreed. "Damn it! I've got
to try! Even if there's no way we can get through, even
if there isn't time, I've still got to try!"

"Then let's go!"

"I'll need clothes. A gun, something."

"We've got clothes. And weapons."

"All right! Let me tell Sara—"

"No! She'll fight it!" Sissi said. "The danger, you know.
You probably won't come back. What can you say to
her?"

After a pause, George decided she was right. "I won't
wake her up."

He tiptoed back into the room to the bedside of the
woman he loved beyond all else. How could he say good-
bye? He couldn't. He didn't. He pretended he was coming
back. Without waking her, he kissed her hair and whispered his parting.

"Take care."

Then Jackie and Jillie.

"Grow up fine."

"They'll be safe here," Sissi said in the hall.

A few moments later, they were on the rooftop of the hospital. George was dressed in silk shirt, leather jacket, leather shorts, and soft boots, a weapons belt around his narrow waist. Guss thought he looked astonishingly like Harry Borg. He lacked Harry's girth of chest and thickness of arms, but his lean height was equal to Harry's. And there was something else. Even with the glasses, he had the look of a warrior. The sharp brown eyes, the gray-shot brown hair, the thin, almost cadaverous cheeks made him look dangerous, even lethal.

Running for the doctor's plane, Guss felt a twinge of envy. What was there about these humans? Were they all warriors? He, Guss Rassan, never looked like anything but what he was—a whiss of a sissal player.

Once in the aircraft, Sissi said, "Fasten the belt. If you haven't flown with Guss, you haven't lived."

"I'm a *good* pilot!" Guss protested.

"That's it! Too frassin' good!"

"She swears a lot," Guss apologized to George.

"I like her."

George had never seen such a craft. It was round, almost saucerlike, and small. But there was room for five. It was luxurious. There were softly glowing dials. There was only the single wheellike control. George did not believe there was any way the thing could possibly get off the roof, let alone stay in the air.

"It really flies?" he asked.

"Really," Guss said.

He took the craft straight up, like a cannon shell fired at the sky. George sank into the seat. He suffered all the g's he could take. Then more. And more. When they leveled out, he was just barely conscious.

"Good God almighty! What *is* this?"

"A Triss-nass," Guss said comfortably and with pride.

"It's got a four-buss ossross and two-shaft vess. Climbs faster and flies higher than most police craft."

"I believe it!"

He had been squashed flat; he pushed himself up and looked down. "How high are we?"

Guss checked a dial. "We could go orbital."

"I'd rather walk." Sissi said weakly.

So high, so fast, so effortless—George was dazzled. "You folks build some kind of a plane!"

"And it's two hundred years old," Guss said immodestly.

"Two *what* old?"

"Hundred years."

"You've got short years or something?"

"Same as yours—once around the sun."

"Then your planes wear well; I'll say that for them." His admiration was honest. "What's a new one like?"

"Like this," Sissi said. "It's the newest we've got."

"You're kidding!"

"Whatever that means."

"Means he doesn't believe you," Guss explained.

"Then *you* tell him."

Guss was checking instruments, looking down to the distant, dark landscape stippled with tiny specks of light. "It's true. We haven't built a new model since this one."

"But why? A craft like this, and you quit building 'em two hundred years ago? What's wrong with it?"

"Nothing," Sissi said.

"What's wrong with us?" Guss said. "That's your question."

"So I'll ask it. What's wrong with you?"

"I don't know the answer. Loss of interest, apathy . . ."

"Decadence," Sissi said. "Mental deterioration."

Guss shot her an injured look, as if she'd hauled a family skeleton out of the closet. But he finally shrugged.

"She may be right," he said. "Some of our deep thinkers say so, anyway. They say we went fat, complacent, that we stopped striving, stopped trying to achieve, that we got lost in trivial pursuits, decayed. All right, something sure as Osis happened. We're not the race we once were, say, two thousand years ago. History says we peaked two thousand years ago. We've been going downhill ever since."

"You and the Roman Empire," George breathed, awed.

"Harry said something about them," Sissi said.

"Yeah? Well, they were great once. Then they rotted away."

"That's us—rotting away."

Guss checked the view below against the dials. "Looks like we're home. Hang on."

George had time for only a quick breath before the craft flipped upside down and dove for the ground, again like a cannon shot.

George groaned. Sissi screamed faintly.

George's inside, gone weightless, suddenly became lead as Guss leveled off, seemingly only inches above the surface, and then raced in a wide circle, zipping up and down to follow the topography. When he stopped, he couldn't have stopped faster if he'd flown into the face of a cliff. They were going, and then they were not.

George knew the seat belt had drawn blood.

"You should fly with him when he's in a hurry," Sissi said.

"No, thanks."

"Just showin' off," Guss said. He was staring at what seemed to George to be the main residence of a country estate. It was rather Disneyland-ish in architectural design, with a dash of Charles Addams thrown in to give it a sinister, threatening look. It was glowing faintly in the darkness. The spires of India and the square strength of ancient Egypt were artfully blended. The small light at the entrance seemed to offer an invitation to approach, to enter—if you were brave enough.

"My family owned this place," Guss said, almost in apology. "And so did I, before all the trouble began."

"Can you kill?" Sissi asked George. "Living things?"

"I have."

Guss moved then, stung by Sissi's question into a kind of desperate activity and opened his door and got out. When the others were at his side, he tried to keep the edge of hysteria out of his voice.

He failed. "We'll have to kill them, you know. The Guards."

"Or they'll kill us," Sissi added.

"You're right," Guss almost whimpered.

"Let's go," George said quietly.

"Now," Sissi said.

Guss ran straight to the door, his long mouth gaping, his forked tongue streaming back, screaming silently with fear. Weapons drawn, he and George stood with their backs against the wall on either side of the door. Guss reached and shoved the door open, quickly. Nothing happened. George, remembering those purple beams that drilled neat holes in outer walls, knew he had never spent a longer thirty seconds waiting for anything. He saw Guss looking at him, asking, even pleading, for another push, and George gave it.

"Go!"

They went in together, shoulders bumping, their weapons trained before them, insides cringing. But again nothing happened. They had to keep moving—there was no time for wondering, for searching. Guss led the way through the arch, into the room that held the Gateway.

And there it was, the clean lines of it outlined with thin black scoring, the surface of it gleaming silver.

Unguarded!

Guss had a moment in which to enjoy an exquisite feel of triumph—and then Sissi's mental cry of despair tore it all away.

"Trap!" she wailed.

An instant later there was a crackle of high energy and the smell of ozone, and Guss and Sissi and George, who had braved themselves to the very threshold of success, found themselves surrounded, as if in a bottle, by what looked like a barrier of glass—but wasn't. Not even the combined purple bolts of their very powerful weapons could scratch it.

After trying, they dropped to sit cross-legged on the floor.

Guss was silent. Never had George seen anyone so defeated. He saw Sissi take Guss's hand to comfort him.

"At least we're still alive," George said.

"But we're out of our sanctuary now, Mr. Bushby." Sissi looked at him. "Now they'll execute us."

Suddenly a powerful beam of light pinned them, like three bugs under a microscope.

CHAPTER 22

Harry Borg gave the sergeant and the five guards who escorted him back to his cell no trouble at all. As a matter of truth, he had been walking faster than the sergeant wanted him to walk, striding hard, furious, impatient. The sergeant had had to restrain him.

"Slow down, sir!" he'd scolded.

The sergeant was a blond young giant with the refined features and cultivated voice that suggested he might be the scion of a wealthy eastern family and, most probably, a Harvard man.

He didn't know Harry wasn't listening.

Harry had been in contact with his people, telepathically, from the moment he had left Hassad. And they knew the whole story now. They knew about the bomb, the location, and the purpose.

They knew it was now eight o'clock Wednesday morning. They were in the mountains of Colorado. The bomb was due to be detonated at two o'clock in the afternoon of this same day in Washington, D.C.

Their mission: Get there, find the bomb, defuse it.

"My God, Harry!" Lori had cried. "There isn't time!"

"None to waste—that's for damned sure!"

"We're ready, sir," Chad said.

"Stand by."

The sergeant and his men brought Harry to the door of his quarters and made him stand facing the door. A man unlocked the door and then opened it. Before Harry could step through, the sergeant lifted his baton and swung it hard. Harry didn't see it coming, but he felt the impact and the sharp crack of pain. He stumbled forward to his knees on the floor, dazed but still able to hear the voices behind him.

"Why'd you do that?"

"I don't really know," the cultivated voice said. "I think it's because I hate the brute."

"But Cecil, he never did you—"

The door was closed and locked.

Chad's telepathic voice was sharp, concerned. "You okay, sir?"

"Yeah, yeah."

"What happened?"

"My jailer kissed me good-bye." It took a moment for Harry's head to clear, for the room to steady. He pushed to his feet, gaining strength. "Chad?"

"Sir?"

"I'm going to bring Hassad along. We'll need him. Give me five, maybe ten minutes."

"You'll be in touch?"

"All the way."

"Ten minutes, sir!"

"You take this building, clear the exit, and secure the

street. We'll need transportation. Use the gum wrappers as needed—but sparingly. And I'll meet you on the walk."

"On the walk in ten minutes, sir!"

"Sam?"

"Sir!"

"Lori is your post. Don't leave her side."

"I'll bring her, sir."

"Damn it, Harry—" Lori said.

"Do what Sam tells you," Harry said. "Or I'll whack your ass."

His mental voice scorched.

"Sir," she said meekly.

"On the count of two," Harry said.

A concealed pocket in his heel gave him a very small but very powerful derringer-type weapon—a gift from the Jassans, though they were not aware they'd made it. Another pocket gave him folded gum-wrapper-like foil—another gift. A small fragment torn from the foil and inserted into the crack of the door provided an opener.

"One!" he said to Chad.

He stood away from the door, focused his mind on the foil: "7-delta-777-tau."

The telepathic code detonated the foil. The door blew off.

"Two!" Harry said to Chad.

He heard and felt the thud of the door to his cadre's quarters giving way, and thought no more about them. They would manage. He had his assignment—and only ten minutes. Long strides carried him into the hall, then back along a route he knew very well toward Hassad's quarters. A guard appeared, startled, frightened, to block his way. The guard tried to draw a sidearm. A flash from Harry's tiny weapon knocked him flat.

The guard would probably live, but he wouldn't move again for several hours.

Harry dealt with two others in the same way before reaching the floor above, giving them the same chance of recovery. It did not trouble him to know only his shots were merciful, that the shots the security guards would use against him would kill outright.

The rules were his own. They went with his territory.

He found Ahmed Hassad at the bar of the room where he'd left him. It seemed as if Hassad had been waiting for him. But he didn't take time to ask about it.

In that first instant, he ignored Hassad. His charge carried him, a rolling bombshell, under the fire of the automatic weapons in the gunports, a bombshell from which shafts of purple light flashed, striking three gunports in rapid succession. The guns went silent instantly upon being struck, as if the gunners had suffered a sudden change of mind.

And they had. They were unconscious.

Harry Borg rose from the floor in one slow, powerful movement, a giant coming to life, growing as Hassad watched.

Hassad's black eyes glittered.

"You insist on dying," he said to Harry.

"Think you can kill me?"

"I know I can."

Harry's laugh was a deep, derisive rumble. "Show me."

Without taking his eyes off Hassad, he put his small weapon in a secure place. Hassad reached up, took hold of the back of the collar of his silk shirt, tore the shirt from his upper body, popping buttons, ripping cloth, and threw the remnants aside. He swelled his chest, worked his shoulders.

"My pleasure," he said.

He moved slowly to Harry's left, cat-lithe, graceful, powerful. His chest and arms were heavily grown with shining black hair that spoke of strength and virility; his shoulders and arms were corded with muscle; his neck was a column.

Harry was shirtless, too. "You're going with me," he said.

"You're a fool. We'd burn out there."

"I'll find the bomb and defuse it."

"Not enough time. Five, six hours at the most."

"If I can't, we'll both burn."

They were talking quietly, their attention fixed on each other's eyes, watching, waiting, like two cannons, arrayed, muzzle to muzzle, lanyards gripped, ready to fire, turning slowly, steadily.

Hassad fired first. He drove in low at Harry's waist.

Harry bounded straight up. Hassad caught nothing but air; he curled, tumbling, to come erect. Harry landed balanced, leaped, and kicked Hassad in the face. Hassad was driven back against the wall, his beautiful nose broken, blood streaming down over a crushed mouth.

But Hassad proved to be tough. He was rolling away when Harry drove in, twisting like a cat. Harry's maullike fist missed. Hassad pounded Harry a fierce blow on the side of his head just behind the ear, knocking Harry sprawling. And when Harry rolled out of it, he found Hassad a distance away, crouched, a gleaming ten-inch blade held rapierlike. Hassad lunged, reaching to pierce Harry's belly.

Harry twisted, arched, and the blade sliced upward, scoring his side, glancing off his ribs. Blood flowed. Harry's move had brought him above Hassad. The back of Hassad's neck was briefly exposed below him. Harry chopped down with the hard side of his hand, striking at the base of Hassad's skull. Hassad's thickly corded neck saved his life, but he fell with a crash, stunned. Harry kicked the blade away, caught iron-claw fingers into Hassad's hair, and dragged him back to the center of the room.

"Now, you bastard!"

A powerful fist under Hassad's jaw straightened him. A second equally powerful blow into Hassad's belly, under his rib cage, folded him. Any of the three blows he'd suffered would have been enough to subdue Hassad. But Harry didn't stop.

The severed finger of a child had earned Hassad more. And he got more.

The kidnapping of Lori had earned him more.

And he got it.

The beatings he had ordered for Harry had earned him still more.

And he got that, too.

But the horrendous crime of ordering the blast from hell that would destroy life on earth was beyond mortal man to punish.

That Harry left to a higher authority.

He took Hassad, still conscious enough to stumble along—though a bloody, nearly toothless mess—to the front entrance of the building. Along the way, he saw evidence that his young men had passed that way before him. The sergeant's prostrate body here, a broken door there, broken glass doors, several more bodies, women standing with frightened, stunned faces, staring, unable to move.

Hassad was known to them. His present condition was not to be believed.

"Believe it!" Harry growled in passing.

Chad was waiting at the building exit. On the sidewalk, an open-sided buslike conveyance was parked, and Eddie, the smooth-moving black, was at the wheel. Sam, enormous, his young face untroubled, waited beside the conveyance. And sitting inside it, just at Sam's elbow, was Lori, almost out of her mind with anxiety.

"Harry, your side! You're bleeding!"

"Scratched," Harry growled. He shoved the battered

and bloody Hassad into the conveyance. "This is the other fella."

He turned to look about. There was a crowd gathered, held at bay by uncertainty and, of course, by Arnie, who was facing them away with a challenging stare, and Homer, who held an automatic weapon he'd liberated from one of the fallen security guards.

Harry saw the faces of the crowd clearly. And he was to remember them.

Sirens were screaming in the distance.

"Move out!" Harry ordered quietly.

They rolled down the citylike street, past buildings, past intersections, heading for the portal and freedom. But it was not to be easy. When they reached the first roadblock, a mental code, sent by Chad and Homer, detonated gum wrappers before and behind them, and the security guards manning the roadblock went out of business.

At the next roadblock, Harry dug hard fingers into Hassad's hair, showed two shocked guards the face of Hassad and the gun he was holding in Hassad's ribs, and they pulled back. Harry saw them pick up microphones as his conveyance continued on. In a few moments, they were approaching the portal. The guard station, three hundred yards inside the portal, was manned by four guards. They were outside the guard station, braced, weapons leveled, blocking the way.

"Who's got these?" Harry asked.

"Me and Eddie," Arnie said.

"Go!" Harry told him.

Two exploding gum wrappers flattened the guards.

Arnie was relieved. "I was afraid I'd forget the code."

"How about the gate?" Harry asked.

"The left side's mine," Chad said.

"Mine's the right," Homer said.

Staring at the last barricade that stood between them and the free and open world, Harry knew that he could blow it open and that they would be able to continue on without pause. But he remembered the faces of the crowd he'd seen a few moments before.

"Hold it," he said.

Chad and Homer looked at each other, shocked, puzzled.

"Harry!" Lori said. "What's wrong?"

"Changed my mind."

Behind them sirens screamed closer. While his men looked at each other, Lori looked back and saw approaching security police. "We'll be caught," she wailed.

"Only seems like it," Harry said. He got out of the conveyance, and dragged Hassad out after him. When the security guards braked to a stop and piled out, they found Harry braced, one hand in Hassad's hair, holding Hassad's battered but still recognizable face up to them, the other holding a weapon pressed into Hassad's side.

They stopped at a little distance.

To Hassad, Harry said, "Tell them to open the gate."

"They can't."

"Then you open it!"

"I can't. Only Hassad can open it."

"What the hell?"

"I'm not Hassad."

Harry was stunned, unbelieving. "You're lying!"

"I'm a double," the man groaned. "He's got two."

"Liar!" Harry was furious.

"He's telling the truth." Hassad's voice was amused.

Harry's gaze was jerked toward the guard station doorway. There was Ahmed Hassad, unhurt, amused, smiling.

No! Harry was not to be deceived again.

He threw aside the battered hulk he was holding and strode to run his hand through what proved to be another hologram. The image was framed in the doorway of the guard station, as detailed, as lifelike, as Harry himself. But was it Ahmed Hassad? Or another double?

Then he found a difference. The body hair showing through the open shirtfront was shot with gray. The man he'd just beaten was younger, the hair shining black. He cursed himself for not having seen it sooner.

This was the image of the real Ahmed Hassad.

The real Ahmed Hassad was somewhere else being photographed, untouched, unhurt.

"Bloody coward!" Harry roared.

Hassad smiled. "You can't beat me, Harry Borg. No one can."

CHAPTER 23

The room had four walls, a ceiling, and a floor. There were no windows, certainly—all the walls were smooth— and there was no door they could see. But there had to be a door. How else could they have gotten in?

The light was everywhere, because the walls were softly luminous, giving the captives stark, shadowless faces.

They were sitting on the floor against a wall, Sissi between Guss and George, their legs drawn up until their chins almost rested on their knees. Guss held one of Sissi's hands in a comforting grip, and George held the other. They had not spoken to each other in an hour or more.

All the talking had been done.

They had tried again and had failed again. What more was there to say?

They waited now for the executioners to come. As nearly as they could tell, they had been in this room, waiting, for thirty-six hours. Maybe less. Probably more. Time becomes distorted when you're waiting to die.

Guss and Sissi had retreated behind the shields of their gray inner lids. The tips of their delicately forked tongues flickered out only when they were used to touch the tongue of the other in a comforting caress.

George envied them. They had each other. He looked down at Sissi's eight small and delicate fingers twined in his own, felt their reassuring pressure, and knew she was trying to share herself with him, to give him the support that she and Guss were giving each other.

"Good people," he said aloud.

They didn't hear the voice, though a flicker of tongue tips said that had felt the vibration. It was the only true sound there had been in the room since they had arrived. George was only beginning to accept telepathic communication as normal; to him, the implant in his brain was still like a new and unfamiliar toy.

They went on sitting in the featureless, silent room.

It was Guss who finally spoke. "It's today," he said. "Has to be."

The gray membranes over Sissi's eyes slid away to reveal that her vertical pupils had opened to near circles, the dark and liquid inner depths holding concern. "What's today?" she asked. "When they come for us?"

"When the bomb goes off," George said.

"Oh!" Sissi squeezed George's hand, trying to give him comfort. "We decided not to talk about that," she said to Guss. "It's no use."

"You're both right," George said quietly.

"I'm so sorry."

"We asked for it, didn't we?" George said. "Building all those warheads. Couldn't miss, when you come to think of it. Bound to be a maniac push the button, sooner or later."

"Not *a* maniac," Sissi said. "*Another* maniac."

"What d'you mean?"

"What kind of a race would build a device that would eventually destroy them?"

"A race of maniacs," George agreed.

As Guss lifted his head, his inner lids retracted, and he seemed to have emerged from somewhere hidden. "I could have saved them," he said.

"Guss!" Sissi pleaded. "Don't start that again!"

"I had two chances," Guss said. "Failed both times!"

"It doesn't help to go on saying it."

"You didn't fail," George said. "You're a hero for trying at all."

"Come on, you two!" Sissi said.

They fell silent again, and tried not to think. But try as they might, they could not keep their minds away from their immediate peril. When would the executioners come? And how would they be killed?

George thought they might be hanged or put against a wall and shot. That was the way it was usually done where he came from. Guss, knowing his kind better, knew it would be either the Converter, which would turn them into a product that would fertilize crops, or a slow, live dismemberment, if it were thought a lesson should be taught to possible future offenders. Sissi was sure it would be dismemberment, because that was what she dreaded most.

And they went on sitting against the wall, knees up.

Condemned.

Another hour . . . then another . . .

Then an opening appeared.

Two Vessan Guardsmen came in. They were in a hurry, crossing to the three on the floor. "Come on! Come on!" They pulled the prisoners erect and urged them toward the opening.

Guss and Sissi looked at each other, and they held hands; they were both frightened, George knew, but they didn't whimper. They walked close together for support, but they walked. And George followed them, thinking, A pair of heroes!

He did not feel at all like a hero. He was leaving Sara and the children.

"Take care of them," he whispered, hoping someone would hear.

A long hallway seemed endless, a path to nowhere, a path without turning, softly lighted, featureless, going on and on.

Then, suddenly, a blank wall barred their way, forcing them to turn right, and a short distance farther on, a Vessan Guard of higher rank stood impatiently in another doorway.

"Hurry!" he called.

The guards behind Guss, Sissi, and George shoved them on, urging them to a great speed. When they reached the doorway, they were pushed again, stumbling, expecting the worst.

They found—Los Ross?

Los Ross, who had begun it all with his discovery of the bomb, who had persuaded Guss to make the journey to save the humans, and who had finally brought them back—facing execution with them?

"You, too?" Guss moaned, agonized.

Los Ross looked near death. He was as gaunt as a skeleton, his color ashen. His yellow eyes, red beacons now, told of hours and hours without sleep. His glasses, still askew on his muzzle, had one cracked lens. And his smock was very soiled with a pocket torn and hanging open.

But there was still fire in him.

"Hurry!" he said.

Guss couldn't cope. "Los, name of Osaris! What is this?"

"Later, later."

George's mind was numb, bewildered. He could only follow along as they were hurried through another opening, into the outdoors and toward an aircraft. It was the same craft they'd used before: Sassan's! And the Vessan Guards were waiting for them to enter it.

"Hurry, hurry!" Los Ross kept saying.

He was obviously not a prisoner. He was urging them along with as much vigor as the guards. He even seemed to be in charge! Sissi was squealing a high-pitched, telepathic noise, a mix of joy and hysteria. Guss's sputtering was beginning to sound happy, but fearfully happy, as if he were afraid to believe what was happening.

Was it a reprieve of some kind?

George felt much the same way: It just wasn't possible.

John Wayne and the cavalry? Galloping in at the last minute, colors flying, bugles blowing, the Indians running for their lives?

Come *on*!

Not in real life!

But what else could it be?

"You take the controls!" Los Ross said to Guss.

Guss, shaking his head in wonder, got in, and the Vessan Guard closed the door for him and gave him a salute— from the outside! Guss turned to watch Sissi and George climb into the other front seats. The back seats, he saw, held a huge case of electronic equipment with just enough room for Los Ross, who climbed in beside it.

And their weapons were there, too. Even Sissi's sword!

"Los! What happened?" Guss said.

"Take us up!" Los Ross said angrily, impatient.

Guss took them up. Straight up.

"We're up!" he said then. "Twenty thousand meters."

"Take us back to that point where I rescued you. Can you find it?"

"Just south of Nessi—I can find it."

Sissi was catching on. "Why, Loss? Are we going back?"

"Back?" George was startled.

"Yes, we're going back—if you want to." Los Ross's head was almost lost in a helmet from which sprouted antennae and wires that connected to the electronic device. "I didn't think to ask if you wanted to."

"Go back to my world?" George asked, unbelieving.

"There's still time," Los Ross said. "If we hurry."

"To find that bomb, you mean? And defuse it?"

"To find it, yes. Defuse it? That's up to you."

"Christ Almighty!" was all George could think to say.

"Well?" Los Ross asked worriedly.

"Well what?" Guss asked.

"Do you want to go back?" Los Ross asked. "There's still a great risk, you know. I mean, if you can't defuse it in time, and you're there—" He didn't need to finish.

"Guss?" Sissi said. "Again?"

Guss looked at George. "What d'you think?"

"Hell, yes!" George said. "I'm willing! More than willing!"

"Sissi?"

"If *you* want to."

Guss took a deep breath and let it out slowly. Then he shook his head and laughed a silly kind of laugh. "One more time," he said. "If I keep doin' it, maybe I'll get it right."

"You do want to go, then?" Los Ross asked, still anxious.

"Oh, yes!" Sissi said.

"Let's give it a shot," George said.

Guss had the craft in level flight, the speed approaching a streak. "Give me a chance to be a hero, and I'll go for it. Must be I've got hero blood." He glanced at Sissi. "Y'think that's it?"

"That's it," Sissi said. "The fact the alternative was the Converter had nothing to do with it."

"Me?" Guss scoffed. "Afraid of being turned into fertilizer?"

"Not afraid," Sissi said. "Petrified!"

Guss looked at George. "She's right, you know."

"Two of us," George said.

Sissi twisted in the seat to look at Los Ross. "We thought you had been executed! How in the name of crass did you manage this?"

"I used blackmail," he said.

And that, he went on, was putting it as nicely as possible. Since the Jassans as a race had retreated so far from their peak of scientific accomplishment, they had come to think of the very few who were still capable and striving in that area—Los Ross and no more than fifty others— as some sort of wizards, capable of unimaginable sorcery. And the head of the Jassan State, President Moss, was certainly one of these.

"I frightened him," Los Ross said.

He'd insisted on an audience, and he had gotten it— as a last gesture before his execution. And he had told President Moss that he had set a trigger at the ancient Museum of War at Tross, where all manner of incredibly powerful devices were stored, and that he would pull that trigger and detonate those devices unless he was allowed his freedom and the right to do as he wished about the crisis in the world of humans.

"You can do that?" Guss interrupted, shocked. "You can blow us up?"

"No, I can't. But Moss doesn't know I can't."

Sissi squealed with laughter. "You monster!"

"The reason he gave permission," Los Ross went on,

"is he thinks I'll be burned up with the rest of you—and good riddance!"

George was looking at Los Ross with stunned admiration. "I'm grateful beyond words that you would do so much for my world, my civilization. I can't imagine why you would. You hardly know us!"

Los Ross took a moment under his weird helmet, puzzling. "It's the right thing to do," he said, almost defensively. "Is that a reason?"

"What?"

"Because it's right?"

"Only the best!" George said softly. "The very best."

The craft tipped suddenly as Guss began the tight spiral that would bring them back to ground level, and in a moment they were at rest again in a barren area among low hills. During the descent, George had seen what would have been, in his world, the Pacific Ocean, and a shore that was very similar to the shores of southern California. The terrain was not very different, he realized then, from the area northwest of Los Angeles.

"Well?" Guss said. "This is it."

Los Ross was busy at the dials on the case of electronic gear. "Hold on!"

He pushed a button.

Only George could hear the loud *crack*! The others smelled the pungent odor of ozone and saw what for an instant seemed to be an opaque vapor, which cleared to reveal the living room of George Bushby's home. They— along with the aircraft—had arrived.

"Kee-rist!" George gasped.

It was a bad fit. A wall had been broken and furniture crushed. There were even two police officers crawling in the wreckage. They had not been hurt, but they had been frightened almost into insensibility. They fumbled for sidearms, for walkie-talkies.

Guss cursed in alarm.

"Zat!" Sissi exclaimed. "We're trapped again!"

"In my house!" George said, still dazed.

"But of course!" Los Ross's tone was that of a person done a severe and unjust injury. "It was the only POP I had! Except that other one, the first one. And that one wasn't big enough!"

"What in Osis is a POP?" Guss wailed.

"Point of Proximity!" Los Ross was really hurt. "I didn't have time to find another."

"We're locked in," George said.

He was watching the police officers outside the window on his side. One of them had recovered enough to use his hand radio, and George could tell by the movement of his lips that he was talking rapidly.

"We'd better go back," he said.

Guss was peering out, looking at the ceiling. "What d'you build these places with?"

"The house? Wood, lumber made from trees."

"Thank Rass," Guss said.

The police cordon, on a twenty-four-hour watch outside the residence since the disappearance of the Bushby family—thought to have been kidnapped by creatures from outer space—had just received word from the men stationed inside the house that some kind of a gigantic flying saucer or something had suddenly materialized in the living room of the Bushby residence.

"Believe it or not," the patrolman had said.

They hadn't believed it. A spaceship in a living room? It couldn't happen!

But just to be on the safe side, they were playing it cool.

And what that meant was that they were trying not to panic and do or say the wrong thing, until they had double-

and triple-checked and had bucked the report upstairs to higher brass.

"Says it's a spaceship. What? Hell, I dunno!"

"Jeehosaphat!"

The roof of the Bushby residence had just opened up like a suddenly blossoming flower. Sure enough, the officer on the inside who had made the report had been on to something. Because, right before their very eyes, spewing out of that opened flower of a roof, shooting straight up into the sky, was a flying saucer kind of a thing.

In a blink it had disappeared from sight.

But they still didn't believe it. It couldn't happen. Not in real life!

"But Godfrey mighty!" a young patrolman protested. "There it was! And there it went!"

Inside the craft, flattened by the g-forces, George Bushby was trying to recover. He was vaguely astonished that his first thought, as he saw his roof go flying in bits and pieces, was to wonder if his homeowners insurance policy was going to cover that kind of damage. Sears was great for fine print and exclusions. Probably come under Damage by Alien Spacecraft, paragraph b, .2) Roofs...

"... eight ... five ... zero ... seven ... seven ... zero ... zero ... nine ..."

Los Ross was giving Guss numbers that Guss was punching into what had to be a computer. George was quickly jarred back to immediate concerns.

"Think you can find Hoboken?" he asked.

"The bomb is not in Hoboken," Los Ross said. "It's been moved."

"Where?"

"Another city. A Washington?"

"Washington, D.C.?"

"South of Hoboken? About—four hundred kilometers?"

"That's D.C. Our nation's capital!"

"That's bad."

"Couldn't be worse!"

"We'll stop it from blowing up," Sissi promised George.

He had turned in his seat. "Y'got a fix on time and date?" he asked Los Ross.

"I'll check," the scientist answered.

Guss had the craft on course at a very high altitude. Since the ground beneath them was obscured by a cloud cover, it was hard to estimate speed, but George thought they were traveling faster than he'd ever traveled before.

But was there still time?

"Your date," Los Ross said, "is the ninth day of the fourth month."

George didn't need to ask the time—they were flying straight at a sun that was well above the clouds. It was late morning of Wednesday, April 9. Around nine o'clock.

A sudden new and shocking thought hit him.

The joint session! Margaret Thatcher would be addressing a joint session this afternoon! When in the afternoon? One o'clock? Two o'clock? The President, the Joint Chiefs, both houses of Congress—all would be there. "That's it," he whispered. "That's the target!"

He could hardly breathe.

CHAPTER 24

Harry Borg looked terrible.

He was naked to the waist, and his right side, from below his arm almost to his lean waist, was raggedly painted with blood from the knife Ahmed Hassad's double had used in an effort to gut him, missing by only that much. Harry's dark blue eyes glinted with controlled fury; his bearded jaw was outthrust. Massive chest, thick corded neck, fists mauled tight—he was enough to frighten a tank.

But Ahmed Hassad had nothing to fear.

Standing in the doorway of the guard station, being confronted by Harry Borg, was a hologram of Hassad, while Hassad himself was somewhere else in Globe One, unharmed and out of harm's reach. And that was the fact that was infuriating Harry.

Ahmed Hassad thought it was because he had defeated Harry again, for the last time, and because Harry was now his prisoner with no possibility whatever of escape. And he was relishing that victory.

But Harry was not defeated.

Ahmed Hassad had escaped punishment—that was what infuriated Harry Borg. It was punishment Hassad had earned a hundred times over, punishment Harry had risked death to administer, punishment he thought he *had* administered, only to find that Hassad had let a double take the punishment for him.

But Harry was not defeated. And neither was he so infuriated that he had lost his cold-minded view of what had to be done and how he was going to do it. There were several considerations in his mind, carefully balanced: the time there was left, the possibility of succeeding, and above all, what had to be salvaged from failure, if failure was to be the final result at the end of this day.

"I'm going out of here," he told the image of Hassad.

"Like hell you are!" Hassad said, smiling.

"You're going to open those gates," Harry said. "Or I will!"

"You can't!"

Without turning away from Hassad, he spoke telepathically to Chad. "Any foil left back down the tunnel?"

"Crew?" Chad said.

"I've got one," Arnie said.

"I've got two," Sam said.

"Blow one beyond the crowd," Harry ordered.

"That's mine, sir," Arnie said. "On your count."

Harry aimed a pointed finger down the tunnel. "Look there," he said to the image of Hassad.

To Arnie, silently, he said, "Blow it, son."

Arnie sent the mental code.

The foil detonated. In the confines of the tunnel, the result was a deafening blast of sound and a compression shock wave that all but knocked the security guards to their knees.

"I've got a bigger one to blow your gate," Harry said.

"Don't be a damned fool!" Hassad's voice was suddenly ragged.

"Without the gate, you'll burn with the rest of us."

"Listen to me—"

"Your people here will die," Harry said. "There'll be no one left to start a new civilization. Keep the gate, and if I can't find the bomb you can still start over."

"Damn you!"

"Open it!" He was lifting his arm to point at the gate.

"Wait!" Hassad yelled desperately. "You win!"

Chad's sharp "It's cracked, sir!" confirmed it.

Harry was still staring at the image of Hassad. "You're going to give me a plane, Hassad. And all the help you can while we're in flight."

"Yes! Yes!"

Hassad's mind was quick, give him that! He'd read the situation, measured the odds, saw the best hope for survival. And profit.

"For God's sake, hurry!"

Harry turned away. He strode back to the conveyance and spoke to Sam. "Out!"

He turned to Lori. "You, too, sweetheart."

"Harry!" It was almost a scream. "Harry, no!"

At Harry Borg's nod, Sam, who had left the conveyance at once on Harry's order, reached in with a big hand, lifted Lori out, and held her, struggling, at his side.

"You're not going to leave me, Harry!" she screamed.

He caught her chin in a big hand and looked into her eyes. "I am going to leave you," he said. "And the baby."

"I don't want to be alone here—or anywhere!"

"If I win, I'll come back."

"No!"

"If I lose, you'll be safe here. You and the rest of the people here will be the start of a new race."

"Harry, please!"

Harry looked at Sam Barnstable, knowing it hurt the big youth to obey. "Sam?"

"On your count, sir!"

"Hold on to her."

"Sir!"

The big lad put both arms around the struggling Lori as Harry turned away. One stride put Harry back in the conveyance, which Eddie drove, tires humming, through the big gates. Harry did not look back. He did not see Lori collapse into Sam's strong and comforting arms, nor did he see the big gates close and seal them safely inside.

"Some bitch!" Arnie muttered. "I couldn't a done that."

"What?" Homer asked.

"Leave 'er there."

Neither of them was looking at Harry Borg.

"We're coming back," Harry said, flint-faced.

That flat, implacable statement was what they needed. There could be no thought of failure. There could be only an absolute determination to succeed. The challenge lighted their faces.

"Better believe it!" Arnie said.

And they were on a roll.

"What help are we gonna get from Hassad?" Eddie asked. His face alive with eagerness, he was pushing the conveyance to its very limit toward the airfield.

"All he can give," Chad said.

"Why?"

"Jassa," Chad said. "He wants us to win. We're the key to Jassa!"

"The key to the mint!" Arnie, said, joyful with the thought.

They had the airport in view now.

"Begins to look better," Homer said.

Hangar doors were open, and a sleek business jet was being drawn out on the runway. By the time they had come to a careening stop under a wing, there were men settling in on the flight deck—pilot and copilot—putting on earphones, flipping switches.

The crew members were disconcerted only a moment to discover they had been boarded by a pirate, naked to the waist, side caked with blood, gleaming gold in his ear, eyes burning with cold dark-blue fire.

"Where to, sir?"

"Washington, D.C., son—and don't spare the horses."

There were perhaps four hours left.

The cloud cover broke somewhere over Kentucky, and by the time Guss got the Triss-nass to a hovering position above Washington, D.C., the sky was clear and the visibility was unlimited.

Looking down from their altitude of sixty thousand feet, George could see the city detailed clearly. There was the Potomac River, a winding glitter. There was the Pentagon squatting solidly on the far side, unaware, sleeping. There on the near side of the river was the green length of the Mall, marked at one end by the Lincoln Memorial and at the other end by the Capitol building and its two satellites, the Library of Congress and the Supreme Court Building.

It was so beautiful. And it was his.

Never had he felt the bond as strongly. Not before Vietnam, or during Vietnam, or after Vietnam. This beautiful city was not just a city where politicians gathered. This beautiful city was the heart of the country, his land, his people. This beautiful city was the beating heart of his America.

It *was* America.

So peaceful.

Had Pearl Harbor been like this, so blissfully unaware of the disaster presently to occur?

Looking down, George had a vision of what this disaster would be. He saw the sudden, blinding, all-consuming flash of light, saw the horrendous blast strike out, leveling all that stood erect, saw the roaring column of smoke and sucked-up dust and debris erupt from ground level and burgeon into the sky, felt the searing heat that melted flesh and steel and concrete, saw thousands and thousands and thousands of people, his people, swept away in screaming agony...

"Where *is* that bomb?" he pleaded.

"I have it...yes!" Los Ross said.

"Where?"

"On the screen."

On the panel before the front seats was a TV-like screen and turning back, George found that it held a picture of the ground below. The gridiron of streets expanded rapidly as a telescopic process functioned. He could see the early morning traffic, then individual cars, and then a truck. The truck was parked at a curb on a street that led through a park area. There were no buildings nearby.

"A delivery van," he said. "A big one."

"You sure the bomb is there?" Guss asked.

"Very sure," Los Ross said.

"Put us down," George said. "We can take it."

"Look at this first," Los Ross said.

The picture on the screen changed, replacing the van with an involved electronic circuit diagram.

"That's the circuitry of the bomb," Los Ross explained.

"It doesn't *mean* anything!" Sissi said.

"It means the bomb will be detonated by an electronic signal."

"From where?" George asked.

"I don't know," Los Ross said. "I'll try to find it."

"How long'll *that* take?"

"A few minutes, a few hours—I don't know."

"Hell!" George said. "We've got nothing—"

"Zat!" Guss yelled suddenly.

Their aircraft bounced, almost flipping on its back, filling with a loud roar. It took them a moment to understand that interceptor aircraft of the United States Air Force had just reached their elevation, ripping a hole in the sky close to them, then racing away for turning room to come back.

"Hang on!" Guss cried.

He took their craft up, straight up, seeking refuge in higher altitudes beyond the reach of the interceptors. And he found it at a hundred thousand meters.

George was smashed flat by g-forces again. "We've got to go back down—I've got to get that bomb!"

"They'll kill us," Guss wailed.

"Won't let 'em." George's voice was quite, cold. He had struggled erect in his seat again.

"Easy to say!" Guss said.

"Go way out off shore. Come in fast at ground level— you can do it. I know you can. Stop near the truck, let me out. Then come back up here and wait for Ross to find that detonator. That's your job—the detonator. Find it. Disarm it."

"What are you going to do?" Sissi's yellow eyes were wide, fearful.

George squeezed her hand. "Drive that bomb as far out of town as I can get."

"It might explode!"

"Not if you find the detonator."

He looked back at Los Ross. The scientist seemed to have forgotten them, or he was ignoring them, his head in the helmet of electronic gear, the eight fingers of one hand flying over the keys of a computer, the other turning dials, moving slide bars carefully, searching.

"I'll come with you, George!" Sissi said.

"Stay with Guss. Kill the detonator."

"I'll need you, Sissi!" Guss said.

"Come on, Guss!" George said. "Get me down there—fast!"

And he meant *fast*. But he didn't mean *that* fast. One moment they were fifty miles above Washington, the next fifty miles above the ocean, then the next moment they were skimming waves, and the next they were veering to avoid the looming spire of the Washington Monument. And then they were at a dead stop on the ground in a park area.

"Told you," Sissi moaned. "He flies crazy."

George got himself together and functioning. "God-almighty!" was all he could say about Guss's flying.

He found he could see the truck through trees at the curb a hundred yards away. JOBE'S STATIONERY was lettered on the side of it, and he could see the head and shoulders of a man in the driver's seat. Then he saw a battered Mustang ragtop pull in behind the delivery truck and stop. There was one man in the ragtop, a black. George was suddenly taut and fit again.

"Stay loose," he told the others.

In another moment, he was out of the craft.

And then the craft was gone.

Harry Borg was finding he was proud to be an American.

After he had told the pilot of Hassad's jet where to go and how much time to take to get there, he'd asked for a patch to the FBI. He got it as quickly and as easily as calling a friend.

He expected a lot of idiot hassle.

He expected to be called a crank, ridiculed, told to hold, and all that nonsense. "A bomb is going to be exploded in Washington? Well, now, sir, you tell us all about it. Give us your name first, and your address. Don't hang up..."

After all, he was saying that a nuclear bomb had been planted.

He was asking that an event of the size and importance of a joint session of Congress, before which Prime Minister Margaret Thatcher was to make an address, with the President there, the Cabinet, the Joint Chiefs—he was asking that *that* be canceled. And all those people scattered to safety.

What a crashingly impossible thing to say, to ask!

And, when asked, to be believed.

And, if believed, how long would it take to go through channels, to get the authority to act? A couple of hours? Twelve hours? Too long.

But he got none of that.

He got sharp voices and clear minds. He got the feeling he'd connected to a well-oiled, smooth-working, very efficient machine. There were a few bad moments, to be sure, but they were very few. The pilot's ID, a corroborating call from Ahmed Hassad, who was now a patriotic American backing Harry Borg in these moments of great national need—Harry snorted at the bitter irony of that and put it aside for future settlement—and Harry found he was in business.

He was given flight priority. Within minutes, Air Force jets were off their wingtips, flying escort. He was assured that the President, the Cabinet, Margaret Thatcher, her entourage, and the Joint Chiefs would be airborne within the hour, going far out of harm's way. And that as many members of the Congress as could be reached would be spirited to safety.

But that left the city, didn't it? That left the millions of people who lived and worked there to die if the bomb could not be found and defused in time. Those millions of people could *not* be allowed to die.

The bomb—now code named "Tiger"—had to be found and defused before two o'clock.

Harry spent the first hour of that tormenting but inescapable time needed by even a fast jet to fly from one coast to the other stretched flat on an improvised table studying the accounts of the search Hassad's people had made, while Homer used the craft's first-aid kit to repair the wound in Harry's side.

"Where'd you learn to sew like that?" Arnie asked.

"Lose a lot of stock if you can't sew," Homer, the farm boy, told him. "Barbed wire, y'know."

"Cross-stitches, even?"

"Purty, ain't they?" Eddie said.

"This Jessica Jones sounds like a psychopath gone schizo," Chad, who was also reading reports, said.

"Got to be."

"What're they talkin' about?" Arnie asked.

"She's bonkers," Homer said, nipping a thread. "Living in a world of her own making, out of touch with reality."

"Learn that on a farm?" Eddie said.

"Read a book."

The cabin public address system, humming all this time, the patch to the FAA and the FBI open and working, came quietly to life with the voice of the man who was the FAA link.

"Mr. Borg, sir."

"Right here," Harry said.

"We have a new problem in the Washington area."

"New problem?"

"Unrelated to Tiger."

"Not interested."

"An unidentified flying object has been confirmed over Washington at an elevation above one hundred thousand."

"A *what*?"

"Steady, sir!" Homer said. "Hold 'im, Annie!"

Harry subsided under the combined weight of Eddie and Arnie, though he was suddenly stiff with excitement.

"A UFO, sir," the calm voice of the FAA man went on. "Confirmed by Air Force interceptor craft. Another sighting occurred in the Los Angeles area at oh-eight-three-zero."

"Where in L.A.?"

"San Fernando valley, a community called Hidden Road."

"I know it," Harry said.

"At a residence thought to have been invaded by aliens." The voice of the FAA man faltered saying the word "aliens" but went on smoothly again. "They allegedly kidnapped the family living there."

"God almighty!" Harry said.

"Sir?"

"Those aliens are friendlies!"

"Sir?"

"I said *friendlies*!" Harry was struggling under the combined weight of Eddie and Arnie as Homer worked to finish the suturing. "Those aliens are friendlies. Don't hurt them! Take care of them!"

"They kidnapped a family. Murdered one man, wounded another."

"Dammit!"

Homer managed to finish.

Shoving to his feet, Harry strode to the microphone, the better to yell. "I know about that killing in Reseda!

That was in *my* apartment! I don't know *all* that happened there! But I know the aliens, and I know they're friendly!"

"But sir—"

"Evans of the FBI," another calm voice cut in. "Why do you say you *know* the aliens?"

"I was *there*!" Harry yelled. "In their land!"

"Control yourself, Mr. Borg—"

"Dammit! Don't attack them! They'll blow you out of the sky!"

"We have not attacked. Repeat, *not*! We can't keep them in sight. We want accurate information, Mr. Borg. If you have it, please expedite."

"Yeah, yeah. Coming right up! Let me think a minute."

He needed more than a minute.

"Y'hear that?" he said telepathically.

"*Is* it a Jassan aircraft over Washington?" Chad asked.

"Got to be Jassan," Homer said.

"Or one helluva coincidence," Harry said.

"Coincidence, my ass!" Arnie said.

"I'll give you odds it's Guss." Eddie said.

Harry stared at him, his dark blue eyes hot. "You son-ofagun! *I* wanted to say that, but I was afraid to. Why did you say it?"

"A feeling. A hunch."

Harry grabbed the young man's shoulders. "Two of us! Let's hang together!" To the others, then: "How about it? Is it Guss?"

"Wishful thinking," Homer said quietly.

"As much chance to be Vessan Guards," Chad said.

"Or Ussirs," Arnie said.

Harry snorted. "You and me, Eddie—against these turkeys."

Eddie showed his white teeth in a quick grin.

Chad still had to play devil's advocate. "Why now?"

he asked. "If it's Guss, how would he know about a bomb Ahmed Hassad put in place?"

"I don't know how," Harry said. "But why else?"

"Another coincidence?" Homer asked, smiling.

Harry grinned. "Arnie's ass!"

"Any connection between the Jassans and Jessica Jones?"

"Couldn't be!" Harry said. "It's not Jassan kind of work. I mean, nuclear bombs? Hell, no!"

"Ussirs, maybe? Those green suckers are tricky."

Harry gave that some thought and decided not.

"Look at this," he said. "The aircraft is Jassan. Guss, maybe, but friendly Jassans in any case. They know about the bomb—don't ask how—and they're here to stop it. Can you buy that?"

"I want to," Chad said.

"Homer? Eddie? Arnie?"

"Sold," they said.

Harry went back to the normal speech.

"Mr. Evans? You still there?"

"Yes."

"Then here's the story on the aliens..."

Jessica Jones was not communicating.

She had closed herself in the office of the old two-story cement-block building that housed Jobe's Stationery, away from the people she had gathered to help her, to sit in an almost catatonic trance at the battered desk. She sat like a thin, storklike bird, bent a little forward, her long face drawn thin, her thin shoulders hunched, clutching her elbows.

On the desk before her was a powerful radio transmitter.

She could detonate the bomb from almost anywhere.

Her solid gold wristwatch lay beside the transmitter. The watch was not evidence of hidden capitalistic yearnings, though having been wealthy all her life, she could well afford such trinkets; it was a trophy, stripped from the wrist of a wealthy Italian industrialist who had been held for ransom, and who had died, not incidentally, after the ransom had been paid. The watch said it was one o'clock.

She had plenty of time.

On a shelf just beside the desk was the shortwave radio that had been used by the business to stay in touch with the delivery truck. It was old and cranky, and sometimes it worked and sometimes it did not. It had worked enough to assure her that Manuel was parked on H Street near 8th and that Ali, in the Mustang, was parked behind him. They were waiting for her to tell them exactly where to leave the truck. They trusted her to give them plenty of time to get safely away in the Mustang before she detonated the bomb.

They were waiting her command.

But she didn't give it. She was savoring the moment.

Her vision of what was to happen at her command had blown her mind. The fragments of reason left to her could not, while she was in this state, decide that she did *not* want to stand at the center of the blast. The thought beckoned. She could see herself rising out of that white heat, ascending straight to the heavens, a shining figure of truth and justice realized, with white robes, perhaps even wings—a shining sword certainly.

But the finality made her pause.

Even after this glorious stroke, there would be much left to do, many wrongs to right, still more downtrodden to be uplifted. Who better than she to do it? Wasn't it her obligation?

This delicious choice held her immobile.

Should she surrender to the joy of immediate exaltation? Or should she force herself to live and continue her work?

And so she sat, gripping her elbows, staring, enthralled.

The group she had gathered to help her waited in the room that held the printing presses: Vladimir Kolankov, the KGB agent assigned to assist her in whatever terrorist activity she might indulge, though he pretended to her to be a *discarded* and insanely bitter KGB agent; Sandra Hope, the gigantic black woman whose misfortune of being both male and female had driven her to hate all things; Sri Singh, the Sikh, the cobra of a man who had been cast out of his own religious family and had become a traveling murderer for hire.

Kolankov, who could see Jessica through the glass of the inner door that separated the office from the pressroom, had a long-barreled silenced revolver centered on a spot just above Jessica's right ear.

"She's talkin' to Manny?" Sandra Hope asked.

Her face shining with sweat, she was sitting on a stack of cartons holding paper, a small machine pistol in her lap, her thick fingers playing a nervous tattoo.

"Not talking, just sitting," Kolankov said.

"Fifteen, twenty minutes, she's jes' sittin'?"

Sri Singh, his lathlike body coiled down in the squat native to his land—buttocks on heels, arms crossed on knees—his turbaned head still, watched Kolankov with a flat, black stare. He flicked the safety of his automatic rifle on and off.

"The memsahib is not sane," he said softly.

There was a green Cadillac waiting in the alley to take them all a safe distance from ground zero, though these people were not aware that the bomb in the delivery van was nuclear. They had been told it was a reconstituted World War II aerial bomb, enormously powerful, terribly destructive, but no more than that. They had been waiting for Jessica to get word from Manuel and Ali that the bomb was in place so that they, too, could speed away.

Jessica Jones had heard that the bomb was in place, but her ecstasy still consumed her, held her.

"She puts a finger on that toggle," Kolankov said, "she's dead."

CHAPTER 25

Walking quickly but not hurriedly, George Bushby crossed to the street, approaching the convertible from behind on the driver's side, caught the door handle, pushed the latch button, and opened the door in one smooth motion. The driver, Ali Rajah, was too startled to be frightened before George Bushby killed him swiftly and silently.

There was time to be only mercifully sudden.

An elderly pedestrian walking a mini-poo down the block, waiting for the little beast to make up its mind, saw a tall man open the door of a convertible, reach in and probably shake hands, close the door, and move on— nothing of interest, nothing to be concerned about.

A terrorist had lost his life.

The dog-walker might have thought that interesting, but he didn't know.

Manuel Alvarez was listening to a Spanish-music station on a hand radio. He had the sound turned down so he would not miss the voice of Jessica Jones when it came again over the CB, a cursed thing that might or might not be working. Twice it had failed in the middle of a sentence to come back scratching, squawking, a moment later. *Madre de Dios!* A man could go insane with the waiting.

She had said go here. She had said go there. She had said to wait.

How much of it could a man take?

Another five minutes, and he would leave the truck here. It was as good a place as any...

And suddenly the door at his elbow gave way, and he all but fell into the arms of a man who put a funny-looking gun in his mouth. A man with the cold, furious face of the devil.

Manuel wet himself.

He had been living on the edge of mortal terror for more than two hours. To be driving a truck carrying such a bomb was bad enough. The señora had told him it would destroy an area of three blocks, and who was to say it could not go off by accident at any moment? There could be an unavoidable pothole; there could be a fool running a stoplight. So many things could happen. A policeman could stop him for any of a dozen reasons and then discover he was wanted in Arizona and California, and in Colombia, France, and Paraguay. And what then? Prison for a thousand years! Or the señora could decide to make him a martyr for her cause and explode the bomb while he was still in the truck. That was not to joke. She had not been in her best mind these past few days. All this had been in his mind as he had sat waiting, and then to have the door suddenly give way as he was leaning on it, causing him to fall half out of the seat into the arms of a thin devil who put a funny-looking gun in his mouth—he could not help himself. His bladder opened.

Fear so intense burned out his mind. He did not hear

the man say, "Back in the truck—slide over." He heard nothing, thought of nothing. He tumbled back into the truck, clawing for the gun he'd had lying on the seat beside him. He got the gun, turned with it—and he died.

"Hell!" George said. He shoved the dead body across the seat, where it slid down onto the floor, got in behind the wheel, started the engine, and started rolling. "Go! Go! Go!"

A quiet man, a capable man, a brave man, a man who had seen months of infantry combat duty in 'Nam—even *he* could not think clearly at this time. His mind was consumed with the awful consequences of a nuclear bomb exploding so near the Capitol Building. Burning with the knowledge that each second wasted meant a million lives lost, he was driven by panic at nearly white heat. He wanted to drive the bomb as far into open country as far as he could, letting nothing delay him for even a moment.

"C'mon, baby . . . c'mon, c'mon . . ."

He talked to the truck, to the traffic, to the spotlights, holding his wire-tight nerves with all his will. He couldn't see into the interior of the truck, but if Los Ross said the nuclear bomb was there, it was there, some kind of a torpedolike thing, some kind of a shining, sleeping evil genie that could burst out at the touch of a button in the hand of a madwoman somewhere distantly behind him.

At any second—the next one, or the next, or the next.

"Give me time! Time to get out of range!"

Out of range of the transmitter.

What would that be? Ten miles? Fifty miles? A hundred miles?

Fifteen minutes . . . a half hour . . . an hour . . .

Please! It was a fervent prayer.

He knew Washington, knew the city and the main streets. He had taken over the truck on H Street, near Mount Vernon Park. Straight ahead would take him to

New York Avenue, left there would take him to 14th Street
and Highway One, across the George Mason Bridge, across
the Potomac, past the Pentagon—into the open Virginia
countryside.

Was that plan the best of possibilities?

By no means.

He was a man running from the devil: A terrified man,
dragging his devil after him.

Looking down from an elevation of a hundred thousand
meters, the humans' capital city seemed no more than a
dot near the edge of the sea, cut by the silver thread of
a river, connected to other dots by the thin, almost invisible lines of highways. And where in that dot was there
an electronic box the size of his hand? True, Ross was a
wizard, but even a wizard has his limitations, and finding
such an infinitesimal collection of wires had to be utterly
beyond magic. Beyond even miracles.

"Stop squirming," Sissi said. "He'll find it!"

"I've got to squirm!" Guss said. "I'm scared!"

He was at the controls, the pupils of his large yellow
eyes thin vertical slits almost closed with anxiety, his red
tongue a forked blur, tips curling. Sissi, sitting beside him,
seemed more in control. But she wasn't, really. She kept
fussing with her combat uniform, making sure the Red
Flame Brigade patch on her shoulder and on her overseas
cap were just right, that her short sword and her holstered
esso were easily accessible. While her golden, vertically
slitted eyes and forked tongue told of extreme inner ten-
sion, she did have herself more securely in hand than
Guss: She didn't shiver half as much.

Los Ross, in the back seat, his head lost in a huge
helmet sprouting wires and antennae, his supple eight-
fingered hands stroking keys, turning dials, moving slides,

his broken-lensed spectacles askew on his muzzle, seemed the most in control. A scientist, he had the ability to concentrate on whatever problem was before him to the exclusion of all else.

He was now looking for a collection of wires.

The Triss-nass was extremely comfortable at this elevation or even higher. Sasson, the surgeon, could afford the very best—soft, tiss-covered seats, lovely fragrances from emitters at widely separated positions to give a surround effect.

But neither Guss nor Sissi could appreciate the comfort.

Their minds were humming like tightly strung wires.

Time was ticking by.

That human, George Bushby, that tall academic with the kind eyes—absolutely mad with courage—was sitting right on an enormous inferno, knowing it could erupt at any instant.

And then there was *their* task! They had to go into the strange, foreign, frightening world of humans in a few more minutes and *kill*! Oh, yes! They would have to kill if they were to stop a human who was so insane that she would destroy her own race.

"I believe I have it," Los Ross muttered.

"You do?" Guss yelled, startled. "You found that box of wires?"

"No."

"Then what d'you mean, you found it?"

"I found radiation—significant amounts."

"Radiation!" Guss was suddenly furious. "We want wires! A detonator! What good's radiation?"

"Look at your screen," Los Ross said, unperturbed. And while Guss looked at the screen and the centering of cross hairs, Los Ross explained: "Anyone who works in close proximity to a nuclear device without extreme

precautions will almost certainly be contaminated. I was
looking for an unusual source of radiation, and I found
it—there!"

The cross hairs held as a magnifying process expanded
the screen image diameter after diameter until it became
an area a quarter of a mile in circumference, then a block,
then the roof of a building.

"The humans who built the device are there," he said
quietly. "And so must be the detonator."

Guss and Sissi studied the picture.

"Entrance . . . entrance," Guss said, searching.

"There!" Sissi said, pointing to a closed door beside
an air-conditioning unit. "Must be."

"It is an entrance," Los Ross said as he scanned the
interior. "A stairway, then a level of living quarters, then
at ground level machines and humans—severely contaminated, heavily armed, extremely dangerous."

"Going down," Guss said.

He flipped the Triss-nass, and they shot downward.

Into what, he was afraid to think.

Harry Borg and his cadre had arrived at Dulles Airport,
raced to a helicopter provided by the FBI, and were once
more in the air, this time flying low over the nation's
capital. There had been no time to question the help Harry
and his cadre might provide—any help, however small,
had to be accepted—or to ask what the chances were of
finding the detonator. The odds against finding it in time
were so remote as to be astronomical. Which is not to
say they were groping blind, by any means. They had
"leads" developed by Hassad's security force. Jessica
Jones had been known to have lived briefly in an area
near Union Station. Her employment record showed print
shop experience—handbills and political pamphlets had

been her life—and it was reasonable to think she would seek familiar ground when returning to a city.

What slender threads!

They had no way of knowing if their threads were right or wrong. All they had was an area of the city; all they could see below them was the sea of building tops, thousands of them, none more significant than any other. Something specific was needed to designate a small area for search. Hopefully a block. Better still, a building.

"Come on!" Harry urged, staring down at the rooftops.

He was speaking to the hundreds of men and women in offices throughout the city who had been set to frantic labors by the FBI, searching out locations of print shops, of apartment houses likely to be a refuge for Jessica Jones, of car rental firms, of police records of known terrorists. There were a thousand police at work, some on standby alert, some racing to destinations already given them as possible places where the bomb might be.

None had been told that the bomb was nuclear and that he or she might be incinerated at any second by a searing holocaust. They were all doing their level best; the knowledge that they might die while doing it would not speed their efforts more.

The man at the communication center in the helicopter, wearing earphones to cut distracting noise, spoke up as he patched in the cabin speakers. "Update on the aliens, sir."

Harry was at him like a starving tiger. "Yeah? What is it?"

"Radar had them at three hundred thousand feet, holding motionless."

"I know that."

"They disappeared."

"Damn!" Harry yelled.

"Radar thinks they descended," the voice on the cabin speaker said. "No confirmation."

"Why the hell not?" Harry was outraged.

"They move too fast, sir. Hold on—" A moment's wait, then the voice returned, sounding almost apologetic. "Radar reports them back in position, holding."

Harry threw up his hands in monumental disgust.

"Five minutes elapsed time," the speaker said.

"Five minutes? They were down five minutes?"

"Gone five minutes. 'Down' unconfirmed."

"What's it mean?" Harry asked helplessly.

"Sir?"

Harry found Chad's young, cold gray eyes on him. "Why would they descend and go back, sir?" he asked.

It was a rhetorical question, though Harry didn't realize it. "How the hell would I know? The radar goofed—"

"To disembark passengers, sir?"

"Jesus holy Christ!" Harry yelled. "That's it! Got to be!"

He turned to yell at the speaker. "Couldn't radar get a fix, *any* fix, on where the ship went—if it came down?"

"I'll ask radar."

Harry waited, and waited, and waited.

And the minutes ticked inexorably away.

Jessica Jones sat at the desk in the dusty office of Jobe's Stationery as she had sat for the past thirty minutes, unmoving, a thin stork of a woman, her gaze fixed, unseeing, her elbows held in long, clawlike fingers.

"A witch!" Kalenkov cursed. He still had Jessica's head in the sights of his pistol.

Sandra Hope had gone to the door to rap on the glass twice to no avail.

"Dunno if she's freaked out or what."

Her machine pistol was in her hands, and she was ready to use it—on anything or anyone. Her belly was rumbling with anxiety and fear, and her eyes were wide and rolling.

Sri Singh had not moved. He was still coiled, cobralike, on his haunches.

"Five minutes more," he said. "No longer." He tipped the barrel of his automatic rifle suggestively.

Jessica Jones was not freaked out. She was fully aware, if in her own peculiar way. Her gold watch told her time was running out. She knew she must choose soon:

Stay, and detonate the Hand of Jessica when the joint session had convened? Rise up to glory at her moment of triumph?

Or accept her responsibility, her duty to live and carry on her work?

If she chose to stay, she could detonate the device now, in one minute, five minutes, an hour. It was so powerful, the city would be destroyed and all with it, including the Prime Minister, the President, the Cabinet, the Joint Chiefs—all, wherever they were, and so much more.

But that would be premature. It would lack the dramatic rightness of a detonation at the very moment Prime Minister Thatcher said, "Mr. President, members of Congress, I come to you—"

Then! That would be the correct instant.

She would wait.

There was still time to take her people, get in the car, and go.

Her people had rapped on the door twice.

She would make the choice in a moment or two.

Guss put the Triss-nass down on the roof of the building that housed Jobe's Stationery with a suddenness verging

on collision. He spilled out one side, Sissi the other. Los
Ross, scrambling into the front seat, took the controls and
vaulted the flight craft back into the sky. If anyone had
seen the action, they wouldn't have believed it. But no
one saw it. And two slightly different looking individuals
who had not been there before were there now.

Guss raced to the roof door and found it locked. He
was not prepared for a locked door.

Sissi had seen a more serious concern on the image
screen just before the descent, and she moved to deal
with it. She ran to the roof edge, peered down into the
narrow space between the buildings. There was a long
green vehicle waiting there, just by an exit from the building on which she was standing.

She wasted no time. She aimed the esso carefully
and drilled a hole the size of a baseball through the
forepart of the machine, killing it. The purple beam made
no sound.

"Sissi! What're you *doing*?" Guss yelled.

She crossed to him. "It was an escape vehicle. They
could take the detonator with them. Then what could we
do?"

"Zat!" he said. "Why didn't I think of that?"

"Open the door!" she said.

His mind began to function again. He turned and drilled
a hole through the door with an esso beam, taking out
knob, lock, and all. The door opened easily then, and
they hurried down the narrow stairs, almost stumbling,
Guss first, then Sissi.

"Careful!" Sissi warned.

Guss's charge was again a panic-filled one, though it
carried him straight on into what he knew to be mortal
danger. They were in a short hall that dead-ended at a dirt-
streaked window. There was a door on the right. It, too,
was locked, and it, too, gave before the purple ray, reveal-

ing living quarters, mean and dirty, more for storage than for comfortable living. In his haste, Guss brushed against stacked boxes, and two of them fell with a thud.

The thud didn't mean anything to Guss. He could only feel vibrations.

But to those waiting tensely in the pressroom downstairs, the thud was ominous, frightening.

"What the hell was that?" Kolankov demanded.

"Upstairs!" Sandra Hope said, alarmed.

Kolankov stood frozen, looking up, face alert.

"Someone up there," Sri Singh said.

Kolankov ran to the bottom of the stairway and looked up to see Guss starting down. The Jassan's unusual appearance might have caused Kolankov to pause the fateful second that spared Guss's life. Guss, as startled as Kolankov, fired one shot wildly. The purple beam narrowly missed, drilling a smoking hole in the wall behind the Russian bull. Kolankov jerked backward, fired a wild shot, missed.

Guss retreated, shoving Sissi back.

She stood against the wall, golden eyes wide and wild, her esso in her hand. Guss moved suddenly to the stairwell again, fired blindly, pulled back barely in time to avoid an exchange shot from Kolankov's silenced pistol. Guss knew he had been fired at only because the door frame splintered.

"Oh, Guss!" Sissi wailed. "We're caught!"

"What a liss!" Guss groaned.

He pressed his back against the wall beside Sissi, his golden eyes no less wide and wild than hers. And at the foot of the stairs, Kolankov was in the same position and the same fix. Only he had an additional complication. Instead of the police he had expected to see, he had seen a man with a lizardlike face who had fired a ray gun— what the hell was going on?

His face was suddenly shining with sweat. He was afraid to move.

Guss was afraid to move.

And in the office, storklike in the chair, the detonator just at her fingertips, Jessica Jones had about made up her mind.

"Guss, Guss," Sissi whimpered. "We've failed again."

In the helicopter, only a few blocks away, Harry Borg urged the men of his cadre to greater effort.

"One more time," he said. "Harder!"

Chad, Homer, Eddie, and Arnie had gathered around him like football players in a huddle. Their expressions were intense with effort—a fourth-down-and-goal-to-go effort. And, all together, they gave it their best.

They yelled together telepathically as loudly as they could. *"Guss! Come in, Guss!"*

Then, together again, another yell: *"Jassa! Come in, Jassa!"*

It was their fourth concerted effort. The other men in the helicopter, watching them, were baffled. They could hear nothing. But they were seeing the strained, intent faces of men doing something with desperate strength. If not yelling, what?

Harry and the young men had no time to tell them. They tried again, yelling telepathically as hard as they could.

Below them, her back against the wall of the cluttered living quarters, Sissi suddenly began screaming.

"Harry! Harry! Harry! Oh, Harry's here!"

Her excitement, her relief, was exquisite pain.

"Harry! Harry! Harry! Oh, my Osaris! Harry! Harry!" Over and over, babbling, jumping up and down.

Harry was just as excited, just as relieved, but his voice was flat, sharp, demanding. "Sissi! Where are you? Come back!"

"Harry! Harry! Oh, my Osaris! Oh, Harry! Harry!"

"Sissi, dammit!" Harry roared. *"Shut—the—hell—up!"*

Chad, Homer, Arnie, and Eddie were pounding one another's shoulders, yelling aloud. "We found 'em! We found 'em!"

The other men in the helicopter were sure they had gone mad.

Guss grabbed Sissi, clamping his hand on her muzzle. "Harry!" he yelled wildly. "It's me, Guss! I'm here!"

"Where?"

"In a building—in a building—"

Sissi fought free. "A square building! Gray roof. There's a door—we burned it open. There's a vehicle beside the building—in a passageway. I killed it."

"Square building, gray roof, door on the top burned open, car in the alley."

Harry was relaying the description to the pilot.

"Two levels—"

"Two-story."

"The vehicle is green—"

"Green car in the alley."

"Got it!" Arnie yelled suddenly. "Green car in the alley! There!"

The helicopter wheeled, dropped like a shot bird.

Inside the building, Kolankov was furious. They had waited too long! Sri Singh had run to the car to start the engine and found that it would not start. He had run back inside as the hammering, thunderous beat of the helicopter had rapidly approached. Even as he had told Kolankov they were trapped, the helicopter had passed overhead, had turned.

Kolankov, cursing, fired up the stairway again.

Jessica Jones, brought jarringly to reality by the thunderous sound of the helicopter, had come out of the office, the detonator in one hand, a machine pistol in the other.

Sandra Hope, her eyes white and rolling, screamed, "We gotta run, we gotta run!"

"Can't run!" Sri Singh said. "Car's dead."

"We must!" Jessica's voice was a whip, lashing.

She worked feverishly, setting the dials on the detonator. Once the detonator was set, only the toggle need be moved forward, and she would have a threat that would hold an army at bay.

Outside the building, the helicopter sat at rest in the street, blades dying as the doors burst open to spill Harry Borg and his four fighting men onto the pavement. They ran crouched, two for the alley, two for the street side, and Harry for the front entrance.

Sandra Hope's machine pistol spewed lead, shattering the glass of the front window, driving Harry belly-down in the street. From that position, he traced a row of bullets across the remaining glass of the front window, waist high, lifted, and ran again.

Chad and Homer, at the door in the alley, found it locked and put their backs against the wall on either side as the door suddenly shook under fire from the inside. Holes appeared. Splinters flew. The instant the burst stopped, Homer kicked the door, broke it half open, and Chad kicked and broke it clear open. Backs against the wall again, they waited out a second burst.

Eddie and Arnie worked up against the street side of the building to take command of the far front window. And the FBI men—there were three of them, quiet and fiercely capable—had fanned out on the street, and were advancing slowly, crawling under the fire.

Suddenly, it was a standoff.

* * *

At the head of the stairway on the upper floor, Guss was frightened to the point of paralysis. His golden eyes were as wide and as wild as eyes could possibly get; his long, forked tongue, gone limp, was hanging out the side of his mouth.

But no amount of fear could hold him now. He had failed twice, and he was *not* going to fail again!

He turned away from the wall with a crazed mental groaning, burst into the stairway, and ran, stumbling, down the stairs.

"Guss!" Sissi screamed.

He didn't pause.

She ran down the stairs after him.

Guss burst into the pressroom.

He saw machines—he saw humans. He saw a crowlike female look up from a device she was holding, saw her stare directly at him with startled, frightened eyes, saw her lift a weapon—he knew she would kill him.

He put a purple beam through her chest and killed her.

"Osis forgive me," he moaned.

A purple beam from Sissi's esso crossed inches before Guss's face and struck down Sandra Hope just an instant before that miserable woman fired at Guss.

At that moment, Harry burst through the front door, sending glass flying. Vladimir Kolankov had turned to run for a rear door. Three long strides, and Harry Borg leaped and came down on the back of the running man. They crashed to the floor, weapons lost, and began tearing at each other's throats.

Harry wanted him alive.

Chad and Homer came in to find Sri Singh stretched facedown on the floor, unhurt, shivering, his automatic rifle thrown far to the side. Chad left him for Homer, and headed for Jessica.

She was dead. But Chad knew her at once from the

descriptions. The electronic box lying on the floor at her fingertips had to be the detonator—what else would it be?"

Chad went to it, bent to look at it. His skin crawled.

The hand of the devil! All the evil man and devil could devise, just there, in black plastic and shining metal. The lives of millions of human beings, the land, the forests, the cities, the earth itself—just there, under that off-on toggle switch, at the mercy of a single deranged human mind.

He dared to pick it up.

A tall young man, not yet fully grown, white-haired, wide of shoulder, strong face deeply tanned, eyes gray and cold, he stood on strong legs and held the evil thing in both his hands.

Carefully.

Firmly.

Securely.

He looked up to find that Harry was standing, Kolankov unconscious at his feet. He didn't know how long Harry's eyes had been on him. There was something in Harry's expression that spoke of deep thoughts, though Chad wasn't sure of that, either.

"Is that it?" Harry asked quietly.

"This is it."

"In your hands, son. All our lives. Take care of us."

"Sir."

"I know you can. And will. You and all the others like you."

Then he turned to a pair of frightened aliens. "Hello, Guss. Hello, Sissi."

"Harry!" Sissi wailed, and ran to him. He caught her in his arms and held her close.

Guss, staring at Harry, sank slowly to the floor. He drew the gray film across his golden eyes, withdrew his long tongue, and became still.

Harry was concerned.

Sissi was not.

"Fainted," she said. "He's a big coward."

She wasn't serious, Harry knew. He hugged her. "We all should be as brave."

George Bushby heard the first sputter of the truck's engine while driving a steady fifty-five miles an hour on U.S. Highway One. His hands were frozen on the wheel. His right leg was stiff with the effort he had exerted to keep his foot from flooring the gas pedal.

He had seen two highway patrol cars. To exceed the speed limit would be to invite almost immediate arrest, which would use up all the gain in distance that high speed would get him and much, much more. And so the nerve-wracking self-control, minute after minute, mile after mile.

How far did he have to go to be safely out of range of a hand-held transmitter?

God only knew.

In his mind, without a moment's relief, was the awareness of the bomb just behind him, the thought of the enormous blinding, flashing, searing ball of pure hell waiting for release. He knew he would not know of the explosion when it came—if it came. He would be alive, and then he would not be alive—that quickly and with that certainty it would end for him.

Mile after mile, minute after minute.

And the motor sputtered finally, out of gas.

So it was finished. He had done all that mortal man could do.

Quivering then, with sweat drenching him, with fatigue beyond enduring draining all his strength away, he guided the truck to the shoulder. When the truck finally stopped, he let his hands drop from the wheel and sat, slumped, staring sightlessly through the window.

No use in getting out. No use running. He could not

possibly, on foot, get far enough away.

Later—he did not know how much later—he heard a tap on the window. A highway patrolman was standing there, beckoning. George rolled down the window.

"Step out, sir," the patrolman said.

George realized then that there was no traffic on the road. Only himself in the truck and the patrolman and the car.

"What is it?" he asked, dazed.

"The area is cordoned off, sir."

"You know—you know about the bomb?"

"Yes. And I know about you—and what you've done. I'm to take you to a safe area." There was respect close to reverence in the officer's manner.

"Thank God," George whispered.

"Yes," the patrolman said. "But thank you most of all."

It had not been difficult for Los Ross to find the truck containing the bomb once Guss had brought him back to the rooftop with signals from their own transmitter, and the FBI and the state highway patrol had moved with smooth efficiency. Twenty miles of U.S. Highway One would remain closed until the bomb could be removed by those who knew about such things.

George Bushby got out of the truck.

His legs almost gave way, but they did not quite. He braced his shoulders and walked firmly to the waiting open door of the patrol car. The officer waiting there thought it somehow right to come to attention as George entered the car.

And, before he closed the door, one more thing:

A hand salute.

CHAPTER 26

How does a nation say thanks?

How, in all honesty, when all things are considered, *can* a nation make a public display of its vulnerability? Or, for that matter, reveal to other nations—in particular, adversary nations—that there may very well have come into their hands, when fully examined, the means with which the world might be controlled, for good or evil, with a power beyond any yet dreamed about?

How could a nation, indeed?

The answer was, of course, "With great care."

And so a lock of secrecy was immediately imposed.

Guss, Sissi, Los Ross, George Bushby, Harry Borg, and his cadre were taken to Camp David, to be held there in luxury and thanked lavishly.

But, necessarily, there were certain restrictions.

Guss, Sissi, and Los Ross could not be allowed the use of their Triss-nass until the government was sure their safety was secure. The fact that the government

wanted to examine it for any secrets of value was not
mentioned. Nor was the fact understood that the government would not be able to hold them against their will.

Harry could not go to Lori, nor could she come to him
just yet—the debriefing, you know? A matter of only a
day or two, and a matter of extreme government importance, it had to be tended to first, didn't it? Of course it
did. They could, however, meet by means of big-screen,
two-way television.

"Harry," Lori screamed delightedly on seeing her husband. "You all right?"

"Just fine, hon. Just fine."

"What you did! You and Guss and Sissi! Outa sight!"

"Aw, shucks!" Harry answered, pretending to kick dirt.
"Nothin' any red-blooded American boy wouldn'ta done."

"Harry, have they thanked you?"

"Thanked us? They've been lickin' our hands till they've
rusted our wristwatches!"

"So come after me!"

"You have Sam with you?"

"He's here. No one dares come near me. The other
lads?"

"They're with me—all fine."

"I want *you*, Harry! I want you to come after me!"

"I'm gonna! I'm gonna, honey! But I've got this
debriefing, you know? Only a couple of days, they say.
And they say you're as safe as in God's pocket, there in
Hassad's care."

"Safe?" she yelled. "He's the guy! He's the one—"

"Hold it!" Harry cut her off sharply. "Right now, I'm
the number-one hero, and he's number two. Believe me!
I can take him hand to hand, but here in Washington he
outweighs me billions to one! Dollars, that is. So button
your lip."

She understood. "Lip buttoned, sir!"

"Good girl!" He wanted to kiss her so badly that it hurt.

And she knew that, too. "Soon, Harry?"

"You better believe it!"

The other lads—Chad, Homer, Ernie, and Arnie—were fine, as Harry had said. They, too, were called heroes; but they too had to suffer "debriefing." Chad insisted upon and got the use of a telephone, which proved to be more tantalizing than helpful. The image of Illia before him, her voice whispering the few words of love she'd learned, her soft, fur-covered body so vivid—it was the stuff of madness, surely. He could hardly say it, but he said it: "It'll be a day or two, honey—hang in!"

Ros Moss, that dried-up, sour, recalcitrant old essan who held the office of President of Jassa, a tyrant in the eyes of many, who wanted no communication whatever with Earth, no chance of being infected with the problems of the human race, proved to be not without kindness. Nor without an accurate report of what had almost happened on Earth, and who had prevented its happening, perhaps to the benefit of all the universe.

And so George Bushby was called to a telephone to hear a voice: "George? Is that you?"

"Sara! For the love of Mike! Where are you!"

"I'm home! Those funny-looking creatures brought us here to our house and left us. If you could call this a house anymore, with the roof broken. I just got here. With Jackie and Jillie. And when I saw our roof, I had all sorts of trouble finding you and getting those stupid people to let me talk to you. George! Our house is a wreck!"

"Oh, my gosh! Oh, Sara, baby—" George couldn't say more; he was crying.

But Sara could say more; she was outraged. "Do you hear me, George? This house is a sight! What did you *do* to it? For goodness' sake! You can look up and see sky everywhere!"

"Hey, Pop!" It was Jackie. "We got cops all over the place!"

"Daddy," Jillie said. "Tippi's here, too. And she's got her finger on, all fixed up like new!"

"Let *me* talk!" Sara said with exasperation. "George? George, are you there? Why don't you say something?"

"I'm going to! I'm going to!"

"I've got to call the girls of my bridge club! And I've got to get to the store, George. We haven't got a thing to eat in the house."

George Bushby was wiping tears.

In the almost palatial luxury of their quarters, Guss and Sissi and Los Ross had just received word, through Ross's equipment—his refusal to surrender it was being honored for the moment—that their violations of Jassan national security would be reviewed upon their return with all consideration taken of their selfless motives.

"Means we'll be safe," Guss told Sissi. "I think."

"And does that mean you'll—you know, you and me? Like you said?"

"Sissi! My word is my bond!"

"Yeah. Sure. But you're also a male."

His long, forked tongue came out, searching for hers. "You're the only female I'll ever care a whiss about."

"*That's* what I wanted to hear!" Sissi and joyfully.

Joyfully, because a whiss is the most there is...

About the Author

Ward Hawkins, born and raised in the Northwest, began his adult life with a high school education and a wife, and his professional career with the hammer and spikes of a heavy-construction worker. He took to writing as an "easier way," sold to pulp science-fiction magazines, *Thrilling Wonder*, etc., went on to the *Saturday Evening Post*, *Colliers*, the *American*, etc. When they went bust, he moved to L.A., joined the Writers Guild of America, and began writing for the motion-picture and television market—*Rawhide*, *Bonanza*, *High Chapparal*, *Little House on the Prairie*, *Voyage to the Bottom of the Sea*, etc.

He lives now in the L.A. area with Adeline, the only wife he has ever had, near his children and grandchildren, plays golf to a five handicap, and writes only what he enjoys most.